I Ain't Got

no

Business!

The R Series ... Rated "R" for Roxanne

By

Camille St. Charles Mississippi

ISBN: 978-1-733-7907-3-4

Book Project Manager

The Master Communicator's Writing Services

Houston, Texas

Contact: sunneygirlsalutations@yahoo.com

Photo by Tammy Harvey Studios

The model on the cover is Ayrika Rayne Jones.

TABLE OF CONTENTS

Anything by Steve Wonder Is Fine with Me!

With Your Love!

Oragami!

DEDICATION!

Thank you, God, because your timing is just right. Thanks to my family and friends that listened to me, as I spoke about some unrealized dreams. I welcome and enjoy all the fun that this new world has offered me during the revelation of Roxanne's many sagas. Happy to know that the last thread holding me together did not come undone! Special thanks to my personal ESAD., because no matter where I go, there they are offering me more crazy guidance!

Re-Introduction

After all is said and done, I'm so glad Mr. Akheem Fulwad made his debut into my life. It took a long time to get here, but I'm thrilled to know that he gives me all the loving shelter I can handle. It's true my life looks pretty pleasing from the outside. However, little does anyone know that some days it's actually a bundle of shit. Now that all the shame and drudgery is behind me, I can smile.

Secretly, I want to shout about how well things have turned out. I am a little scared to, though, because Trouble always waits to fuck with my family and me. So, I just hold my peace, count my blessings and get on with the art of living. Part of me knows that just around the corner, heartache and bullshit are whispering my name as I run to it. Still, while the sun is shining on me now, I will just smile.

My sweetheart just dropped what he was doing and flew me out to Texas. I was in LA at the auto show. He knew that I needed to see him because after all the sexual tension between us, it was time to seal the deal. I giggle to myself when I think of how we agreed not to have sex for ninety days. Akheem came with this novel little plan, because, he told me, I needed to get my past lovers out of my system.

He told me that he does understand that I am a woman with needs, but he wanted to consume me with no sexual strings to anyone else attached. We kept our hands to ourselves, but for me, it was hard as hell. I found it hard to give up sex because there are days when I am a sex junkie! I got so excited when I was in his company, but his hands never explored my body in that way.

This man would not even offer me oral pleasure. I wanted to beat his ass. Truth be told, I have never had a man tell me that even though I had a sexual need, he was going to force me to self-cleanse my desire for sex. He was a man of his word because he forced me to talk most of our time together. Part of me thought that maybe he was an inexperienced lover. Yes, he is younger than I am; I just thought that I was more than he could handle.

Not everyone can handle a full-figured woman like myself. Maybe he was in the gym working on his stamina and building up his strength. I thought that maybe he was powerlifting when he wasn't in my company. I gave it no thought because the more he kept his hands to himself, the more I withdrew in my mind!

However, when he flew me to Texas, there was no more beating around the bush. First, he was shocked that I had no pubic hair, so there was no beating around the bush for real. When he finally got his hands on me, he had to put out a three-alarm fire in my body. Akheem was beyond skilled in the lovemaking department. He was a tantric sex practitioner and he had me all tangled up in many different positions.

It took a lot to get me to come to Texas to be with him, but I would run into his arms gladly from then on. We would sit on the side of the bed, looking up at the stars through the window. I'm delighted that I said yes to him and made my way to be in his company. I giggled to myself as I gave thought to my encounter with Trevor 24 hours ago. Look at me now, in the lap of luxury with Akheem. I had a small pain in my chest while at the LA auto show. A small part of me that thought I might be crazy to entertain Trevor. Still, there was something so intoxicating about him. He did not seem as if he wanted me to be perfect, he just liked me. But he was crazy as fuck, and I *know* crazy. I might not be an expert on most things, but Crazy is part of my name.

***

Shit, I was mentally revisiting several crazy conversations with my mother when I was younger. She would often tell my sister and me our Crazy should make us happy in one form or another. She mentioned we needed to accept the Crazy part of our heritage. We all have a hint of Indian in our blood. I guess some black people find it charming to know that in their DNA, there are other ancestral makeups in their family lineage. But Crazy runs rampant through our family, and we should embrace it like she had!

I'm not being offensive or disrespectful to the native people of the land. This was just a thing in my family that we all hated, until we got older and saw it for what it was. Because everyone knows that Crazy, true Crazy has been alive forever. It is a spirit that takes you out of your body and makes you do and say all manner of Crazy things. To me, it's like being told that you are Bat-shit Crazy but not willing to look at it!

You see, our grandmother gave us all a glimpse of what pure Crazy looks like and we would run from it! She was so Crazy; her family gave her an Indian nickname! I guess our grandmother showed an outstanding ability to give Crazy a run for its money. Our mother had her own nickname in the Crazy arena as well. Then she carried on the tradition with us, because she needed to arm us! In my family, Crazy would and could chase your dreams away or help you find them. The choice was always yours; here are the names used in my family on my grandmother's side!

1. My Grandmother (Ms. Eva)/Born Crazy
2. My Mom (Sara)/Still Crazy
3. Me (Roxanne)/Running Crazy
4. Maxey/Tread Lightly Crazy
5. Cherokee

Here's the truth about Cherokee—that girl already had to fight behind her name. She is Crazy personified, confrontational, assassin-like tendencies, renegade spirit, *and* she drives around with an authentic Cherokee tomahawk under the front seat of her car. People like that do *not* need another title draped at the end of their name. My mom and grandmother could never find a true Indian name that captured Cherokee's essence. My sister already had an uphill climb with being Crazy. I guess my mom did not wish to add insult to injury, so we only call her Cherokee to her face. However, behind her back, we know that she is a fucking lunatic.

***

I smiled to myself while sitting on the side of the bed, looking at the captain of my heart. Akheem does not even know that I am Crazy. Maybe, somewhere down the road, he might stumble across the Crazy aspect of me. But for now, we are going to be gentle with one another. I deserve to be worshipped as if I am royalty. I remember the feelings over this weekend that this man has given me. The trip to get me here, how he stepped in to guide me to a delicious life with him. How my business is popping, and how he makes feel as high as a cloud. Damn, this man chases all my fears away and the sex with him—delicious! He is devoted to me enjoying myself with him and passion is his middle name.

Akheem's new residence was now located in my heart as we held hands and walked into the shower, while all three of my angels showed up! They stood over by the sink and watched me with smiles on their faces. I knew that they were there to give me more shit, but this time they did not say anything. They just broke out into their own rendition of my special song that played in Heaven whenever I started to pray to God. They started to sing "Roxanne" by Sting and The Police. I smiled as Akheem placed his right hand on my rear end and gave me a tug!

"Rocky, I'm sure that we will be great together, but I need to know if you could offer me our own 'until'. I know that I love you, and I'm sorry that our first lovemaking session was rather quick. I pride myself on being a three-hour lover—maybe next time I could build up more stamina for you."

I remained still and silent because I could not believe his words. I reached over to turn the water on, and stopped. I called his name and turned to look at him as he was about to step into the shower.

"I already love you, my Akheem, and I know that we will be great together. There is no need for you to feel inadequate about anything that we do together, because I wish to savor my time with you. To me, your skills as a lover are great and if our sessions get any longer, then maybe we should both consider becoming cross-country sex partners. You have already given me several dangerous orgasms and with them total bliss. We have experienced our own version of 'until'. I already know what I have in you, and Akheem, that is more than enough for me."

I turned on the water as we stood under our own showerheads. I allowed water to flow across my body first, while I turned my back to him and began to cleanse my body thoroughly. Akheem just watched me and adjusted his water to his liking. I turned back around to catch a glimpse of him cleaning his body.

He said, "Be very, very quiet because, I'm in the process of hunting down this fine-ass duck!"

I looked down at his penis and began to smile, because I knew of a nice and snug crevasse that I desired him to hunt down and explore. I knew that we were about to be involved in another round of trailblazing sex. I had it my head that I was going to pump him as if he was a container of glue, as he would be stuck to this pussy. Since we were already done with our first-round title match, I was aware we would have to establish who the winner was by the end of the weekend. I placed my hands on his anchor of a dick as he smiled. He moved closer to me as I gave him an innocent look.

"Akheem, can I anticipate this to be a shorter session in the shower, or will we need to step out into the bedroom to finish, because I am ready for round two, if you are?"

Akheem's eyes lusted for me as mine did for him. He leaned me in the corner and began to place his cock inside of me, satisfying my hunger for him. I damn near lost my footing as his engorged and extended penis followed the road to my rather hot and steamy pussy once more! My body was confessing all manner of shit to him! Akheem walked inside of me and was determined to make me scream.

My body chimed a perfect tune as his body struck repeatedly to find gold inside me. His actions made me happy as I removed all the past years' sorrow from my body. This man was the pot of gold at the end of the rainbow, to me. I guess that no matter how I looked at it, I now knew my role with him. I knew I did not have to beg him to love me. I was willing to surrender myself to him and only him.

While this man pleasured me in the shower, I said *yes, yes and yes* in my head. He made my pussy confess whatever sins I might have committed or planned on in future. I became lost inside my desire for him, all while locked inside that shower, as he sent me over the edge of gratification over and over again. As the water rained down on us, he had me pressed inside a tight-ass corner. He was offering me comfort and helping me feel expensive. You see, sometimes in the past with Michael, I felt like spare change. Michael made me feel as if I was a fucking afterthought by the end of our marriage.

Some days there are moments when I regret how I thought he made me feel. The truth of the matter is I didn't love myself enough. I never gave *me* too much thought, because to me, *he* was the gift. My love, my Akheem treated me better than my ex-husband had ever done. I didn't regret anything with him so far, and I welcomed what was to come.

Akheem began to laugh while I moaned with pleasure at his actions in the shower. He gave me nothing but good loving. While the sounds thrilled him, he proceeded to ask me one last question.

He reached over and touched my face, saying, "Rocky, is it *duck season* or *rabbit season*?"

I smiled at him and said, "Akheem, it is indeed *fuck* this *duck season!*"

CHAPTER 1

THE SEX WAS SO SPLENDID!

Mr. Fulwad and I spent a wonderfully indulgent weekend together—nothing short of glorious! We had given each other permission to have our way with one another, all while wrapped up inside this luxury hotel in Texas. We explored each other's bodies repeatedly I was pleased more than once with my new lover Akheem, and I was thrilled to find out that he was more than a typical male. The sex was as splendid the first time with him as it was when we satisfied our hunger for one another seven more times during our getaway.

I only remember him making me upset with him once during our exclusive, fun-filled weekend. He said that he wished I would not lose any more weight. I have always heard that I should be smaller for any man to really want me, so I could hardly believe it when he told me that in his mind and eye, I needed to be just a little *larger* for him. Well, I told him in no uncertain terms that my ass and I are a package deal. If my somewhat smaller body type did not please him for any reason, then it could be that he might need to experience a new delight with someone else other than me. I then whispered that I would not be offended if he did not embark upon a relationship with me.

The smile faded from his face as my words lingered in the air for a moment. I wanted him to know that I was here right now, so he had to deal with the Roxanne standing before him. I know that I must have caught him off guard by my un-movable comments about myself. I thought, how *dare* this motherfucker inform me that he needs me to be a little larger or fluffier?

Nevertheless, he sees his world from a different vantage point while he performs some unspeakable act on me, both of us making each other smile. Maybe he wants me to be just a little bit larger than I am, or maybe Akheem is trying to figure out what he can get away with as he talks to me. Once we got back on the same page, I knew that we were both capable of loving one another. Our time together was great as we made each other scream repeatedly!

I awoke to our last day together wrapped in his arms, almost swallowing up one another in our loving embrace! I found myself singing in my head as I got out of bed, my mind having been eased for now. I was aware that my troubles were in fact waiting for me to get home, but I kept singing this song over and over in my head! It was "Lovely Day" by Bill Withers.

I was so involved inside my own love affair that I felt as if I was dancing inside a fairy tale. I knew that I needed to enjoy my last hours with Akheem. I went to the bathroom to freshen up. Although I had taken a shower the previous night, I planned on taking one more before we left for home. I put on a nice outfit to wear to breakfast together, because I wanted to blind him with my beauty. While he laid in bed napping, I called down to room service and placed an order for a light meal.

His comments pleased me almost as much as his elongated penis did! Then, as we were finishing our last sex session for the weekend, Akheem thought it would be quaint if we made love while standing up! Although, I hadn't had sex standing up in some years, I was eager to try it out! As we were about to get started, I thought I felt secure enough with my body and myself to be adventurous with him, so I decided to give him my all.

Akheem positioned me in a corner and began to work out his unresolved issues in the sexual arena. My body and my legs were not used to being pulled in so many different directions as we joined as one! Akheem is what some people call a Power-Fucker, just like Sissell. He was raiding my pussy as he traveled in and out of my body! He enjoyed delivering powerful thrusts into me, and the fact that I was nimble enough for us to stand up and have sex made him excited about screwing me.

He held my leg in place; I began to shake with pain from a massive leg cramp! He thought I was having a sexual cosmic merger with him because he thought he was making me happy. He thought that he was helping guide my soul towards the conscious meditation of us being one spirit as we came together! But in all actuality, I was losing blood flow to my leg and about to fall out of this corner that I was wedged into

It would have been selfish of me to make him stop at this point … his whole state of existence was instrumental in him reaching his perpetual universal orgasm! I do rather enjoy watching him cum because his eyes tear up as he looks at me! I enjoyed seeing him reach his bliss. Since we were not going to see one another for the next 14 days, what was a little pain among lovers? Once we were done and he was no longer pounding the shit out of my little glory and me, I fell to the floor and began to cry.

I had to give him a gentle reminder that I was 7 years older than he was and my body doesn't work like his does. He offered to give me another massage, as I lay on the floor while he worked out the kinks in my leg! Then he made me scream with extreme ecstasy on the floor as he manipulated my body to another heartfelt orgasm! He laid hands on me and I became weak all over! This last orgasm that he helped me achieve almost eclipsed all the others. There was no place left on my body that he had not explored, and I was literally *and* figuratively worn the fuck out!

Once my body had calmed down from the rush of this last orgasm, I lay on the floor listless because my momentum was gone. I knew that we needed to be preparing ourselves to make a swift exit out of this town, so we took our last shower together and repacked our clothes. I smiled as I looked over at Mr. Fulwad, who was placing his gun back in its holster and repacking his luggage. He blew me a kiss and I grabbed it out of the air, placing it on my lips. I asked him if he was tired.

"Rocky, I don't have the chance to get tired. Many people want a part of me, and my job requires that I be ready to go anywhere that the company wishes at a moment's notice. I feel great to have had a chance to spend some time with you. I am so grateful to you for helping me rejuvenate my mind, body and spirit! I can't wait to spend more time together. Knowing that you have great stamina to keep up with me makes me overjoyed. If I can be honest with you, your stamina turns me on more and more. It's like you've cast a spell on me! To answer your question, Ms. Roxanne, no—I am not tired! I'm just now getting my second wind with you. I plan on doing more for you, with you and to you in the future, if you stay around."

I didn't open my mouth to ask any more questions of him, I only made sexy comments as we finished our packing. I was happy with my time with him, which wasn't disrupted by anything or anyone. I felt like a new woman as we both got on his company jet, on our way back to our crazy lives. Akheem and I held hands as we flew back to Sacramento. We kissed all the way to my town and it was hard for me to get off that jet. I found myself falling more in love with this man. I had to wait 14 days for him to fine-tune my body once more. I didn't mind, because I knew that we would talk every day!

Despite my contentment, a crazy thought came to me. I smiled to myself, trying not to be mean-spirited. I suspected Akheem could cause me all manner of trouble, because he had my heart at his disposal; he could break it anytime, if he chose to. Now that I had my own point of reference about him, I realized I could break his too.

Sexually, I was willing to wait for our next adventure. As we made our landing in my town, I replayed the weekend in my mind. I began to smile and offer up great praises because he was just what I needed. I was thrilled that we enjoyed so much pleasure, knowing that we'd had sex 11 times over our three-day adventure. It made me feel like a young girl again.

When the jet plane landed, Akheem wanted to know whether we had an exclusive contract with one another. I guess he wanted to make sure I wouldn't be sharing the wealth of my body with anyone else. Both of us came to find out that exclusivity had its own special privileges! Akheem got off the jet and walked me over to the car. He had a member of the staff secure my luggage in it. Cherokee came to the airport to collect me. She suggested that Akheem and I stop acting like adorable adolescents, as we both kissed like fools even in her presence.

"Hello, Ms. Cherokee, and how are you doing today?" Akheem said.

"What's up, *Full*-Wad?" replied Cherokee.

Akheem and me looked at each other and began to laugh. He was aware of the drama that was always around the two of us. We'd both talked about our families that weekend, gaining a better understanding of how we both saw ourselves inside our families. He held my door open as I got into the car, and leaned down to kiss me once more. He held my left breast and gave it three firm squeezes, telling me that he would talk with me later that night. Cherokee pulled out before he himself took off, as I smiled.

We did not say a word until we got to the freeway. Cherokee was the first to speak because she could not take the silence and I was enjoying being still. While she tried to ask me about Mr. Fulwad, Carly Simon's "Nobody Does it Better" came on the radio. I began to sing along, smiling as I looked at my sister.

I could not believe that I was singing about Akheem until Cherokee told me to shut the fuck up! She made me aware that she had no problem pulling my car over and beating my ass while we both laughed our asses off! I was thrilled to have found

8

a new love. Even though it is hard to admit, I do now understand that some things are better left unsaid.

I told Cherokee all about my weekend in Texas. I did my best to give her all the sordid details of my sex life with Mr. Fulwad. Cherokee and I shared several laughs as we made it to my house. She wanted to come in and go over some details about the upcoming wedding. I was totally exhausted from my weekend. We went over several more details for her wedding and it suddenly occurred to me that my sister was scared! I could tell by her voice how much.

"By the way, how is your man doing?" I asked.

She looked at me and began to weep. I moved closer to her, rubbing her back. Cherokee continued to cry for a couple of minutes. Then when she was ready, she responded to my question about her fiancé, explaining that she was unsure if she loved him until death did them part. Cherokee was unsure how to be in love with anyone for long periods. After a certain number of exchanges with a man, her feelings began to decline.

She had no point of reference to pull from in her life, and I was the only person besides our grandparents who had maintained a serious relationship throughout her life. It was

9

apparent that I did not do such a great job of keeping my family together. I was at a loss for words to say to her, because I was no longer in a committed relationship with my husband. Some unfortunate shit had happened to us, to cause us to call it quits. I asked her to tell me how Learnard Rankin, Sr. (The Pastor) really made her feel.

She told me that The Pastor made her feel remarkable, that she didn't have to be the villain when she was with him. When he asked her to marry him, she thought that he was playing a trick on her. No one had ever loved her enough to offer her a glimpse of a dream.

Wow, I thought to myself. Here was the heart of the matter — my sister didn't know how to love this man, so she is scared. She had no clue about how to give and take in a relationship. They did not have to worry about money, but love was what she didn't know, nor how to give him that part of herself no one has ever wanted to discover. I felt optimistic about the upcoming marriage, so I softened my voice to encourage her.

"Well, well, well, Ms. Cherokee! You are not as hard as you pretend to be, and I am proud that you have this relationship with The Pastor. Your relationship with him will require more from you than you have ever given in the past! It just seems kind of funny that here you are, looking seriously at love for the first time in your life! You better give that man the best of you. If you can offer me up some of your tears for him, it must be your heart telling you that you must give him that part of yourself you have kept hidden for years. You can no longer be selfish or stubborn all the time. Tell me, are you tired of being alone?"

She moved her head up and down, letting me know that she was tired of walking by herself through life. I told her that I did not have the answer for her; only she and The Pastor knew how they felt about one another. It would not likely be a walk in the park, but if she loved him, it would feel right in her soul. My sister's life had been so full of turmoil, I truly believed that it was time things went well for her. I advised her that the benefits of love and life have no specific time limit or agenda, so if she loved her fiancé right now, then she should enjoy her time with him.

I made her aware that there were no guarantees for anyone. Cherokee noted that she wanted to love The Pastor until her love evaporated! I reached down, picked up her hand up and kissed it. I told her that if she felt that strongly for him, she better grab hold of him and love him until they both evaporated!

11

I stood up and told her I needed to rest, because I was worn all the way out, and my body was doing its own countdown. I also needed to call and check in with my children.

Cherokee gently said, "Thank you, Roxy, you said just what I needed to hear."

I knew that my sister was pleased that I could be there for her while she wrestled with her own truth! I knew that good times were in store for her because she did deserve her own version of happiness. As she was walking out of my house, she turned around and asked me whether I was still paying for her honeymoon. I told her that it would be my honor to do so! A big smile spread across her face.

"Roxy, all I want to do is to be happy ... a skill I never learned. The Pastor is offering my soul some shelter, and I like the feeling. If I seem scared to walk through the rest of my life with him, I am, because loving him reminds me of all my past failures. I do not like to revisit some of my past mistakes. There have been many, most of which you are aware! I fear sometimes that someone is playing a cruel joke on me; but I do love that man. I have so much guilt from my past mistakes that travels with me in my mind. Knowing that I do not wish to give the bad side of me to him only allows me to see more of my complicated past. I am tired of being broken-hearted. With him, I suspect that I can be happy."

I suggested to my sister that she couldn't run away from her past, but rather she should make peace with it. Next, I suggested that the things that do not serve her and her life right now she should consider leaving behind, because she had no room for any more errors. I asked her to show me a woman without guilt and I would show her a truly fucked-up man! I urged her to make peace with her past, so her life could flow in a more positive direction. As I spoke, my body was settling down, because for me sleep was right around the corner.

I walked her to the door, suggesting that if she truly wanted to be happy, she had three options open to her. She should either continue to let him live with her and just play house. Or, she could give herself as close to completely as she could to him, because he seemed to accept her past. I then alluded to my final option.

"Maybe he expects you to love him with all your heart. If you cannot love him just the way he is, then maybe you should take up gardening. Prepare for the rest of your life to pass your crazy ass by!"

I was about to call her a spinster, but kept my mouth closed while we giggled at the door. I hoped that I'd made her feel better about her new life and the possibilities in marrying someone she loved. I only wanted her life to be a lot easier than it had been. I did not think she was asking for too much. She wanted to make sure that she could love this man until they were no more! I guess Cherokee was feeling like she had spent all the love that GOD gave her. She was unsure of what her life was going to be with her new husband. I tried my best to get her to retire her past, and stop beating herself up over some of her unfortunate experiences. Knowing that The Pastor wasn't jaded by his love for her made me believe that she was due for her own happy ending.

CHAPTER 2

WRITE IT DOWN!

I reached over and hugged Cherokee I thanked her once again for picking me up from the airport, and said I'd see her later this week. I kissed her on her cheek and watched her walk to her new car. I stood there as she drove away. I locked up my house and set the alarms. I was saying my good-byes to this crazy, long day. I began to walk up the stairs and said a prayer for my sisters. I pulled my suitcase behind me as I listened to the stillness of my house. I reached my bedroom as I was ending the prayer for my sisters. I placed my suitcase in the corner of my room. I removed my clothes and plugged in my cell phone.

I walked into the bathroom and ran myself a bath. I removed all my make-up and brushed my teeth. I did not ignore how tired I really was, so I knew that I would not be lounging around inside the tub. All I wanted to do was end up in bed before the clock struck midnight! I had decided not to talk for long with anyone on the phone. I took a hurried bath and got out of the tub. I walked into my room with a towel around me. I opened my dresser drawer and pulled out some sleepwear. I sat on the edge of my bed and told GOD that I had had a beautiful weekend.

After I called to check in on the kids, I called my Akheem. I told him that I was nearly asleep, but wanted to speak with him before I allowed myself to drift away. He was pleased to hear me on the other end of the phone. He implied that he wanted to hear the magic words from me before we hung up the phone. I was unsure what he meant, so I told him I loved him.

"That is sweet, Rocky, and I love you too—but that is not what I wanted to hear. You mean to tell me that you don't remember our secret code?"

I mentally rushed through the Filofax inside my head. I must have forgotten something important to both of us. I was becoming pissed off at myself, because I could not, for the life of me, remember what in the hell I was supposed to say to him. Akheem implied that he was not going to hang up until I told him what I needed to say! I was getting pissed off at him and myself, wondering how he dared to quiz me while I was so tired. I did not stand a ghost of a chance remembering a word or phrase right now.

He was unaffected by the obvious distractions that I was trying to put up. I was hoping he'd give me a hint, but he was not budging. He just sat on the other end of the phone and waited for the right answer! Then it dawned on me what he was waiting to hear.

"Mr. Fulwad, it's Duck Season ... and good night, handsome."

"That's right Rocky, it is Duck Season. I will speak with you sometime tomorrow, so go get some rest for that lovely body of yours!"

I thought I heard him say good night, beautiful, as I hung up my phone and laid down to rest. I promised myself as I was going to sleep that I was not going to be naughty in my dreams, nor was I going to be a bitch tomorrow. I smiled and began to giggle! I told myself that I should stop lying to the universe and take my happy-go-lucky ass to sleep—and that was just what I did. My body was speaking to me as it told me goodnight, sleep placing me under its spell.

My alarm clock went off suddenly, waking me from a beautiful night of sleep. I asked GOD to have mercy on my tired body and me. We had a standing Monday morning meeting, and I had not seen my team since Thursday of last week. I knew that everyone would want his or her own piece of flesh. I needed to be ready for whatever they might bring to my attention. I was hopeful that this meeting would go smoother than the last couple of meetings we had. I was in no mood for any nonsense, as I prayed for a great day, slowly wiping the sleep out of my eyes!

I opened the garage and stepped into my car, plugging in my cell phone so I could use it hands free. I started my car, backed it out and made my way towards the street. I was on time and thrilled. Knowing that my dealership had not seen me in almost a week made me feel as if I had been on a welcome semi-vacation. I knew that it was time to get back down to business because I wanted to know if there were any new discoveries made about the in-house security breach.

I'd made my way onto the freeway when my cell phone rang. I turned down my music and prepared myself to do battle. I pressed the button, looked out the window and spoke.

"Good morning, this is Roxanne."

It was Michael on the other end of the phone and I let out a long sigh. Mentally, I whispered to myself to leave my conversation with him alone.

"Good morning Mrs. Sager, this is your husband Michael speaking! I need to know do you have time to talk with me about our kids."

I responded to his comment by reminding him that I was his *ex*-wife, and yes, I did have time to talk with him as I drove to work. Michael wanted to know whether the problem involving my mother and Anthony was resolved, or whether there was there any more damage waiting to be inflicted upon our son.

I hoped that all the trouble with my mom and our kids was over for now, but one could never know what was waiting on the horizon. Even though I was sure that all the problems were behind us, Michael was still a little concerned about the event; so, I did my best to persuade him that everything was going to be just fine. He allowed the strangest comment to flow from his lips, as though he had been drinking or was trying to bring me to my knees, for some strange reason! I knew that he was not a drinker anymore, so I just removed those crazy thoughts out of my head as I drove myself to work; but I had this funny taste growing in my mouth as I waited on more bullshit to flow from him.

Michael suggested that if we were still married none of this would have happened with the kids! I let out a wicked laugh at his statement, because he was talking to me as if he was a fool. I told him that we could never be sure if he would have been able to be there for our children during this unfortunate situation with my mother, but all those troubles were behind us, as far as I was concerned.

It had been my fault not warning my mother about blocking the jabs to her head from Anthony while he slept; but I did not wish to revisit what could have been. I continued to pour salt inside his wounds by informing him that he'd made his choice over seven years ago when he began to date, then play house with Olivia, and then bless themselves with a child. The things from his past no longer entertained my mind. It no longer entertained me to talk about what could have been. I lived in the present now, and there was no room for me to look back on our life! We had a lot more things to talk about.

Michael did not enjoy the fact that I'd passed the point of talking about our lost love for one another. I then gave him a gentle reminder that he had the kids for Christmas day, he should be by my house around 3:00 p.m. to pick them up that evening, and he needed to bring them back on the 30th because both were in Cherokee's wedding to The Pastor. This was going to be our second holiday without him there, and I wanted him to be ready for his time alone with the kids.

I smiled to myself as I felt like we were oceans apart for now, because he took for granted what we had when he had me. So, now the other life that he thought that he wanted does not taste as sweet as he had dreamed it would be! It is unfair to ask us to start over once more, so I asked him if he needed anything else from me. I was done with our conversations.

He told me that he would bring the kids back home on Saturday evening since Gloria would be back on Friday. I told him that if he wanted to drop them off ahead of time, it wouldn't be a problem for me, but my words did weren't well received.

"I want to spend as much time with my children as I can. I will bring them back when I told you that I would. I pray that one day, Roxanne, you will no longer hate me!"

21

I allowed the sound of my voice to offer him a smile on the phone, but my eyes were beginning to tear up! I told Michael that I would speak with him later. I hung up the phone and pulled onto my dealership parking lot. I turned my car off as I wiped away several tears. I knew that I didn't hate him. It's just that we'd gone as far as we could in our relationship. Maybe now he was really feeling the pain that the whole family felt when he dismissed us and started a new family.

I began to mentally sing Guns 'n' Roses' "Welcome to the Jungle" because I knew that some shit or the other was waiting for me. I said a prayer and checked my face before I stepped out of my car. I was pleased to be back home with my team. I was in cruise status, when I walked through the door of the dealership as I smiled to everyone I saw. Everyone was readying him or herself for our meeting, so I ran to the restroom and then grabbed some files from my bag. I was encouraged by the response of my team as I approached the boardroom with tons of hope for a great day.

I sat down at the head of the table, remembering that it had been almost two weeks since we were all together for our Monday morning meeting. Knowing that I had made several notes about things I wanted to address during this session only made me anxious for our meeting to get underway. I did not wish to mistreat anyone on my team, so I just sat there as we all reacquainted ourselves with each other.

Each department danced through their report from our last meeting. All of which did not concern me in the least, because I had my own thoughts on what I wanted them to address. I was making notes when the meeting turned from being a show of positive reinforcement for one another to one that could bring things to a halt. I was not alerted that the shit was about to start, but, as I began to focus more and more on the culprits, it became clear to all of us that things were about to take a turn for the worse.

Incomplete Maggie felt that it was her turn to have the floor. I folded my arms as she presented her complaints about how she felt things had gone wrong while I was out of town. She was not happy with the job that The Pastor had done in my absence. She told us all that we should never all be away from this dealership at the same time.

"The Pastor is a jackass in a well-tailored suit, and none of us like the way he ran this dealership while you were gone,"

23

Maggie charged. "Furthermore, I believe it was careless on your part, Roxanne, to leave such an idiot to handle the day-to-day goings-on. Maybe you should consider finding a replacement for him."

She was not afraid to tell me that he did not do a good job as far as she was concerned, and how I should reconsider allowing him to marry my sister. Then she decided to make me aware of some more news about him and her dislike for him. Maybe she thought that she was informing me of some devil inside of my dealership. I was aware of the skills that The Pastor brought under this roof. It could be she felt I should know about their displeasure with him running things.

"Roxanne, no go, no happy! Never all three gone! Jackass in tailored suit. No one likes him! Not do good job. Reconsider him marry sister. Took long lunches! Not needed here anymore. Speaking for team! Prefer, don't allow over."

Now, to the untrained ear, she might have sounded like a fool. But this was how she spoke. I had to attempt mindreading as I filled in her words for sense. Once she'd finished, it took me a couple of seconds for my mind to recalibrate her statements before we could move forward! For clarity, here's the translation.

"Roxanne, he took really long lunches and is not needed here anymore," Maggie continued. "I'm speaking for the team when I tell you this! We would prefer if you didn't allow him to be over any of us soon."

God bless Maggie for trying to speak on behalf of the dealership, though, because this old woman was just sailing by on the grace of God as far as I was concerned ... I knew that she caused chaos here at the dealership. She was part of the scenery here, which was why she was afforded more leniency than any other character here on the lot! She was also my grandmother's best friend—another reason I kept this troublemaker around, having promised my grandmother she would always have a job with me.

The Pastor stood up, once Incomplete Maggie concluded her analysis of his leadership abilities. He told us that he took offense at her statements about his performance as he spoke up for himself.

"How dare she present such a biased opinion of my work here at the dealership? Baby sister, I object to Ms. Maggie having anything to say about my performance! Especially considering she has never supervised anything or anyone, nor will anyone give her a chance to run anything! In my opinion, Maggie is jealous. She has nothing nice to say about anyone, and is a walking example of what an old fool looks like! What more can she do to cause more chaos for all of us? I think that I did a fair job of taking care of things, despite not having formal training, *and* we made a profit on all of the cars sold!"

Then he added that it troubled him to know that she is never happy about anything for anyone. His words were true, but I had a dull ache growing in my head.

Well, needless to say, Incomplete Maggie did not sit still as The Pastor expressed his displeasure with her statements. Bo held her hand while she stood up. I knew that it would take me several minutes to get our meeting back on track, while allowing Maggie to speak her piece. Incomplete Maggie was not shy about expressing her thoughts. I watched the two of them go back and forth about how the other one was such a poor example of a leader, and how I should consider relieving the other one of their duties.

All of us listened as they both spoke of the sacrifices, they both had to endure, working with one another. I swallowed several times before I realized it was time for me to break it up. It was no longer charming how they both went after each other for their shortcomings. All I could think was that I'd found myself in a senior citizen edition of the popular show "Law and Order".

When each of them paused to catch their breaths, I knew it was possible for an intervention to take place. If I did not get a handle on this situation, things would be derailed. I had never experienced the stern side of The Pastor. Maybe he'd grown tired of doing battle with that crazy-ass woman while I was gone. I was hopeful that they would both grow tired, sit down and *shut* the *fuck* up!

Erica jumped up, growing tired of both Maggie and The Pastor. I watched her as she was wearing a rainy-colored blue dress with matching heels. She was becoming undone listening to them both bitch and complain. The dress she wore captured my attention. It flashed before our eyes, just like neon sign did! While she tried to gain control of the room, I became fixated on her dress! When she asked them both to take a seat, a smile danced around my lips. She was trying to show that she could still be masculine even while wearing a dress. Mr. Lady (Erica) was showing the rest of the team that she could oversee any situation.

I just sat there and waited for my turn at bat. I felt as if I was waiting in vain for the room to calm down. That is when I pulled out a notepad and wrote down three pivotal words. These words kept repeating over and over in my head. I wanted to convey their importance to everyone. I looked at my employees and felt a flicker of hope arise in my mind. I was thinking that these three words could free all of us. I knew that there would be some skeptics. I was willing to show them that I was serious about my three words that were burning a hole in my mind.

Members of my team were growing tired of this scene. I knew that Erica could not command the type of respect that I could. That is when I placed my right hand on her left arm, cleared my throat, and spoke.

"Thank you, Erica, but I will handle things from here. I appreciate you trying to guide Maggie and The Pastor out of another misunderstanding. You and I have different tactics, because I am unsure that they want me to throw everyone out of this boardroom. Most times, your method of talking to our team seems to work. On some occasions like this one, though, I need to rely upon DIVINE intervention! I have a couple of things that I would like to say. Once I am done with my segment of this meeting, all unanswered questions and comments will have a home and a place to be answered. I have just enough time to present on what our day-to-day existence could look like from the other side of the coin!"

With my last comment, Erica sat down. Isabo began to rock in her chair because she knew that the grievances, I was about to air wouldn't be things my team saw coming. Since they had pushed this meeting a little bit too far, I was about to lower the boom on everyone in the room. That was the sacrifice offered up for all of them! I stood up and looked at my watch because I did not wish to show signs of weakness. I asked everyone whether they were finished speaking about whatever was on their minds. Everyone shook their heads to signify they had. I looked around the room and made eye contact with each person, wanting to be sure that they were all done before I regained control of this motherfucking Monday morning meeting.

"Well, if all of you are sure that you are all done, I will begin! First, let me start off by saying that I was rather pleased at how well you pulled together as a team while we were absent from the dealership. The sales and the profits that you made this weekend will be reflected in your upcoming pay, and I believe that all of you will be pleased! I am troubled, however, at how easily you pick each other apart. I am implementing a new rule here at Rox Sager Lexus from now on. I need all of you to take out a piece of paper. This new rule will not only become a legend at this establishment, but will be institutionalized and committed to everyone's memory! I will wait until you can write it down!"

CHAPTER 3

FEAR IS A GREAT MOTIVATOR!

I watched as everyone scurried to find a piece of paper while I kept a shit-eating grin on my face I and looked down at my fingernails. Once everyone had pen and paper in front of him or her. I continued laying down the law.

"The next time any one of you should open your mouth to express any form of displeasure that you might be feeling towards your co-worker, you will need to be mindful of the repercussions that you may unwittingly unleash upon yourself. It is my job to let you know that this line of negative action will no longer be tolerated on these premises! And it would be to your advantage to remember these three little words!"

I looked over at Incomplete Maggie, giving the impression that I came up with these words just for her. Knowing that no more than four words would be spoken by her was somewhat challenging. This would streamline our daily exchanges, making my choice easy for me to deliver. I knew that this phrase would not cause her any harm. I guess I was developing into a new creature that did not enjoy any measure of bullshit!

I then turned around the pad that I had written on, telling everyone to write down what it read! The notepad had three words written on it, reading, "LORD SAVE ME!" Once everyone wrote down the words, I explained that no matter what they saw here before them, we were a *team*, no matter what! I promised that the next time someone was compelled to talk or speak negatively about a co-worker, I would not only fire the person in question, I would fire the person who felt obligated to bring it to my attention.

"Just so that all you *motherfuckers* are clear upon this subject," I went on, "we are our brother and sister's keepers here on this premises. I do not give a good fuck what all of you do in your personal jaded lives. But while you are here working for me, when you set foot here at Rox Sager Lexus, you must understand that we all are a team. I need all of you to survive, so we *all* can prosper. I do not like to feel helpless as you speak ill about one another. It came to me as I was watching all of you talk badly about your team members. So, to cut down on the chaos and confusion, if you see one of your team members having a difficult time in a certain area, it would be to your advantage to help them improve or keep your fucking thoughts, concerns and comments to yourself and get out of the way!

"I will no longer tolerate any nasty comments from any of you. If you are not clear about what I have just shared, all you need to do is *fuck up* and say the wrong thing to me about a co-worker! You will find yourself standing on the other side of this building with them! You and your co-worker could be facing the unemployment line in a couple weeks together, if we do not get this small problem under control. Everyone knows that misery loves company. You will have a companion to travel with whoever wants to walk down this road from now on! So be mindful of what you say about one another. I will be watching and waiting!"

I licked my teeth as I looked all around the room and decided that I was not done with the lot of them. I tilted my head to the side and made eye contact once more, before continuing.

"Before we finish up with our meeting, I would love to hear all of you repeat the phrase for me to be confident that you know how it goes. So, whenever all of you are ready, you can repeat it on three: one, two and three!"

I could tell that they were thinking I'd lost my mind. Maybe they would pull together and act as a fierce, fighting team, and stop all this unnecessary BULLSHIT. But on the contrary, I was clearer about this new phrase that I was asking them to repeat than I was about anything else. In my mind and as far as I was concerned, The LORD would have to come down to Earth and ask me not to fire any of them. I was serious about them watching out for each other and if I had to threaten them with words from the Bible, then so be it. In my mind, there would only be few reasons why I would allow them to stay if they violated my new rules!

I watched as my entire team repeated, "LORD SAVE ME!" Once I knew that they did indeed understand the ramifications that their unkind words would have upon each other, I said, "Let's continue with the meeting, because it looks like time has gotten away from all of us!"

I informed them that I did not begrudge any of them for looking for employment elsewhere. I understood that I was asking a lot out of them, but I was tired of the backbiting that went on here. If we were going to be a team, then that meant we were each other's keepers! Finally, I wanted to address our last two subjects before we adjourned.

The first subject was our advertisement and the upcoming new car models that would be showing up soon. There were some corporate issues that we needed to address since some things were left undone before we went to the auto show in LA. I wanted to let them know that I did not wish to change anything right now.

"I love the look of our corporate advertisement because it displays such class," I stated. "To me, it appears well thought out and beautiful, but we should also allow the quality of our well-constructed cars to speak for themselves. Now that we are all in agreement with my previous statement, I would like to move on to one last subject. I was thrilled at the number of cars that we sold while we were out of town. Finally, maybe I should stay away a little more often, because we made our projected sales goal. The month has not even ended yet, so that speaks to the great teamwork from all of you. And if there is nothing else that anyone would like to address, then this would be a great time for us to end this meeting on a high note!"

I sat there and looked at everyone. That shit-eating grin appeared on my face once more. I knew they did not know I was bordering on another verbal outburst. I kept still and quiet as I thought about what I had said to all of them. Erica and Isabo hesitated before they stood up to exit. Bo stopped by and asked me not to leave town anytime soon. He knew that he'd have a hard time asking the LORD to save him before he speaks!

I smiled at him as my team exited the boardroom. I just sat back down in the chair and began to laugh! Mr. Chan and his family did not make a sound as I sat still in the boardroom! I wanted to give my staff some of their own medicine, and I found it rather funny that everyone was afraid to express his or her true feelings about what I had said to them. Truth be told, I did not give a fuck about what they thought about my threatening words. If they wished to believe that I would fire them if they spoke ill about a co-worker in my presence, then so be it!

Maybe one day I'd tell them that I was only kidding, but for right now, I knew that being part of a successful team for a long period of time was no myth. I just needed to have control of my dealership. If threats of physical harm would enable them to get back to the business of selling cars, then I had no problem with my tactics of abuse. I have found that fear is an excellent motivator. If my suggestion of calling on the LORD's name before they gave me any unnecessary information about a team-member was effective, then I had no more thoughts about the whole exchange that happened at our meeting.

I remained seated at the table as a scene from one of my favorite movies flashed into my head. It was a scene from the movie "The Wiz". For some strange reason, I was feeling just like the lead character named Evilene, who was a menace to work for in her sweatshop. She would inform her employees that under no circumstances should they bring her bad news.

I sat there humming a verse from "No Bad News", one of the songs that Evilene performed in the movie. I even laughed aloud for a couple of seconds. I heard a soft knock on the door to the boardroom, and called out to whomever it was to enter. I was almost feeling regal and majestic as I allowed this person to have an audience with me. A crazy smile remained on my face as that song entertained my mind, and I looked down at my nails once more. I knew that I had taught my employees a lesson.

While I waited for them to enter my kingdom of my conference room, I still had my head down with a crazy smile on my face. I raised my head and saw it was Lily making her way towards me. I softened my face as I lifted my head, so I could look at her. I cleared my throat before I said a word to her. I still had some harsh tones lingering in my mouth. I did not wish to be harsh to her.

Lily stood next to me. I could tell that she was a little bit nervous to be all alone in my presence. Seeing that I just bullied all my employees to conform to my way of thinking, I could tell that she was scared of me by the look in her eyes. I calmed her fears once I called her my flower, and smiled at her. I saw the tension leave her body as I asked her to sit down for a minute, but she wanted to remain standing.

That is when she began to inform me of some issues that needed to be addressed as soon as possible. She first suggested that I lay off the coffee. I had already finished three cups so far, and knowing that coffee sometimes made difficult to deal with, this was a gentle reminder to me to calm down some more. Then she reminded me of an upcoming meeting with the new head of security for the dealership.

"Ms. Roxanne, his name is Major Morrison, and he would be here on Thursday morning to meet with you and your managerial support staff."

I smiled at her delivery, because she seemed to be stuttering a little. I looked down at my hands for a couple of second while she was speaking. Finally, Lily presented me with a letter from the State of California. I asked her to give me a brief summation of what the letter was about She stated that it was time for me to be re-certified to carry my personal handgun for protection purposes. She knew that I truly needed my handgun to be my constant companion here at the dealership. I knew that I needed to keep my handgun ready at any given moment. I did not wish for anyone to believe I ain't got no business and they could do anything to me ant anytime.

I was preoccupied by what she was telling me. The other things that she had just mentioned did not trouble me like the gun issue. Mentally, I was looking at my schedule for the upcoming weeks, because I needed to address this issue very soon.

I decided to have Eric and Isabo deal with the new man from The Lexus Corp. Maybe they could tie up all those loose ends from the security breach. However, the thought of me not being able to carry a concealed weapon gave me a slight tingle down my spine! I asked Lily how long I had before I had to do this. She told me Friday of that week. That meant that I had to find myself at the local shooting range before the end of the week. My back was to the wall as far as time was concerned. Lily shook her head as we both agreed that I needed to take care of this issue right now.

"What about Eric and Isabo, don't they need to be recertified also?" I asked.

"Ms. Roxanne, Eric and Isabo took their pre-qualification test at the start of this year," Lilly replied. "You have been putting this off for the past 11 months. So now it's down to the wire, and if you do not go, you could lose your license for up to a year. It is imperative that you address this as soon as possible. We all know how much you enjoy having your gun as an accessory item."

Lily and I both laughed at my predicament, because what she said was true. I knew that I needed to fit this new event into my schedule. Sometimes, I get mad at myself for having such poor time-management skills. I was a busy woman, which is why I had no trouble with delegating things to my two co-captains. I asked Lily to clear my schedule for Friday afternoon. I asked her what else needed to be addressed that week, because next week is Thanksgiving.

I knew that I had to go over the menu with Gloria. I also knew that I needed to be on my best behavior and be understanding. This was our first major holiday without our grandmother, and it was going to offer its own special kind of drama, now that my sister invited my father and two new brothers to my house for dinner. We were not sure if our new sister would make an appearance. We needed to prepare for anything that might arise. Trouble enjoyed showing up and beating the shit out of all of us Beaumonts.

Lily pulled out my personal organizer for the dealership. I then asked if I could reschedule anything to after the holiday. She looked over my book and told me that I could wait to tour the banquet hall, in which my sister was going to get married in. I needed to address all the small matters before the time snuck up on me.

"You could go visit the banquet halls when you get off work," Lily suggested. "You still need to go and visit the travel agent, to pay for your sister's honeymoon …"

"Shit, *shit*, SHIT!" I exclaimed.

I've already admitted that I had poor time-management skills. I shook my head at all the things I had to do danced through my mind.

"Lily, how am I going to get these things done? The kids come back on the weekend and I need to spend some time with them, too."

"Ms. Roxanne, you always seem to pull things together," said Lily, "so these upcoming events should not trouble you in the least bit. I will help you get a little more organized."

"Take a seat and work your magic on me, because I really do need your help," I replied, gratefully. "I am tired of being on the run from time all the time. If you could take some time and help me, I would really love that!"

Lily sat down next to me and began to reorganize my life! Not only did she plan my life out into the middle of next year, she told me that I needed to delegate a little more to Eric, Isabo and The Pastor. I was shocked that she had kept her organizing skills to herself. I could not wait to put some of her ideas into action. I wanted to see how smooth my life could run without my always flying by the skin of my teeth! I know it was time for me to live more of a carefree life. While we sat there, I watched my flower bloom a little more, and I was proud to see it.

Once Lily and I redid my schedule, it looked as if I had a better life on paper. I looked at my watch as Lily exited the conference room. The time was 1:45p.m., and I needed to pee rather badly as I grabbed my belongings and walked back to my office.

The first voice message I cleared was from my children. They just wanted to hear my voice and make sure that I was OK. I smiled as I heard both talking to me on the phone, and at that moment, I did not wish to be a grown up. I just wanted to play with them because I liked the people that they were becoming.

Next, there was a message from my Akheem, just checking in with me. He told me that he would be in and out of meetings all day long, but we would talk before the day was over. He told me that he was feeling antsy and was missing me more than he

43

liked to admit. He added that he looked forward to our next adventure, so we should plan another getaway!

I knew that it would work itself out as things usually did. Then the third and final message began to play. I almost lost my breath because it was Trevor on the other end of the phone! He left me a very explicit message and I heard music in the background, possibly some Barry White. My heart began to beat exceptionally fast as he explained the reason for his call; I was stunned listening to his message!

He made me smile briefly while he said that hearing my voice on his phone made him reach down between his legs and give his balls a twist! I guess that old saying is true; the devil was in the details. I realized I had to give my exit strategy from him an enormous amount of thought and care, because I was in love with Akheem. I heard a short knock on my door as I placed my cell phone back in my pocket. I told the person to come in.

Erica and Isabo stuck their heads around the door and said in unison,

"LORD SAVE ME!"

They both seemed silly with excitement, as they repeated the phrase once inside my office, the tears and laughter beginning to overflow. Isabo was the first to speak.

"Roxanne, are you *sure* you want us to institutionalize those three words? To my understanding, you cannot force anyone to be their brother's keeper' but I could be wrong. It's sort of encroaching on everyone exercising their own right to worship any way they choose. Your blatant infringement could cause some unwanted repercussions, if you are not very careful."

Erica was still laughing over this forced issue, no less with Isabo all too eager to inform me that my request to the workers was unconstitutional. She kept laughing and repeating, "LORD SAVE ME"! Although I was aware that my request was going to be challenging, I was hopeful that we could cut down on unnecessary disagreements every Monday morning.

I was tired of going into a tailspin over bullshit. If my request seemed somewhat over-the-top, then so *be* it! Thinking about some fights that broke out during past meetings made me shake my head in disbelief. I was hopeful that I had both Erica's and Isabo's support during this time of transition at the dealership. I just did not need any more bad news from anyone.

45

CHAPTER 4

A BAD-ASS LITTLE GIRL!

Erica and Isabo sat still on their chairs, as I unsmilingly regarded them. I just sat back in my chair and surveyed their faces. When it was apparent that I was not kidding with anyone, the smiles that were plastered across their faces were swiftly replaced by blank stares. I began to count the seconds as my eyes met theirs. I could feel that they were both becoming a little concerned about my behavior. So, I licked my teeth and tilted my head to the right side.

Erica began to shift her position in the chair. Maybe she was experiencing a blockage of blood to her balls, or she had just discovered that she was wearing the wrong type of undergarments under the form-fitting outfit she had graced us with today. Isabo began to break eye contact with me. I could tell that both were scared, like fatted calves. They could sense their impending slaughter, because I showed them my teeth to let them know they could be next if we kept discussing being our brother's keepers!

After seventy-seven seconds of silence, I could no longer stifle my laughter! Once they saw me laughing, both joined in and told me that I should consider learning how to play poker. Because I hadn't allowed my face to give me away. For a moment, both imagined that I was telling the truth. I meant everything that I said in the meeting, because I wanted to give my employees something to think about—it all came down to respect.

Erica put in, "I thought you were kidding about the whole thing, but when I saw you lick your teeth and move your head to the side, I knew that we were going to accept your new policy. We would be thrilled to help you implement it! I can tell you this, Roxanne; you had me scared for a moment."

Isabo chimed in with the same concerns that Erica had just voiced. I was quite aware of the policies that state that you cannot force religious beliefs upon people who work for you. I just wanted to redirect our meeting to show everyone that if I chose to be a bitch. It would be an effortless experience for me. I do believe that I did convey my point of view this morning at the meeting. Erica and Isabo both stood and gave a standing ovation, the sort of praise bestowed upon dignitaries like me. I pushed my chair back from the desk and gave both of my co-managers the royal wave. Once I resumed my seat, both followed my lead.

All three of us broke out into convulsive laughter. It took us 13 minutes to end all our silliness. Then it was time for us to get back on track—we had business to discuss. I gave Isabo a gentle reminder that we would be visiting this fancy furniture store around seven o'clock that night. So, while we were wrapping up new business, I made a mental note to myself to give my mother a call. I told them that I needed them to join forces and deal with the corporate security officer that would be showing up later that week. We all agreed to act as one strong unit to represent the dealership in the best possible light.

We finished our private meeting. I told them both that I needed to leave work early on Friday because I needed to put some time in at the shooting range. Erica suggested that she would handle the man from the corporate office, if Isabo would give a refresher sales course to the employees. They both agreed on what issues they were going to address that week. I cautioned Erica not to be offended, if by chance the Major enjoyed looking at an authentic woman, not a wolf in sheep's clothing. I asked her just to be mindful, if he didn't not wish to have a man-to-man conversation with her. I didn't wish for Erica to suffer needlessly nor be embarrassed, if he didn't not respond to Erica in a positive fashion, depending on her outfit that day.

Erica assured me she wouldn't be offended by the visitor from Lexus' corporate office, adding that wild horses could not keep her from the meeting! I personally was thrilled with her enthusiasm. The reality is that Erica was often unsure how people really felt about her. So, it was my job to be a buffer in some situations that developed. Even though she was always the top salesperson every month, there were times when she had to walk away from a sale. Some people cannot handle the fact that she is a male who enjoys dressing in women's clothing. I wouldn't dismiss her for anything under the sun. If dressing like a woman soothed his savage beast, then so be it!

Isabo finished our conversation by assuring us she didn't mind playing second fiddle to Erica. She was eager to step in at a moment's notice if some type of trouble should arise. All Erica needed to do was give the "please rescue her" signal and she would make sure that she pulled out her cape to stand in or assist her at a moment's notice. I believe that this security breach will be a thing of the past, real soon.

I then asked them for a final favor that day. I wanted to know if they could find it in their hearts not to share the joke, I played on them with the other staff members. I wanted to see if we could make it through the week without someone feeling obligated to inform me of another coworker's inadequacies. If we could make it minus any in-house *bullshit*, I would gladly tell them that I changed my mind about the new policy.

"So, if the two of you could hold off letting the cat out of the bag, I would greatly appreciate a carefree week," I reiterated.

Erica and Isabo agreed to keep my secret. I asked them both if they had any questions for me. They both answered in the negative. Isabo told me that she would be ready to leave with me at 7 o'clock; all I needed to do was stop by her office. They walked to the door and turned around at the same time, saluting me. I smiled as I returned their salute.

The time now was 3:45 p.m. and I still had tons of things to do, but I found I was hungry. The meal that I had consumed earlier that day was only a distant memory. I had a craving for a big-ass egg salad sandwich, and got busy asking Lily to get it for me. I was having a serious fat girl moment because I was not dreaming of a healthy meal. I knew that I would not eat the whole sandwich. I would eat the sandwich filling and the chips, and drink some soda, breaking my cookies into four parts before also eating them!

After I ate and attended to my list of items, it was time to put on the whole armor of the Lord and call my mother. I wanted to find out if she had picked out a doggie companion for herself yet. God reminded me that He is always with me. I had nothing and no one to fear, not even my mother. I picked up my cell phone with joy in my heart, only to hear my mother's litany of complaints about her new toy poodle!

My mother's newly purchased toy was turning out to be a true disappointment as far as she was concerned. He was shitting all over the house! The dog, whose name was Speak-Easy, wasn't enjoying being her pet, either. She'd purchased that dog the past Wednesday and he'd had to have a medical procedure basically forced on him Friday. I did not know the reason she was being so cruel to that dog. I knew that when the time was right, she would help me understand the method in her madness.

My mother had the dog's balls removed and requested that they silence him by slicing his vocal cords too! I guess the dog is *well* pissed off with her by now. That was why he was shitting all over the house. My mother guessed he wanted to show her *some* form of gratitude for not also having his asshole sewn shut! I am afraid that her trouble with that dog is only going to get worse, but she got exactly what she had requested.

"Roxanne baby, was your trip successful, and did you meet anyone new?" she inquired.

I informed my mother that my trip was rather successful as colleagues and competitors surrounded me at the auto show. I felt it was not her business to know if I had come across any interesting new people. I had no problem allowing another lie to pass through my lips. I was almost high as I let those lies dash out of my mouth! I only wanted to keep peace and was quite aware that my mother was looking for something else to sink her teeth in. I did not offer myself up for slaughter, plus I know how to keep my own secrets.

I visualized the ass-kicking I needed to give my sister Cherokee. It was her fault that we'd have to interact with our father and newly discovered brothers and pretend that we were enjoying it. To my mind, spending time with them was not my idea of a great holiday exchange. I would sooner walk into the room and give each one of them a fucking slap across the face than to share a meal with them! If I am called into battle with my father and brothers, I wouldn't run from it.

Nonetheless, I planned on remaining neutral towards all of them. I would be on my best behavior for my grandmother's sake. Still, I knew that sooner or later there would be a disagreement on that special day, so I planned on having my boots already laced up and ready to go! I would not be on the losing side with my family because some days I cannot stand any of them. I guess God knows that we all are crazy. My mind was running almost out of control, thinking of the upcoming family event. Once I regained my composure, I heard my mother ask a question.

"What should I wear, Roxanne?"

She wanted to look beautiful for my father, which made me pause for a couple of seconds. I felt a small fire burning in my soul, but I had to remember that she still loved that man. And no matter how much I might dislike him; I might as well keep my comments to myself.

"Mom, no matter what you decide to wear you will still look like a million bucks. If you would like for me to go with you to pick out a special outfit, just give me a couple days' notice in advance and I will be at your disposal!"

"Thank you, baby," she replied appreciatively.

"You're welcome, Mom!"

She then began to scream at her dog Speak-Easy in my ear! I guess the dog was shitting in her living room. She told me that she needed to go, and we'd talk later this week! I smiled to myself because I heard her say all manner of vulgarity to Speak-Easy as she screamed at it once more. I giggled aloud when she threatened to tape the dog's asshole shut right as she hung up the phone. I did not know why my mother behaved like a bad-ass little girl all the time, but I guess it had been working for her so far in life. I smiled at her comments to Speak-Easy because the dog wasn't sure who was in control of that house. I guess if he managed to survive, he'd discover that he'd be at a disadvantage with her for the rest of his life!

I hung up the phone and decided to take a walk out onto the sales floor. I hadn't seen some of my selling staff since first thing this morning, I roamed around the dealership for almost an hour. I made small talk with some of the salespeople and walked to the repair shop, to say hello to the guys. Once I was done making my rounds, I walked back inside the dealership and made my way to Erica's office. I wanted to know if she was going to have lunch on site or was leaving the lot to have a delicious meal. She politely told me that her wife was bringing her dinner up to the dealership. If I needed to leave early, it was not a problem.

I thanked her for being here for the dealership and me.

"Roxanne, where else would I be?" she demanded. "No one has ever treated me as well as you have, and I rather enjoy being your right-hand woman or man at any given time. Working here with you has been a win-win situation for me."

Erica smiled as I walked out of her office. It amazed me how at home she felt. I knew that I had a couple more phone calls to make, before I departed at the end of my day. I got back to my office and sat back down at my desk. I sat still for a couple of minutes to make a mental note of how I wanted the new furniture in the office to look. That is when this crazy thought jumped into my head.

The thought was of something so silly I was almost embarrassed to finish the thought. I redirected my mind and changed my train of thought. I felt the urge to call my Mr. Fulwad and check in with him. I reached into my pocket and pulled out my cell phone, instructing it to voice-dial him. This crazy feeling was pushing and shoving at me and it wasn't until he picked up the phone on the first ring, I felt an overwhelming rush.

"Doll, I was just thinking about you and here you are calling me to say hello! I was aware that it'd been several hours since I last heard your lovely voice. I have just got to know, what are you doing right now?"

I was not too prideful to admit to my Akheem that I was missing him, too. I felt love and lust for him as my thoughts went to doing dangerous things to him. I found myself becoming so involved with the sound of his voice that I remained silent for several seconds. Akheem had to call my name twice before I responded! Mentally, I just cruised right on into having a needed conversation with him as we explored each other's day.

I told him that I was in my office, enjoying some alone time with him. Since it would be two more weeks before I saw him again, I just wanted to hear his voice before I closed out my day.

"I miss you also, Rocky! But let me tell you once more, I had a *great* weekend with you! You satisfied the hunger I'd been acquiring for you for these past three months. It pleases me to know that I pleased you also. Can I tell you a little secret, Doll— I was a little afraid of finally getting the chance to sexually experience you, but my time with you was *amazing*. I want to let you know that our next encounter will not be like the one we just had. I will try my best *not* to fulfill all of my desires in one weekend, because now I desire to see you *real* soon."

"Well, my question to you is, why not, Akheem? Because *I* plan on fulfilling all of my desires with you! When you finally find out the type of person I really am, you will be amazed, because I have a strong sexual hunger for you, too. I plan on attacking you and your body every chance I get, because, Mr. Fulwad, I don't need you to handle me with care! I wish to grow weary exploring that delicious body of yours. It will not bother me if you think my desires for you are greedy, because they are.

There's nothing you can do about it, except to feed my desire. You tempt me towards madness, Akheem!"

I heard him say, "Wow, Rocky, I see that you're going to be more than a handful. Believe me when I tell you that I am up for the challenge. I must jump over hurdles to satisfy you and that needful body of yours; know that I am the man for the job. We are going to have to end this conversation now and pick it up later tonight or sometime tomorrow, because I am getting hot and bothered by your voice seducing me. It would be to my advantage to get off this phone! I am on my way to another meeting and I do not need to step into the conference room with two guns in my pants, instead of one!"

We both started laughing because this was our first dirty conversation. There was so much sexual tension on the line, and he was tempting me, too. I was delighted in showing him a different part of me, too. I had been waiting for someone like him to show up in my life. He made me feel delicious as his voice trailed off. I realized this man was the perfect outlaw for me, as a sharp little chill ran up my spine.

CHAPTER 5

COMMITTED TO MEMORY!

"Akheem, I'm ready to make whoopee with you real soon," I confessed. "If I must communicate my desire for you over the phone, then so be it. There is always a chance that I am horny for you as your words and the sound of your voice are giving me several big ideas. So you might find yourself engaged inside several long and sexual conversations with me. You were the one who asked me to give you some of my time! If by chance you are not up for the challenge with me, I will dial down my request for you to have your way with me and allow you ramble all over my body."

"Maybe we should continue our private whoopee conversation later tonight," Akheem replied eagerly. "I promise you a conversation that you will not soon forget. We could synchronize our watches for the perfect time. I will call you, so we can continue with our conversation!"

Once I was done talking to Akheem, I got up to use the restroom and prepare to leave. I sat down at my desk and turned off my computer. I pulled out my lip-gloss and applied it to my lips, then there was a knock at the door, I told whoever it was to come in.

It was The Pastor on the other side of my door. I asked him to close the door behind him as I watched him make his way towards me! I prayed to myself that whatever it was he wanted to tell me would not take long, because I had something else to take care of. I did not wish for my evening to get away from me. As I looked up at him, a crazy smile came on my face.

"Baby Sister, I just wanted to stop by and tell you that it was a joy to see how you incorporated God into your Monday morning meeting," he began. "It was sheer genius the way you introduced your three words to be committed to memory, "LORD SAVE ME"! To see how you took control of that meeting was almost flawless, a thing of beauty. And the way you reminded all of us that we are each other's keepers … you don't have to tell me that your meeting was anything but divine

60

intervention, because I believe that THE LORD placed it on your heart to give all of us a reminder of His might and majesty."

I sat there and looked at the peace emanating from his body. It was not my place to tell him that it might not have been divine intervention. I hadn't wanted to hear any more of Incomplete Maggie's or his shit! If he believes that THE LORD gave me those three words to use, then I saw no reason to tell him otherwise. I knew that this man had something up his sleeve. If he wanted to waste my time before he felt the courage to ask for what he wanted, we could play his little game until it was time for me to leave.

I left the figurative door open for him to ask me anything since he was going to be my brother-in-law soon. He needed to find out how to talk to me, but I wouldn't be giving him a crash course today! Maybe he might just stumble upon plain old dumb luck and just *tell* me what I could do for him. I looked down at my watch and I saw that I had 27 minutes to give to him. I told The Pastor that he better get to the heart of this conversation because I had to leave soon. If I could help him with his request, he'd need to let me know now. If he could put some speed behind his request, I would appreciate it more than he could know.

"Baby Sister, all I wanted to do was check in with you. Did you have a great time on your little getaway, or do you not wish to talk about your trip?"

I looked over at The Pastor and told him that I did enjoy my business trip. I did not wish to be impatient with him. The Pastor sat straight up in the chair and told me that he'd conceived of a new idea for my dealership. The asshole that resided inside my mind was gearing up to show itself once more, because his words were catching me off guard. I suspected that this man had never given birth to anything other than a wet fart.

I really liked The Pastor, though, and he was going to become part of my family. I was going to allow him the chance to present his idea to me. He was one of my favorite people here at the dealership, so I smiled at him, inviting him to begin anywhere he would like to.

I was under a severe time constraint but wanted to be fair to him. I sat back in my chair and waved my hand for him to proceed as a smile danced across my face. I know that between the both of us our conversation was going to be a thing of beauty.

"Baby Sister, I thought of a novel move for us," The Pastor enthused. "To begin to offer our entire customer base a mobile detailing service for their cars. We would go to wherever they are in the surrounding city limits and detail their vehicles for them. Of course, they would have to schedule appointments in advance. Also, it would allow us to expand our customer base, plus it would grant us tons of accessibility and advertisements on the side of the cars! This service will only reinforce the integrity of the cars sold here. It could have a lasting effect on where our future customers purchase their cars. I believe that this could be a great business venture for us to embark upon!

"Also, Baby Sister, did I mention that I wanted to financially back this division of your dealership? I understand the risk that I am asking you to take with me. I promise you that this will be such a successful endeavor for both of us. I will purchase and pay for the cost to retrofit the equipment and all five of the SUVs to be used for this business venture. Of course, I know that you will sell them to me at cost and make sure that they have all the proper items inside them to maintain a respectful representation of this dealership!

"I already came up with a name and a business plan. I was hoping that you would like R.S.L. Mobile Details for the name of this new business. I pray that you are not too jaded by your past business dealings to trust me and give me a chance to be part of something big for both of us! Of course, you and the dealership would receive royalty fees for the business. I know that it must be hard for you to trust the stranger in me. All I can ask you to do is to pray on this matter before you give me your answer, say, when I return from my honeymoon with your sister!"

I was beyond impressed with his proposal while being introduced to another side of him! I was really enjoying what I was hearing. I began to stutter as I tried to find the right words to respond to his enormous idea that he had just presented to me. I was looking at the light that was coming through his eyes as he looked back at me. I could tell that he was unsure of what I was about to say. I was replaying his presentation over inside my head. I really did want to understand his presentation, but I did not wish to cut into my profit margin at the dealership.

I needed to investigate his concept for a new business inside the dealership. His idea did sound like a great one.

"Pastor, you have just jammed my mind with very exciting thoughts. I need to consider this new vision for Rox Sager Lexus! I can tell you this; you are a very smart man and you never cease to amaze me with your ability to offer me a new way to look at you! But until I have the chance to think about your proposal, I will hold off with my reply. Thank you for giving me a gracious timeline for after you return from your honeymoon. You have piqued my curiosity and I am unsure of how I feel about this new venture. Let me talk with you about this later down the road. I promise I will have an answer for you *before* you marry my sister!"

The Pastor stood up and extended his hand to shake mine. I stood up and shook his.

"Baby-Sister, I am mad with joy for the success that this new venture is going to bring all of us!" he exclaimed. "If you just place your faith in me, I will not do you wrong!"

I was proud of him as he looked back at me, asking me not to mention this to my sister.

On reaching the door, The Pastor turned around and said, "Baby Sister, I have often heard this song lyric, and I wanted to share it with you. It goes, don't let the sun catch you crying, because some things are just for you and THE LORD to experience! They are not open to debate or negotiation from outside ears and eyes."

And with that last sentence, he walked out of my office. I could not believe that this man knew the title of one of my favorite songs in the world. It is a song that by Ricky Lee Jones, called, "Don't Let the Sun Catch You Crying". I sprang from behind my desk to go after him but as soon as I got to the door, Isabo walked in. We almost ran into each other; my face was lit up with a smile and a tear hiding in my left eye. All I could do was smile as I prepared to exit my office.

Isabo and I left the dealership at exactly 7:00 p.m. each driving our own car. We headed for this classy furniture and business supply company located in the downtown area. I took the quick route while Isabo took her time. As she pulled into the parking lot, I was already inside picking out furniture for my dealership. I was not under any type of time constraint, but I knew what I wanted for my office. I had no problem walking up and down each aisle because when I found what I was looking for, I'd know!

Isabo caught up with me while I was still replaying the conversation I'd had with The Pastor! I decided to bring Isabo in on what he had asked me. She was equally impressed as I was. She told me that his proposal seemed to be a sound business investment. All I had to do was lend my name to his business. I then mentioned to her that he made his wishes clear. He would pay for everything that this new business would need. All I had to do was offer him shelter and a home for his business. He would pay for his own insurance for a year. He promised to show a profit in the next 6 months to a year or he would reimburse me for any trouble that he might have caused my dealership.

"Damn, Roxanne, that sounds like a win-win situation for all involved," Isabo commented. "If you do not have to invest any money, it sounds like you could make out like a bandit. You better have our legal team check into every aspect of his proposal. If things go badly for him and his business, you don't want to be held responsible. It is better to be safe than sorry, plus you should ask Akheem what he thinks about it. It will show him that you value his opinion and will grant him a little more room to walk around in your life! You know how men like to feel as if you are asking them for help, so this could be a great opportunity to draw the both of you closer."

I did see her point of view about The Pastor's venture. Not to mention the windfall that this new business could give all of us. I gave her comments careful thought, walking around the showroom.

Once I came upon a particular place in the showroom, I called out for Isabo and the salesperson to join me. I felt like I had found what I was looking for with this arrangement of furniture. I was standing in front of this massive ensemble and tried to make my way towards the middle of it. I could not believe that God had heard my plea for spectacular office furniture. I was already calculating its costs and what I'd planned on spending. I had no problem investing in my dealership. I just was praying that the price would not remove all the wind from my sails!

There were certain qualities I wanted my dealership to possess and I was about to realize the true price of beauty. As the salesperson walked towards me, he had a smile of success plastered on his face. Maybe he was thinking that he was about to make his sales quota for the whole month from me! He realized that I was his ticket to saving his company while he approached me.

I stood and watched as he licked his lips before he spoke. He extended his hand to shake mine as he introduced himself to me, opened the packet of prices for this furniture. I was proud that I had not fainted at the amount he had quoted me. He had informed me that this set of furniture was on sale. I removed my glasses as he was telling me about the details of that brand of furniture.

Isabo stood next to me while our salesperson Peter translated the advantages for me to purchase this set, since I wanted to re-do every room inside the dealership. I also wanted new furniture for my massive boardroom, but I did know one thing about myself—money was not an object for me at this time. Since this was a business expense, I had already had a set price in my head. I knew that I would not walk away without spending over a couple of hundred thousand dollars. I allowed him to present his selling points to Isabo and myself. I was thrilled to find out that the furniture would only cost me $225,000.00. Then once he was done speaking, I wanted to know how long it would take his company to deliver the furniture to my dealership location and remove my old furniture.

I wanted his company to drop my old furniture off at the local Salvation Army, because it was still in good condition; I just wanted my dealership to have a new upgrade! Peter told me that if I purchased all this furniture from him, he could have my old furniture delivered to the *moon*, if that would make me happy! I smiled at him and sked what percent he would receive from this sale. Peter replied that he would gain 10 percent.

"WOW, so you mean to tell me that this one transaction would give you over $22,500.00 in your pocket?" I exclaimed. I knew that I was being nosy and sort of aggressive, but I just did not care. For that large a bonus, I wondered what else he could give me. "Peter, I feel that I need something more from you. I know that you want to keep my business, so let me know what I can have as a gift from your business to mine?"

Peter responded, "Ms. Sager, for the amount that you are about to spend with my company, I can give you 5 additional accessory items! You let me know what it is that you would like to enjoy at your dealership, and I will make sure that they accompany your furniture, once it is delivered!"

I was pleased to know that he wanted this sale just as bad as I needed to purchase new furniture for the dealership! Now the number five was dancing around in my head. I told Isabo to find a nice piece of artwork for Eric's office and hers. I would locate a lovely piece for the lobby and for my office, as we set out on a massive scavenger hunt of sorts. I went in the opposite direction from her to see what little treasures I could locate. I needed something that capture my attention and maybe called my name!

Before I set off on my scavenger hunt for artwork, I went over my requested items from the sales paper. I wanted to make sure that I had everything I wanted for my purchase. I repeated my request to Peter and watched as he wrote everything down item by item. Once he was done, I wanted to know when I could expect delivery. Since we were ready to rejuvenate the look of the dealership, I was eager to find out when we could start.

Peter told me that it would take up to a week for delivery. He had to send to the warehouse for duplicates of desks and chairs. He wanted to make sure that there were no imperfections on my new furniture. He wanted to request everything new for me and if I did not mind the slight inconvenience of waiting an additional week for my furniture, he could schedule delivery for the day after Thanksgiving!

I shook my head no, because I preferred a Sunday delivery. Peter informed me that his company wasn't open on Sundays. However, if having the furniture delivered on Sunday would guarantee him the sale, he would share a portion of his commission with the delivery team! I told him that we had a deal, as I presented my Black American Express charge card. I shook Peter's hand, telling him I would be right back. I moved past him and started my search for the additional accessory items.

I was not sure what I was looking for, but I knew I'd know it when I found. I began to prepare myself mentally to be bowled over by what I would find. I hitchhiked my way through the furniture sales floor! I came upon a massive mirror that shaped like a tree and I smiled while looking at it. That mirror grabbed my attention and entertained my eyes at the same time. I stood in front of it and gazed behind myself! I knew this mirror was perfect for the entrance into the dealership, because I truly understood the art of placement of lovely things. I practice Feng-Shui myself, and already knew which wall the mirror was going on! Besides, I enjoyed watching people capturing their reflections in mirrors. This mirror was beautiful and I took a tag from that item.

I was off again to find something for my office. I was telling myself that I wanted something I wanted to look at all the time, not something busy, but simple. That is when I found this piece of Asian artwork sitting on a wall all by itself.

This picture offered me an instant pick-me-up as I looked at it! It was a picture of a Samurai warrior and a Geisha sitting on a bench next to a lush riverbed. The warrior was giving the woman his heart, which he was balancing on the end of his sword. Both characters were draped in red velvet outfits that clung to their bodies perfectly. Here was the item that held my attention. Red was one of my favorite colors, and the depiction of the couple kept transporting my mind back to Akheem and myself as I took a tag from it, too. The only item left for me to identify was one for the conference room.

CHAPTER 6

SURRENDER YOURSELF TO ME!

In the middle of searching for my final item, I heard my cell phone ring. It was Isabo. She was requesting my presence seven more aisles over from where I was standing. I told her that I would be right there, and set off to where she was. I looked down at the charm bracelet that Akheem had given me and smiled. I noticed that the time was 9:30 p.m. and was surprised that finding the perfect furniture had taken so long. Here I was, wandering around this big warehouse. I was yet to find out what I was looking for as I stumbled towards Isabo. I told myself that I could only commit to 30 more minutes at the warehouse before it was time for me to call it quits.

While I made my way towards Isabo, I began to dance down the aisles for some strange reason. I began to twirl and sing as I moved. When I got to Isabo's aisle, I was dreaming that I had a glass of champagne in my hand and I was toasting her! I was still proud that I had come in under budget, so I guess that was cause for celebration for me. I danced toward Isabo, who was smiling at me. I was being rather silly, but really, I was exhausted and becoming giddy because of it.

I did a final spin before I got dizzy and passed out in the middle of the warehouse. I stood next to Isabo and gazed in the direction in which she was looking. Isabo pointed at a three-foot tall statue of a woman holding a lantern. All I could do was hold my breath, because the statue looked just like Isabo. It was almost scary looking at that statue while it looked back at us.

This statue consisted of silver-looking glass, but the glass had a hammered and polished look. This was truly a work of art and I could understand how and why it fascinated her. The fact that that statute looked so much like her was uncanny. I asked her what this piece said to her. Any fool could tell that she saw herself inside this piece of work.

Isabo said thoughtfully, "It is saying to me that no matter how lost you think you are in this life; I can help you find your way home!"

"Damn, that was deep, Isabo," I mused. "Did you find something for Eric?"

She informed me that she did find something for him. It was a small statue of two women holding hands. I asked why she chose two women.

"Because Eric really enjoys her wife and she loves dressing like a woman," she explained. "I could not think of a better way to show her love for her wife than to capture them both as little girls. I believe that she will enjoy this work for herself, and since it is not too overbearing, it just looks like something that she would find beautiful! It shows that we appreciate the uniqueness that she brings to all our lives at the dealership!"

"That's a good answer Isabo," I replied, nodding. "Do me a favor and help me find some artwork for the conference room, will you? I am so ready to go home, and it has been a long day. My mind is slowly leaving me while I stay here. If you help me find the perfect piece, we can both leave this place at a decent hour."

Isabo grabbed me by the hand as we set off once more. It was dawning on me that there was an art to finding the perfect picture. I watched as Isabo looked down one side of the aisle. I kept my eye on the other side of this section. It was good to see that we still made a great team. When she showed me a few pictures that she thought were appropriate, I did not like them, so we just kept on looking.

I did not experience the feeling I was expecting, as I told her that I would know it when we found the perfect picture. Knowing that this picture would hang right behind my place at the table in the conference room, I told her that it had to possess a certain type of wonderful. I did not know how to convey to her what I was looking for, so we just kept on walking.

We walked down each row of furniture and accessories I felt that we were about to stumble upon a masterpiece, but we did not find anything that stood out. All I wanted to do was exit this building until I saw Peter, the salesperson, moving toward us. He walked up to me with a big-ass smile on his face. He had a stack of papers in his hand. Peter asked me to step over to his desk to sign several copies. I placed the tickets from all four of the accessory items he was going to include with this sale, so we could be done.

By now, I was crestfallen. I'd wanted to choose all five of my items so they could be included with my order. Although I was not having good luck finding the last item, the evening had been mostly positive. I asked Isabo to keep looking for something that would charm me, and told her that I would be right back. In my mind, I knew that I might have to come back later this week to find the perfect picture. I was not locating a masterpiece tonight. All I could find was pictures of ordinary things, and ordinary would not do for my team and me, because there was nothing ordinary about any of us.

I followed Peter towards his office, my eyes still dancing up and down the walls, just in case. I was giving my eyes a tour, and *that* was when I saw the picture that lifted my spirits! I began to laugh hysterically as I walked towards the picture! It was of three eagles, all involved in some type of bondage!

The first eagle had gold fasteners over its eyes. The second had fasteners over its ears, and the third had a fastener over his beak. All three eagles had their heads tilted in the same direction. Each bird's head was leaning to the right side while they all stood on one leg! I knew that there was a subliminal message for all of us. The more I looked at the picture, the more I saw what it was trying to say to me.

To me the picture quite eloquently stated, Harm No One. It reminded or reinforced the saying from my youth that said, speak no evil, see no evil or hear no evil. The picture offered no distractions as far as I was concerned, because it just simply said to me, "LORD SAVE ME!"

Even though it was cloaked inside a funny picture, I got the message because God also delighted in the details. The picture was just what I was looking for. I alerted Peter that I'd found the final piece of my promised five accessory items! Now, I was truly happy, plus I could end the evening knowing that my request for the gifts to speak to all of us, was met! Peter asked me to pull a ticket off of the picture and I did. I grabbed that ticket and presented it to him as I walked into his office to sign the paperwork.

By the time we were done with this transaction it was 10:25 p.m. I told Peter that I would see him that Sunday morning and thanked him for all his assistance. Isabo, however, wanted to know if I wanted to go have drinks with her. I knew that I would not be great company if I drank tonight, so I declined her request.

"Thank you darling, but no thank you for that lovely offer," I began. "I need to be going home, because I have a lot of things to take care of tomorrow. I need to have my phone call with my Akheem. We must reschedule sometime this week for the two of us to go out for drinks. Thank you once again for accompanying me while I searched for new office furniture. It has been a pleasure to have your company. I will see you around one o'clock tomorrow, because it is my turn to close up at the dealership."

We hugged each other in the parking lot then got into our vehicles. I arrived home in 45 minutes and was so thrilled to park my car in my driveway. Once I was secure inside my house, I set my alarm to secure my perimeter. I placed my handbag on the kitchen table and removed my high heel shoes. I walked to my refrigerator and tried to find a nutritious snack. I had not eaten since earlier that day and was famished. I was not successful in my search. Gloria had been gone for almost two weeks and my food supply was low. I grabbed a container of yogurt, and a bottle of water.

I went upstairs to my room and removed all my clothes as I ate my yogurt. I plugged my cell phone up and wrapped my hair. I drank half a bottle of water, while I started my shower. I pulled out a pretty pair of pajamas and placed my shower cap on my head. I stepped inside a steaming hot shower as my mind and body began to relax. I was aware that I had just finished with one busy day, while tomorrow was going to be equally as challenging. I was so relieved that I made it through, while I began to cleanse my body and inhale all that hot steam. I lathered my body three times, then let the water remove all the soap from me.

I thought for a moment that I heard my cell phone ring. When I turned the water off, I did not hear a sound. I rubbed lotion all over my body before putting on my pajamas. I just wanted to enjoy the smell of that fragrance. It was a bottle of lotion that I purchased in Texas. I began to think about my Akheem more and more. I told myself that I needed to hurry up and call him, so I rushed and found my phone.

I noticed that my cell phone had two missed calls on it. Both were from Akheem, so I hurriedly redialed his number. The truth was I wanted to hear some tenderness in his voice as badly as he'd said he wanted to hear mine! My call went straight to voicemail; I did not have a message to leave for him, so I just ended the call. Right at that moment I received another call. I accepted it and it was Mr. Akheem Fulwad on the other end.

"Rocky, I was becoming concerned about your whereabouts. I am so glad that this third phone call has found you." As he spoke, I was all smiles. I told him that my heart was missing him also.

"I hope more than your heart is missing me," he went on. "I was under the impression that you were missing more than my heart."

I was very quiet as Mr. Fulwad began to talk dirty to me. I must admit that he was doing an excellent job of turning me on. It had been a long time since I had phone sex with someone. I was somewhat rusty for a couple of minutes but once I found my sexy voice with him. I became committed to being as naughty as I possibly could. We both were having a great time talking shit to each other! It was a very sexy conversation. His voice and his words showed me what he was going to do to me when he got his hands on me once more.

If I was the type of person that got off on talking dirty, I might have experienced several orgasms. But dirty talk didn't really turn me on as much as it did him. It showed me another lustful side of Akheem, the side that is mad for sex, because I wanted him *here* with me, rather than on the other end of the phone. All the talk of sex didn't work for me. I was glad to know that Akheem enjoyed himself, however! He wanted to know if I was pleasuring myself while we were on the phone. I could hear the disappointment when I told him no, I was not. Akheem wanted to know whether he was saying the right things, or did I want him to be dirtier than he had been. I smiled as I began to answer his question!

"Akheem, it does not make a difference how dirty you talk to me. I have found that I enjoy real sex more than your explaining to me what you plan on doing to me. Your talking sexy to me allows my mind to think harder about you! No matter how hard I wrap my mind around the sexual tension that I might have for you, I will not climax because I need the real deal for me for me to enjoy myself. So, until I gaze upon you, I am enjoying hearing your voice! I just want to let you know that it is nothing personal towards you. I just need you to enjoy yourself, and hearing you being pleased is more than enough for me."

"Well, Doll, I'm sorry that our little session did not do you any justice. When I see you by the end of next week, I am going to invade your body as if I'm stealing from a foreign country! By the time I finish fucking you, you are going to check your ass into the hospital, just so you can rest!"

Both of us began to laugh uncontrollably. I was becoming moist at how forcefully he was talking to me, and as he continued to describe what he was going to do to my body. I told Akheem that I was getting hot because of what he had just said.

"You are the type of woman that does not wish to play with herself, unless you plan on getting fucked right after the conversation is over with!" he told me.

"That is correct, sir," I agreed, "but don't be cruel with me, Akheem; you only know the parts of my life that I wish to share with you for now. You must learn to be patient with me, and if by chance I am not as experienced in some areas as you might be, the deeper we become involved, the more you will discover that there will be nothing left hidden from you. Before we end this phone call, tell me what you plan on doing to me when you finally see me!"

"I plan on mugging you and your body! Maybe some hostage negotiations will take place. Then, I wish to place your snug pussy inside of a chokehold, all while using my flexible dick to make you surrender yourself to me. Your body will be in a stupor by the time I am done with you!"

"I did not know that your unit was flexible!" I exclaimed, blown away by what he had just said to me, I let out a semi-frightened laugh! I waited a couple of seconds before I spoke again.

"Akheem, do you know how to place me in a chokehold?"

Akheem laughed on the other end of the phone.

"Rocky, have you forgotten that I used to be a cop? I know how to do an assortment of things to restrain a body that is trying to get away from me!"

I was at a loss for words, but I was strangely afraid and turned on at the same time. This was new and uncharted territory that we were embarking upon. I did not know in what direction to move. I was strangely intrigued by what he had just said to me! My mind was sort of running away from the idea of being in a chokehold. I was going to offer myself to him once we were together again, but now I was slightly concerned that this man could hurt me, something so alien to my mind. I wanted to be clear about my position on the subject.

"Akheem," I ventured, "do you wish to harm me, or are you just searching for something to say? Because I want to make sure you know that I do not enjoy violence being perpetrated upon me."

"Good to know, Rocky," he responded, "because I don't enjoy dishing out violence, especially to someone whom I am in love with. So, you need not worry your mind about that subject. If me talking firm to you frightens you, I will never bring up mugging you ever again. It means nothing to me to give up talking hard to you. I just got caught up in the moment, and I humbly ask your forgiveness. Will you forgive me for scaring you, Doll?"

I told him that I forgave him, and that while I very much looked forward to our next conversation, it was time for me to be going. Maybe our conversation had not really sunk into my mind. But before anything else could be said to cause more damage, I felt I should end the conversation. I told Akheem that I prayed he had a good night's rest.

Akheem wanted to make sure that I understood that he was only kidding around. I assured him that I was aware, plus I'd even been thinking that I was way too sensitive. I added that after a good night's rest, maybe I would have a different outlook.

Since I possessed violent tendencies myself, it felt rather strange to be having this discussion with Akheem. I didn't enjoy violent sex of any kind. Since I loved sex just as much as he did, I didn't wish the lines to become blurred for both of us. When I was with him all I wanted to do was enjoy the pleasure that we both brought to each other, and this was not the time or place for this discussion.

I reiterated my willingness to forgive his telling me he knew how to do me harm if he wanted to. I was no longer interested in carrying on our conversation and was trying to back out of it, but he would not let me go!

"Roxanne, was it not *you* who called me today with sex on the brain?" he demanded. "Now, our line of conversation is somewhat inappropriate for you. It seems to me, Ms. Roxanne, that you need to make your mind up about which direction you would like for us to go. I refuse to be jerked around by your indecision. So, from now on, let me know which type of conversation you would like to have with me: I will not take the blame for this misunderstanding between the two of us. You will have to face that you were an active participant during our exchange. And, just so that we are clear, you are not the only one who has hurt feelings. I recommend that you consider giving me an apology also, and maybe I will think about forgiving you. Ms. Roxanne, it is too early in this game for us to be mad at one another!"

There were about three minutes of silence between us then. I heard myself speaking in a soft voice! I did *not* expect our conversation to spin so out of control. I did call him earlier today wishing to enjoy a sexual exchange—but *now*, I was determined to offer him some clarity from me!

"Akheem, please pardon me for being such an ass with you earlier today. I do adore you and I am sorry that we are having this silly little misunderstanding. I have no desire for my careless words to disrupt our feelings for one another. If we could start this whole phone call over, I would surely appreciate it! Because Mr. Fulwad, seldom will you find that I am willing to back down from anything or anyone. But with you, there is no need to fight over words.

"And it is true that I did initiate our raunchy exchange of sexual talk with one another today. But the thing is, Akheem, for just a split second, you scared me by telling me that you were going to mug my snug pussy. I forgot that you used to be a police officer in your former life. I really enjoy you and I do not wish to fear you in the least bit. Because, Akheem, I don't have the time to fear you. All I want to do is be in love with you. I guess that is something I will have to work through. Please allow me to apologize for my carelessness with you, and if you give me some time I will change!"

I paused for a couple of seconds to let my apology sink in. Then, after a 39-second delay, I decided that it was time for me to speak once more. I knew that my meaning had finally gotten through to him; moreover, I was sorry. Sometimes my real feelings could hide themselves inside crazy statements, and I wanted to make sure that we were back on one accord. We just didn't have the time to travel down such unnecessary roads with each other.

My mood was changing as I cleared my throat to speak again. The fact that we were away from each other more than we were together made me realize that I was being somewhat unreasonable, and I needed to make peace with him. I did not enjoy disrupting those happy vibes when I did get the chance to encounter them. I wanted to end our exchange on a happy note. I was unsure what was really bugging me, but I knew that I needed to place it on hold while I was dealing with Akheem. Sad to say this but, for me, Trouble was always right around the corner. Always waiting to do me and the people I loved some harm.

CHAPTER 7

I HAVE HIT THE JACKPOT!

I wanted to show Akheem that I loved him, so I said, "I hope that you will find a place in your heart to forgive me. I feel as if I have hit the jackpot with you. I am sorry for making you aware of some of my feelings about our relationship. Even though I know that my life is not your typical storybook life, neither is yours. There are times when you say the strangest things to me, and in those times, I am frightened. There is still so much we don't know yet about each other. As I've said, I do not wish to be afraid of you, Akheem, but there are times when you chill me to the bone with your cold comments. No doubt when I better understand and appreciate you and your sense of humor, well, needless to say, it will be a great day for all of us. I will feel better about some of the things you say to me and be more mindful of the things I say to you!"

There was silence on the phone once more. We just listened to each other breathe. I guess my confession sort of hurt his heart and stung like a bee! I was hopeful that he had accepted my apology. I wished we'd ended our conversation sooner. I felt that things were in danger of spinning out of control. I was sleepy and needed to cut out the crazy feelings I was having. It was not my intention to derail this exchange. I was leaning on one shoulder as I waited for him to respond to my comments, but in the back of my mind, I suspected things were going to hell in a handbasket. Seconds danced before my eyes as I was hopeful that we could salvage the situation. I was hopeful that our friendship and love affair could continue, as he began to speak.

"So, let me get this right, Doll, am I to understand that I frighten you sometimes? And the fact that I used to be a cop troubles you just a little bit? Do I have that part of our conversation right, or did I misinterpret your meaning? Because the last thing that I wish to do is frighten you!"

I began to count seconds once more because I was becoming upset again. I was not upset with Mr. Fulwad; I was troubled by my own fucked-up comments to him. I knew that I needed to do some fast damage control before things got all the way out of hand!

"How is it that our conversation went from being one of a sexual nature to one that has taken on a shameful undertone?" I asked. "I did not mean to derail this conversation with some shameless concerns about you harming me. The truth is, I have been known to be a violent person, also. But the difference between us is I am just *talking* shit to you, while you *could* make me suffer under your touch. I desire for you to forgive me for being careless with my words."

I tried to laugh, as a distraction tactic, and to let him know that I was only kidding ... but it did not work. Silence prevailed as I tried to clear my throat and offer him a chance to speak his piece. I guess he was stunned on the other end of the phone, so he remained silent for a nice length of time. I began speaking once more when I heard Akheem exhaling on the other end of the line.

"I am not sure where that line of concerns came from," I went on. "The more that I think about it, I don't fear you, Akheem! I know that I could love you with all my heart one day soon! I guess both of us are exhausted and have had a very long day.

93

That is why I am asking you to allow me the opportunity to back out of this conversation. I feel that you are pretending not to be enraged by my comments, so I need to let you cool off because I spoke out of turn once more! If you love me like you say you do, allow us to call a truce for now. Maybe we can pick this conversation up later this week, once we have both had a chance to rest and regroup!"

I felt like I was standing under an umbrella with 25 different holes in it, drowning beneath my own words! I was asking him for shelter as I listened to him on the other end of the line.

"I will speak with you tomorrow, Rocky! Have a good night's sleep!" Akheem said, tersely.

Sad to say, I was reliving several nasty scenes from my past. Scenes where I let my mouth get me in trouble. I was pissed off at myself for talking out of turn once more. I was not aware that I was indeed in the process of sabotaging my relationship with Akheem. I was aware of the rules of disclosure and full disclosure, but it looked as if I had just said some things to my man I couldn't take back, and he was not in the mood to forget or forgive me. This was a new type of Trouble I didn't need, because I knew that my comments to him were uncalled for. I needed to learn to shut the fuck up sometimes, but the damage was already done, since I had hurt his feelings!

I asked Akheem, whether he would forgive me for my comments. His reply was that he would have to get back to me on that! I was trying to cast a lighter air on our conversation, but I was not successful in reaching him; so, before we hung up and ended our conversation, I was going to try to make him smile!

"Akheem, again, I'm sorry for saying the stuff that presents itself in my head. I'm throwing up a white flag of surrender. I didn't mean to sound so unkind. I love you, Akheem, and I do not wish to end our conversation with both of us sulking! I fear that I have hurt your feelings—please forgive me, before we hang up!"

"Well, it seems like it is officially Rabbit Season tonight," Akheem stated. "You just served me up my ass on a platter with your words! Good night, Roxanne!"

Seemed like he had no concerns for me because with his last three words to me, he hung up the phone! I just sat in the middle of my bed, crying and screaming inside! After seven minutes of tears, I pulled my cover back and said my prayers as I lay in bed. I looked over at my clock and saw that it was 1:45 in the morning.

I was at a loss. I just closed my eyes and fell into a daydream-like sleep! I felt my Angels get in the bed with me, but I did not open my eyes to look at them! I just lay there and wished I knew how to travel back in time, so I could undo what just happened.

My clock went off at 8:00 a.m. I knew that this was going to be worse than yesterday. I had to get on with my agenda so I got dressed, did my hair and made my way downstairs. I knew that I needed to place my crazy feelings on hold for now, while I made phone calls to my kids and got ready to hit the road. I looked at my watch and saw that I had missed my window to talk with my kids because they were already in school by the time I was about to leave. I pulled out my organizer and went over what my day would involve. I saw that I had an 11:00 a.m. meeting with the travel agent. I needed to go pay for Cherokee and The Pastor's honeymoon. I told myself that I would call my kids later that day. I knew that I would need them to help lift my spirits before the day was over … a thought that made me smile.

I ate another cup of yogurt and had some green tea. I stepped back upstairs to brush my teeth and check my face. Once I was done with my daily maintenance, I grabbed my handbag and made my way back downstairs. I picked up my keys to leave as my cell phone went off. I saw that it was Akheem calling. I rushed to put my handbag down and answer his call.

"Good morning, handsome, and how are you doing today?" I gushed.

"Good morning, Rocky, I need to talk with you before the day gets away from either of us. I need you to promise not to get upset by what I am about to say to you."

"I promise, Akheem!"

I sat down at the kitchen table and allowed him to speak. He cleared his throat and began to tell me his truth. I felt his hurt that I caused coming through the phone line. Some bad vibes were floating around the airwaves because I was feeling a certain disconnect to him as he spoke to me. I had no doubt in my mind we were about to do battle because I felt this knot growing in my throat, my body bracing itself against the atmosphere raging on the other end of the phone.

"Well, I never knew it was possible, but you shamed me last night!" Akheem began emphatically. "Even though all is forgiven as far as I am concerned, maybe we should reevaluate our relationship. So, for the rest of this week, I will not call you to check in because that is the kindest thing that I can do for the both of us. I hope that you will do the same for me too. I need you to respect my wishes and do this for me; I hope that when we speak sometime next week, you will be ready to continue with this relationship.

"As I said, the last thing that I want to do is scare you, Roxanne. Promise me that you will not call me until next week, and give our relationship the thought and care that you should. Hey, I want you to be sure that you wish to be with me and only me, because fear should not even be a part of our exchange, Rocky. I need you to know that I only have love and respect for you. Do me this favor and let some silence fall between the both of us!"

I was at a loss for words because I thought that we were in the process of enjoying a great love affair. If he needed some time away from me, then I'd give it to him, gladly! I pretended that his words were not hurting my feelings as his words began to linger in my ears. I practiced saying, "I promise" in my head first, before I let the word slip past my lips. I was hopeful that a feeling of compassion would show up, or the Lord would make a cameo appearance and offer Akheem a different feeling about me. Sadly, no such thing happened. This man was taking his love away from me, and it was my fault. It was as if I had lost my luster with him.

"I promise, Akheem!" I managed to say.

He told me he hoped I had a great rest of the week and that we would talk next week sometime. He hung up the phone as my body became cool. I picked up my handbag and walked out the door. I secured my home as I got in my car and backed out of my garage, and simply got on with my day. The tears threatened several times, but I would not let a single tear escape from my eyes.

I knew that I could keep my mind off him, but he did not tell me that he loved me, and I did not get the chance to say it, either. And it could be that he is still so upset with me and maybe I made a bad move with him by showing him some of my frailties. It could be that his image of me was not what he thought but I will grant him all the time that he needs and if he wishes for me to withhold myself from him, I cannot make him wish to see the real me!

I pulled into the parking lot of the travel agency, strictly admonishing myself to keep my head up all throughout the day.

Next, I looked at my cell phone to check my time. I was still on schedule to be at my dealership by one o'clock. I checked my hair in the mirror and saw that a tear was forming in the corner of my eye. I grabbed a tissue and gently wiped it away before it had a chance to form! I got out of the car walked into the agency.

I had an appointment with a young woman named Jo, while I signed into the log and took a seat. Jo came out from her cubby and welcomed me. I followed her back to her desk and sat down. I told Jo that I wanted to give my sister and her new husband an exquisite gift for their honeymoon, one that they would never forget as long as they lived. I added that I wanted to send them on a one-week cruise and give them a one-week stay in a foreign country.

Jo asked me if I had a specific destination in mind, and I told her a Mediterranean cruise and a week's stay on the Canary Islands.

"Wow, Ms. Roxanne, that sounds like an exciting trip!" Jo enthused. "I am sure that the happy couple will enjoy the thought that you have put into this gift. Let's get started and put your wishes down on paper, to see how best to craft this gift for them."

She asked when I wanted to schedule the trip. I told her that the wedding was taking place on New Year's Eve, and I knew that they wanted to leave shortly after the exchanging of vows. I had no wish to leave anything to chance, which was why I was there petitioning for Jo's expert help with these matters. She gave me a big smile and told me to sit back, relax and watch her work her magic! I asked her how long it would take, for her magic to take hold. She asked if I had a spending limit I wanted to adhere to. I told her to pull out all the stops because it was my sister's first time getting married, and I wanted the best for her. Jo cracked her knuckles and asked me to give her 15 minutes!

We both set out to plan the trip of a lifetime for the two of them. I requested that she include first-class air transportation. Helicopter tours over the islands, and spending money for all the ports that they would visit. I wanted travel insurance included in the package. I sat back and watched her place my entire request inside a lovely package and present her findings to me. I was pleased with what Jo came up with! She had scheduled them to leave for their honeymoon two days after the wedding. She also arranged for the Pastor and Cherokee to view a different stage show every night on the cruise ship.

She included shopping tours, food and beverages, and dinner nightly at the Captain's table, and for their stay on the Canary Islands. They were booked into a five-star hotel. There was a daily tour guide assigned to them both, and they had the choice to either dine out at a fancy restaurant, or have a chef privately prepare a sumptuous meal for them, nightly. She presented her findings to me inside a red folder. The whole package with everything, including her commission was at the outrageous price of thirty-five thousand dollars. Knowing that I was not going to help pay for the wedding made me feel at ease. This price did not destroy my train of thought; it only made me wonder how much was going to be enough for Cherokee to have the honeymoon of her dreams.

I did not wish to spend any more time on the gift. I pulled out my personal credit card and paid for it. Jo was overjoyed when the transaction went through, and I signed at the bottom of the receipt! She got up, walked around her desk and hugged me! I took the folder from her hands and stuffed a couple of her business cards inside my pockets. I signed the receipt and told her that if there were any changes of plan, my sister would be contacting her.

I shook Jo's hand and prepared to leave. Jo told me that it was a pleasure doing business with me, and if I had any other travel request, I shouldn't hesitate to call her. I told Jo that she was an exceptional salesperson and I was rather pleased with the outcome, but I didn't plan on paying for more cruises anytime soon!

That is when Jo volunteered, "Maybe I can plan a romantic getaway for you and your husband?"

I politely told her that I was not married, and romantic getaways didn't happen for a person like me. She told me that maybe my luck had finally changed. I shot her a dirty look before I put a smile back on my face! I told her that I needed to leave and thanked her once more for all her help. I placed the folder under my arm and walked out. I could not get in my car fast enough, and drove off as tears flowed down my face.

I was slightly running behind schedule for my evening shift at the dealership. I pulled into the parking lot at 1:15 p.m. I turned off my car, looked at myself in the mirror, and began to threaten myself once more. I told myself that I could not afford to fall apart at work, nor did I have time for tears. I needed to pull myself together and snap back into business mode. I had several other issues to address and if I was very careful with my time, I could squeeze in some time to cry later tonight, once I was home. I exited my car with a smile on my face, remembering in time that I *did* have the good life.

I vowed to keep my head up the rest of the day as I moved to the entrance of my dealership. I began to sing Tupac's "Keep Your Head Up"! My cell phone began to ring as I walked through the door!

I said my hellos to all my employees as I walked inside. I headed straight to my office while I answered the phone It was Peter, the salesperson from last night. I asked him to hold on for a moment. I asked Lily to bring me a cup of green tea, put all my items down, sat behind my desk and began to speak with him.

"Good afternoon Peter, what can I do for you?" I inquired.

He laughed on the other end of the phone.

"Ms. Roxanne, there seems to be a slight problem with the scheduling for the delivery of your furniture."

"What type of scheduling problem with the delivery, Peter? Because to my recollection, we scheduled delivery for next

Sunday! So, in my mind we are still on track with the delivery date."

Peter let out a sort of nervous laugh before continuing with our conversation. He informed me that the delivery date we had put down was not going to work for him and his team because it was the holiday weekend. Most of his staff would be out of town, but if I wanted to have my furniture delivered on the following Monday, it would not be a problem. I then told him that if he could not deliver as promised, then I would just come back into his place of business and cancel the whole transaction.

I made him aware in no uncertain terms that I wanted my furniture when I wanted it! Peter asked me not to be so hasty with my decision. He suggested that he have the furniture delivered to the dealership that coming Sunday. I remained quiet for a couple of seconds before I told Peter that that Sunday would be quite pleasing for my team and I. I mentioned that I wanted every piece that I'd chosen, and if by chance anything was missing, I would not accept the delivery at all. I still expected my five additional accessory items to be included with the delivery! So, if his company could abide by my request, I didn't have a problem rescheduling the delivery date.

Peter let out a sigh of relief because in the world of retail, the customer is always right. Since he promised me something, I expected him to keep his promise. I was aware he was already spending the money from his commission in his head. By my calculation and many other people's standards, $22,500.00 was a nice little commission to walk away with! I was sure that Peter was going to be more than accommodating to my dealership and me.

I told Peter that we had a deal and I would see him and his team at my dealership around nine o'clock Sunday morning. Before we concluded our conversation, I told Peter, "Please, don't make me wait for you!" I offered him a bit of advice while he was dealing with me. I informed him that it would be to his advantage to double and triple-check the truck before it showed up at my dealership. I wanted to avoid any form of misunderstanding. If we agreed on this contract, I would see him on Sunday morning.

"Thank you so much for your help with this unfortunate situation, Ms. Roxanne," said Peter graciously.

"Peter," I replied, "the situation is only unfortunate if you come unprepared to my dealership. I welcome seeing you and your team. Now go on and have yourself a great rest of the day!"

He told me to do likewise before we ended our conversation. I was not trying to be dismissive towards him. But now I had to go out and request that my team show up to help me receive the new furniture. I sat at my desk for several minutes, thinking. I needed to ask my staff to work on Sunday. I was willing to offer them an additional incentive if they showed up to help me. I was willing to offer each employee triple time, because my dealership never opens on Sunday. I knew that it was going to be a chore for them to show up. I was confident that it could be done without too much fuss. I was thankful in knowing that my team would not let me down! Since it was only Tuesday, they had more than enough time to redo their schedules. I was prepared to make special allowances for the time in my head. I began to count seconds until Lily brought in my tea!

Once she gave me my cup, she asked me if I was all right. Truthfully, she was the one who looked sort of *out* of sorts. I refrained from asking her whether she was alright. I guess her personal life was of no concern of mine. We were not friends like that. Lily worked for me and I tried my best to keep to myself — only if she needed me would I open up more. I was unsure what was going on in her life. I told her that I was fine, but I had a question for her. I did not wish to share any part of my life with her because I was a private person. I kept my brokenhearted-ness to myself. I asked Lily if there was any way possible that she could come in to work for three hours on Sunday. I told her the story about the furniture.

I explained I needed her to help keep an eye on everything. Lily's face lit up with my request for her help! She seemed like she wanted to applaud my asking for her help. Lily has such a silent eloquence about herself, but since she is just an employee, I kept her at arm's length. We both did a great job of concealing our true feelings. We both exhibited a convincing show of our lives, but it wasn't overstating it to say that one day we would likely each come undone. But for now, I was thrilled that she had agreed to help. I knew that we would make a great team to whip the dealership into shape on Sunday. I was happy to have her accompany me, if her schedule was not too hectic.

Lily said, "For you, Ms. Roxanne, it will not be a problem ... but what time are you speaking of, because I teach Sunday school for the junior girls."

I told Lily that I did not wish for her to miss helping with church, so it would not be a problem if she did not come.

"Ms. Roxanne, Sunday school starts at 9:30 in the morning and it only lasts for one hour. I *want* to be here to help you with your office, so look for me around 11:45!   I will stay with you until everything is in its proper place, because I know that you value this; I will make sure the office is perfect before I leave!"

CHAPTER 8

MY OWN PERSONAL ESAD!

There was no way of knowing that later down the road I would have a great friend in her. I shook my head yes to her. So much time had passed between the both of us. But for the rest of my life, I knew that I would never forget her, as I smiled and looked at her.

"I welcome your help with this matter, Lily, and thank you for being such a team player. Now that I have purchased everything that I wanted for the dealership, I need to make sure that this redecoration goes off with as little drama as possible."

Lily told me that she would see me on Sunday morning.

"Thank you, Lily," I called again, as she exited my office.

I asked Erica and Isabo to come to my office and both appeared quickly. I began to fill them in on the story of the furniture store, and how they would be here on the coming Sunday to deliver my order. Both guaranteed that they would be able to assist with the redecoration of the dealership. I asked them to petition assistance from all the employees, and if we could get at least half of the employees to show up on Sunday, I believed that we could successfully be done by three o'clock that afternoon.

"I believe we will have more than half the dealership participating," Erica observed, "because the incentive that you are offering is just like saying, pretty please with sugar on it! I believe that we will successfully be done with our mini-facelift for the dealership before our time frame is up!"

She wanted me to describe how the furniture we chose looked. I told Erica that the look on his face would let me know if I got the right things. Erica smiled at my comment as she reminded me how much she trusted my taste. She could tell by the way that I was speaking about the furniture that it was going to be magnificent. Isabo did not want Erica to know about the special sculpture that she had picked for her!

Out of Erica's view, Isabo motioned to me to cut the conversation off. I told them that I had to cut this meeting short because I had a couple of phone calls that I needed to make. I reiterated how I needed at least half of the staff here with us, as we ended our meeting. They both told me that they would inform the employees about our plans for Sunday morning. Erica and Isabo added that it was already done, as far as they were concerned.

I looked down at my computer screen and saw that it was 4:45 p.m. I still had not spoken with my kids all day and I needed to use the bathroom rather badly. I ran to the restroom to relieve myself, then once I returned to my desk, I popped a couple of mints into my mouth, commanding my cell phone to call my children. Franchescia answered, laughing hard, and I could hear some type of noise in the background. I asked her what was going on, and where she was. She told me that she was at a video arcade with her father and her brothers.

"I'm sorry honey, was that a singular or plural use of the word 'brother'?" I asked, incredulously.

"Mom, I used the plural version of the word, because I am here with my father and my *brothers*. You heard me correctly the first time. Before you began the interrogation, we are all having a great time! So, how are you doing today? Are you missing the both of us tormenting you?"

I counted for 17 seconds before I answered her questions!

"Fran, I have never interrogated you and I am sort of offended that you would think that I am doing that! I would not want you to miss out on this golden opportunity to get to know your new brothers, and just so that we are clear, I will interrogate you when you return home!"

Both of us began laughing. I added that I was great. I looked forward to seeing her and her brother later that weekend. I wanted them to enjoy their time getting to know their two brothers. I then asked her to let me speak with her brother.

"Mom, you're going to have to call back," Fran said. "Anthony and Sager are battling one another on some outrageous video game. He told me that he does not wish to be disturbed right now. If you could possibly call back to speak with him later tonight? I will be sure to give him your message."

If her comments to me were not so outrageous, I might have been offended by her putting me off to speak with him! I dismissed her juvenile attempts at being Anthony's secretary. I informed Ms. Franchescia that I would indeed call back. I hope that her brother is free to speak with me then! But if by chance he is still distracted with his brothers, I would simply call him tomorrow. At the end of our conversation, Fran blew me a kiss over the phone line. I thanked her for her lovely gesture, told her to tell her father, I said hello, and that I wanted she and her brother to both have a great night's rest. I was about end our conversation, when Fran spoke again.

"I love you too, Mom, and I can't wait to see you on Saturday."

I let out a small laugh before I said, "I love and miss you, too!"

We both hung up the phone at the same time. My thoughts were on getting myself something to eat because it had been a very busy and long day. I'd only had tea and yogurt to nourish my body and was developing an uncontrollable hunger. My stomach was growling at me. I thought that I had a taste for this sumptuous Chinese chicken salad! Those meals never seemed to disappoint me when I was hungry and today, I was hungry and ready-to-eat!

I had been holding out all day long just so that I could have this meal. I was not sure if I wanted to grab some take-out to eat.

Knowing that I was going to be closing up tonight, I felt like I needed a brief change of scenery. I grabbed my handbag, turned off my computer and prepared myself to leave for a brief escape. I stopped by Isabo's office and told her that I would be back in an hour.

She replied, "See you in an hour, Roxanne! But before you go, I just wanted to ask: are you alright? You seem somewhat out of sorts, and I was concerned about the sadness around your eyes."

"I guess my body was paying its dues from my very long and extravagant weekend. Maybe I have not recouped yet. Also, I have not been sleeping well because my house is empty. And most of all, I miss the background gibberish that has been in my house since I can remember. Sometimes it seems too quiet for me to rest."

"While that explains some of your distance, is there anything else you would like to talk about?" volunteered Isabo.

I told her that I was fine as I walked out of her office. I made way to my car and drove off in a hurry. I ended up at a local Chinese restaurant and placed my order.

I consumed my meal and became lost in my thoughts. I sat in the back of the restaurant and ate my soup without interruption. I was reevaluating my life when my three Angels showed up. They were all interested in why I was dining by myself, why I hadn't learned to shut the fuck up. My mouth would keep asking for trouble if I did not learn how to be silent! Interestingly, my Angels were all dressed in waitress outfits from the 1950s!

All of them had their hair styled in one of those beehive hairdos. Each one had on a poodle skirt with a matching sweater twinset. Even though we were not located at a drive-in movie restaurant or a diner from the past, all three of them also wore roller skates. So, while they rolled towards me, I did not know whether to laugh or cry. I knew that I was about to be lectured as I was looking for a back exit from the restaurant. They had already boxed me into the corner where my seat was, so I allowed them to say their piece.

I knew that my Angels were here to do heavenly business on my behalf. I did not understand why they were so concerned about my disastrous relationships. I came to realize that I might not ever understand what was going on in the spiritual world for me. I just needed to trust that they had my best interests at heart. I was preparing myself for my verbal lashing, but all three of them were smiling at me! I looked at my personal help from the Lord, but I felt hopeless. My ESAD (Earnestine-Samantha-Ann-Danielle) knew that I was a fuck-up and they were here to rub it in my face! My Angels knew my heart and maybe God sent them to calm my spirit.

"Did I think or say something funny?" I demanded. "All of you are looking at me with smiles on your faces. Before we mov forward with this exchange, I want to make sure that I did not say or think something stupid!"

Earnestine was the first to speak.

She said, "Ms. Beaumont, since you are so concerned with what other people see you doing right now, all anyone here is going to see is a woman having lunch by herself. They cannot tell that you are having a conversation with us. I just wanted to answer your question before we got started. We do understand that you do not want to look like you have lost your mind, sitting at this table talking to yourself. So, no one else is aware of us but you. That is why we are all smiling at you, because for a second you thought that maybe you had outgrown us. That was a sad thought for us, that you thought you didn't need us anymore. That idea sometimes hurts our feelings. But it is apparent that you still need us. Look at the mess that you have made of your relationship with Mr. Fulwad!"

"I did not mean to cause any hard feelings between Mr. Fulwad and myself," I explained. "Sometimes I do not know how to shut my big mouth! I seem to keep suffering for that aspect of my personality. Maybe one day I will get it right. I do love that man, but maybe I am not ready for him. It could be that I am just an asshole!"

They all started to laugh at me!

Then they said, "Yes Ms. Beaumont, you *are* a stupid, gaping asshole! But it is our job to help you steer clear of some of your own pitfalls! Believe us when we tell you that you are a piece of work and you need us more than you would ever know. We are hopeful to guide you in the right direction, although it is a challenging road to walk with you. We are still up for the battle, because you do so much good for other people. But for the life of us, we do not understand how one soul like yourself can keep fucking yourself over and over, every time things start to align themselves in proper order for you!"

"Ms. Beaumont, you are wasting your time climbing mountains that you have no need to go up against," said Samantha-Ann. "You keep foolishly allowing your mouth to cause harm in your life. You should be tired of that aspect of your life by now. You are one of those creatures that often deserve to have the fuck knocked out of them. Too often you seem not to learn the lesson, so it is our job to lead you back on the right path. If we allow you to continue down this road that you are traveling, you will unravel; not just your life, but you could possibly destroy innocent bystanders as well, with all of your unnecessary foolishness."

Danielle, who was in the process of rearranging her beehive wig, only looked up at me and shook her head in disgust before she decided to speak to me! I knew that she was going to let me have it, because she seemed to always dislike me. Her eyes began to scold me.

"BITCH, what *is* it that you do not get? Danielle demanded. "Did we not warn you about harming Mr. Fulwad, because there is a bounty on your head should you not succeed with him? You are systematically destroying your life with your beautiful mind, while you offer a refuge to others. It concerns us to know that you are not being mindful of your actions with your own life. You have this strange tendency to save other people, but you remain careless with yourself. You are not covering your own heart, Ms. Beaumont, and it pains us to stand by and watch you be dangerous with yourself.

"So, while you are in the process of rescuing everybody else, you have allowed your mouth to roam and destroy the life of an innocent soul. Mr. Fulwad is an innocent soul with you, and we were being truthful with you when we advised you to take care of him. It was not a suggestion; it was an *order*! We were not playing around, Ms. Beaumont. You better do what you need to do to get yourself back into his good graces! It would be wise of you not to let this discord between you linger until the end of next week!

"We have no problem with cutting you down to size. You deserve to have your ass kicked, because that mouth of yours is your downfall. You wander around inside your own fucking life like you are some sort of tourist or something! It would be to your advantage to pull out some of your tricks that have worked for you in the past! Tricks like being a big ass-kisser or a ball-swaddler. If you don't get back in step with a worthwhile agenda, you will do more harm to everyone else's life than you are supposed to!

"You have the power to stay in our good graces. If you do not get your life back on track, or cause his heart any more problems, well—we will be forced to erase you from this life! Although we are undecided on what to do with you. Make no mistake, we will have you removed from your life in the blink of an eye, Ms. Beaumont! Time-out for offering you idle threats for now … we will have no choice but to act as one and do away with your worthless, stupid and sorry ass!"

I sat there confused as hell with all three of them looking back at me. I was about to risk it all and question them. I was trying to understand what they were trying to tell me. They had lost me when they said I was harming Akheem with my careless conversations with him. They were my Angels and they knew my course in this life. But it seemed to me that they were acting on Mr. Fulwad's behalf instead of mine.

For them to threaten to have me erased caused me all sorts of confusion. I can only speak on my soul's behalf, but by no means do I wish to know what it is like to be erased, until it is my time to exit. I do have a beautiful life, no matter what some people might think! I have so many people who need me, but I wanted a deeper understanding of how I was causing Akheem's life to be altered.

I thought that I would ask them why I am so pivotal in Mr. Fulwood's life. But before I could open my mouth to form the question, Earnestine jumped back into the arena of tearing me a new asshole!

"Ms. Beaumont, how many more times do we need to tell you how special you are? You have so many souls entangled with you that you need to assess how pivotal a role you really play in other people's lives. Allow us to give you a small look at how your soul touches more people than you will ever know. And why Mr. Fulwad needs you more than you will ever know, because you surround him and his life with light. Compared to the life that he used to live, you have offered him and his heart a place to call home.

"We know that you do not know this, but Mr. Fulwad was supposed to pass through this life and move onto the next one when he was shot! He kept hanging onto hope and started praying that he could find someone to make him smile. He wasn't dismissing the life he had with his wife and kids; he just wanted someone who had his best interest at heart. We were aware that he loved his life, but knew that he wanted more. Then he sent a prayer up to GOD and asked for you, Ms. Beaumont! Although he did not know your name, he knew that he wanted someone like you! This man lost everything that was important to him only so he could find your crazy and sorry ass!

"We are sure that you are aware that your life has prevented numerous others from perishing, all for your own selfish reasons. You seem to keep hindering your own ability to move forward. You keep your eyes on your own circumstances, but there is always a bigger picture going on behind what you think you see. We prayed that you had learned to be more mature in your understanding of how this world really works! That is why we are telling you, that you are making everyone pay the price for you not keeping your eyes open and your mouth shut!

"That is why we are here, to give you a brief glimpse of how your fate has intercepted several souls in your path. Your random interlude with some of the people in your life has saved them from being evacuated from this life without experiencing someone with a kind heart and soul. You are that soul, Ms. Beaumont, even if you do not recognize it. You are a wanted person and you have danced with more souls than you care to acknowledge. Let us revisit the past 24 hours in your life, so you can see what we are talking about. Then and only then might it ring true to you, how truly needed you are!"

I just sat there because I knew that they were speaking of my family. I knew that my family needed me, but I never knew how deeply they did. I then started humming the song "What A Difference a Day Makes"—24 little hours, even though I did not know who sang it. Next, Samantha-Ann took over where Earnestine left off.

"Ms. Beaumont, we are not talking about how much your family needs you. We are speaking of non-family members, and in that way, you can see how badly we need you to get in step with the plans God has for you! First, allow me to tell you of someone that you offered hope to. It was a beautiful thing to watch unfold, even though you were not aware of it.

"Let's go back and revisit your exchange with that woman named Jo, whom you helped out of a dire situation a couple of hours ago! Remember, Ms. Beaumont, she is the one who worked at the travel agency! Jo was about to be fired because she had not made her sales goal in over nine months. Her boss had already prepared the paperwork for her departure at the end of the day! But the fact that you stepped in and pulled her back into the work force, only made her more valuable to her place of employment. You're the angelic interruption that her life and soul needed. Now she can float through the rest of this year and be at peace, while she continues working. She has made her quota for the whole year with your one transaction!

"You gave her such a great reminder of what it is like to have someone be kind to a stranger, because you never know whom you are really dealing with. The fact of the matter was that you could have told her that you needed to think about your gift to your sister, but you did not. You reached past your own self to give a gift of love, which helped *her* also. Let's not forget Peter, the man who works at the office furniture store. Your actions saved him and his company from being consumed by a bankruptcy case. You offered his company a chance to regain their footing while he was at his wits' end yesterday. He had everything to lose. He had to make the choice to call it quits, but your lucrative purchase gave him back his company's independence!"

I just kept my mouth shut as they continued to talk with me. I did not wish to feel what it was like to be erased by them! Once they were done speaking, I asked several questions for a stronger sense of clarity. Then Danielle took the floor, so I placed my eyes and ears on her. It came to me that they always spoke in the order of their names. They were always my own personal ESAD, my own Eat Shit and Die, or Earnestine-Samantha-Ann-Danielle! I never paid any attention to that fact about them, until now. I heard a soft voice call to me from far away. I looked around the diner but there was no one looking in my direction. I thought that maybe my mind was playing tricks on me once more as I smiled to myself.

"Last but not least, Ms. Beaumont, let's not forget about Lily," Danielle went on. "This is your second time at rebooting her life. You offered her a new life when you paid for her rent for seven months in advance, so she could move out of her sister's house! And when you sent Bo over to pay a little visit to her then brother-in-law, to fuck him over like he did her! Well, that was the bridge that she needed at that time in her life. And today, Ms. Beaumont, you offered her another bridge of help!

"However, you passed up the chance to have a great friend in her. Her saving grace from you came when you requested that she come by to help you on Sunday! You had a teachable moment with her, when Lily asked you if you were alright! You missed another opportunity that GOD was presenting to you! But later, you rushed in and helped guide her to safety once more. You see, what I am about to tell you, Ms. Beaumont, is breaking a promise that all of us took when we signed up to be your Angels!

"We are not supposed to interfere with other souls while on their journeys. But you need to know this. By not allowing Lily into your life, by not becoming friends with her, you have altered her path. You will not like what is going to happen to her if you do not mend your ways with her, because she needs you.

"You need to find a way to reach out to her before it is too late! Lily has been so lonely for the past couple of years. She is so lonely, in fact, that she has concocted the idea to take her own life this Saturday night! There is a mental cancer growing in her, because she has been a sort of outlaw in her own life. Informing her sister of the harm that her husband had done to her has caused a rift between them. Understanding that no one would come looking for her, she knew that she would be able to follow through with her plans to end her life!

"But when you asked her to show up on Sunday, you pulled her back into the land of the living. She left out one very important detail, because there is no Sunday school class that she teaches! It was all a lie because she didn't want to trouble you or cause you any pain in suspecting how lonely she really is. Ms. Beaumont, you gave her something to live for, something that most souls long for, a sense of purpose and direction. Someone to need and to be needed by someone, is one of the things that makes a soul happy. GOD only knows why, but she admires you!

"Not to mention that she wants to be your friend, but you keep her at arm's length. We need you to let her in along with others, because it does not interest us how you find satisfaction, Ms. Beaumont! We could care less if you got the idea in your head to go out and fuck a stiletto-wearing simpleton. It's not our place to judge you, but when you hinder a soul from its greatness, then we have a problem!

"So, go ahead and fuck that savage bastard from LA, if it pleases you, even though you never have allowed Mr. Fulwad to find out about your little escapades. We don't care if you choose to cast pearls before swine. Mr. Fulwad is your diamond, Ms. Beaumont! You might not see it now, because you have become used to second-rate emotions from your mates. But Mr. Fulwad is different, and there are several other people eager to meet you further on down the road. You just need to get your head on right, because you really should be tired of being careless with your own self."

CHAPTER 9

POWER STRUGGLES

As Danielle spoke to me, I felt awash in helplessness as tears rolled down my face. I knew that I was in the presence of GOD, because the sun still shone while I cried. I never dreamed that Lily was lonely. I did not know that Akheem was my peace on Earth right now—I realized that all any of us ever has is right now. I guessed that my Angels being so honest with me turned out more demanding than they expected. I knew that I could not allow Lily to kill herself. If I needed to rescue her from herself, it was no problem for me. I liked her and I loved that man. I sat still and kept my mouth closed until I was told I could speak. All three of them were staring at me. Maybe they were waiting on me to say something stupid, but I was still replaying some of the things that they said to me.

I waited for 55 seconds before I said a word. It was news to me that love was my passion on Earth, and that I was needed by other souls for them to pass through this life! I was aware that I was not the wisest person you would come across sometimes. But at this moment all I wanted to do was go sit in a corner! The enormity of what they had presented to me was overwhelming. I dried my eyes before I spoke. I was trying to get my bearings. I wanted to fully understand and admire the fragile gift that was given to me.

"Ladies, thank you, because you have just changed my life," I ventured. "No matter how badly I try to destroy my life, I will not damage another soul. Since you three have seen fit not to have me erased today, I am inclined to believe that you don't see me as hopeless. I promise to do my best not to destroy another innocent soul while I am here! I need you to do me a favor and allow me the chance to repair the problem with Akheem and myself.

"Let me claim my own miracle with him, and since he does not wish to speak to me until next week, I will use the time to prepare the proper words to say to him face to face. Please allow me to grant him his wish. I want to find a cozy way into Lily's life, and that is going to require some thought on my part, but I know that I will reach her. I am also so proud to know that I could help total strangers along my path. It lets me know that I indeed have a spiritual agenda. If all three of you could hold off with erasing me for now! I believe that I could do a better job of helping my family and friends in this life without the possibility of being swiftly escorted from it!"

I was hopeful that they would allow me to move at my own pace with Mr. Fulwad. But there was a sense of urgency with Lily and I needed to strike while the iron was hot. All three of them agreed to my conditions. But I was issued a warning about Mr. Fulwad! I had until the end of next week to get us back on track with each other. I could not manage to clear a path back to him by myself. If I didn't, then, they would remove their hands from me and I would be just another lost soul, walking around this world all alone.

My Angels reminded me that GOD had his hands on me. Unlike some people, once GOD removes himself from you, your life no longer has meaning. It is as though you have been ERASED! I told all three of them, don't write me off so soon, simply allow me the chance at righting several of my wrongs to those who do not deserve it!

My Angels informed me that it was time for them to go. They all became transparent while sitting at my table! I looked down at my watch to see how long I had been gone. My mind was riding its own merry-go-round! I could not believe that I had been gone only 45 minutes. The time that I spent with my Angels felt like several hours, but they had only been in my presence for 15 minutes. The server was standing at my table with the bill! I was aware she was there, but she did not register in my mind because I was thinking of how much I had to get done! I paid for my meal with a smile on my face, and then it came to me. I would ask Lily for help and invite her and other employees over to my house for Thanksgiving dinner! I needed to get back to the dealership before she left for home! I wanted to ask her in person to collaborate with me and help me become more organized.

I left a generous tip for the server as I walked out the door. I got into my car and called the dealership. Incomplete Maggie answered the phone, as I repressed a frustrated sigh.

She said, "Rox Sagar Lexus."

"Maggie, allow me to invite you over for Thanksgiving dinner, next week at my house."

"I will be there," she assented.

I said, great, and added how I looked forward to having her over. Then I asked her to speak with Lily.

Incomplete Maggie said, "You just missed her."

I asked Maggie whether Lily had a cell phone. "Yes, she does!" came the reply. A pause of seven seconds followed. I smiled and said,

"Maggie, do *you* know Lily's cell phone number?"

"Yes, I do," came Maggie's reply.

I was having a hard time concentrating on traffic. I wanted to be nice and let her go through her normal routine of bullshit, but I did not have the time to play with her. I raised my voice and asked her to give me Lily's cell phone number. Maggie let out a sigh and asked me if she could help me with my problem.

"Maggie," I said, teetering on the edge of rudeness, now. "If you do not give me that number, you will find yourself uninvited to my home for dinner!"

Predictably, Incomplete Maggie gave me the number—but in four-number increments, with the last increment being three digits. Altogether, she gave me ten numbers. I asked whether I needed to dial the area code before I called her.

"I don't think so," Maggie replied.

By the time I concluded my exchange with Incomplete Maggie, I was pulling back into the parking lot of the dealership! I was screaming inside my head with frustration. However, I thanked her for her help. I made a mental note to collect all my employees' cell phone numbers just in case I needed to get in touch with them personally. I parked my car and made my way back to my office. Both Eric and Isabo were waiting for me to return. Eric reminded me that he would be off tomorrow, but he and Isabo would take care of Major Morrison from the Lexus Company on Thursday. Isabo informed me that she would be off on Saturday, but she would be there to help all day long on Sunday! I asked both of them to wait for a couple of minutes, because I had something to discuss with them.

I informed them that they were welcome to come over to my house next week for Thanksgiving dinner. Next, I asked them both to forgive me for handing them over to deal with someone from corporate office, but I had other issues that required my personal attention. I told them that I normally I would've dealt with Major Morrison, because I was not an irresponsible business owner. I trust that they would guide us through this uncharted territory. I would take the helm and steer my dealership towards success if they found they were having a hard time handling this matter.

They thanked me, adding, "OK, but we are still here if you need us. Don't hesitate to ask us for help!"

I was glad to know that I still had their support, but this was my dealership. I would find out what was going on with this meeting scheduled between my dealership and the corporate office. I watched as Eric and Isabo walked out. The sales staff were still on the job, as there were plenty of people looking to buy a new car. I left the staff to handle all the sales because I had a very important phone call to make; I was wondering what to say to Lily.

My mind was set on the task at hand while I sat down at my desk and turned on my computer. I felt almost afraid to call Lily, but I knew it was something I had to do I dialed Lily's number and she answered. I apologized for calling her after business hours. Lily graciously said it wasn't a problem to talk with me while she was on her way home.

I began to invade her phone with my petition and plea for her help in securing a caterer for Thanksgiving dinner. I told Lily that it would please me if I could have her assist me. I also extended an invitation for her to join my family and me for Thanksgiving dinner. My disclosure about what I needed her to do for me might have been overwhelming to an amateur. I knew that Lily could handle everything I was asking her to do. I was going to tie her life up with mine, so much so that she was going to beg me to release her or at least give her some days off, by the time I was done with her!

She responded to my request with bubbly laughter, advising that she knew of the perfect caterer for my event. She added that she would be overjoyed to enjoy Thanksgiving dinner with me and my family! I noted that she slipped into helping me with such ease and asking was not complicated for her at all. Maybe I was the one who was fearful of asking for help with something. Now that I know I had Lily involved in my life, I would find a way to ingratiate myself in parts of hers. The last thing I wanted hanging over my head was to be penalized for not helping a lonely soul out who was under my professional authority. I could tell that she was happy on the phone, and I reminded her about our plans for Sunday at the dealership.

Lily chirped, "It would be my pleasure to help you with the small remodeling of the dealership, Ms. Roxanne. Maybe I could even come just a little earlier to help remove your paperwork from your desk and organize your things for you!"

I told Lily whatever time she could give me as appreciated, because I was aware that she was a busy woman. I valued her carving out this time to assist me. I mentioned to her that I also needed to pick her brain for some key pointers that would help me to become more organized. She gave a high-pitched laugh, which made me smile. I told Lily that I must be going now, but I welcomed seeing her tomorrow, and we ended our conversation on a high note. I felt like I'd made some headway with her, and now that I knew that she needed me, I would relentlessly include her in some of the goings-on at the dealership and in my life!

I pulled the projected sales to close out the year, looking at the screen for a couple of seconds, a slow parade of numbers dancing before my eyes. Before they could distract me all the way, I realized that Bo was standing at my door. I motioned for him to come in. I asked him to have a seat and tell me what was on his mind. I already knew that this was not going to be a sweet-as-candy conversation. He had a look on his face that was sort of chilling to me. I watched him close the door and take a seat in front of my desk. He almost crashed into my seat, seeming somewhat out of sorts.

"Please forgive me for barging in, Ms. Roxanne, but I need to speak freely with you," Bo announced. "It is apparent to me that I am not doing a good job of hiding the love and rage that I feel for your sister Maxey! She has refused to marry me and even though I have asked her on three separate occasions, she has turned me down. I find myself always begging her to give me some type of consideration and allow us to join in holy matrimony. I am thinking about her and the baby, and I want to do more than just pass some time with her.

"I love her, but she is not giving any thought to my request. Ms. Roxanne, I feel as if she is laughing at me! There could be an argument made that I might not be as smart as she deserves. I am determined to show your sister that she will *never* find anyone to love her and our baby as I already do! I want to give her all of me, even if she believes that I do not deserve her because she is way out of my league. It could be that she is looking for her own, personal Superman!"

I just sat there and looked at him. I could tell he was growing weary of pursuing my sister with his whole heart and soul, to no avail! I was thinking to myself that Bo had turned one of those corners in his mind where he'd vowed to be the man to make my sister proud. I believe that he was mentally selling himself short, because he was a very smart man. For him to come here and proclaim that he desires to marry my sister makes him still more valuable. I knew he just needed some guidance and direction because his time with my sister gave him purpose, despite his past.

"Bo, you need to practice more patience with Maxey. She has a different set of circumstances before her, which caused her to be a little more cautious than normal. Dealing with her heart and her accepting your proposal will happen once the time is right for both of you. You cannot force a heart to love you; it takes skill and time for her to release herself to you. The baby offers another set of rules for both of you. Since you don't have any children yet, it is going to be exceptionally challenging for the both of you—so if it means slowing down just a little bit, then so be it.

Be the bigger person and allow her to tell you when she is ready to say "I do"! You never know, Bo; it could be any day now, or not until next year! Just hang on in there and I promise you; I will speak with her about her intentions towards you, because we do not want you to feel overlooked, or used. Do me a small favor. Give thought to falling in love with my sister and the new baby just a little bit more, and from there you might be able to show her that you are a keeper! Because I already know that fact for myself ... I would not trade you for another person for all the tea in China!"

Bo smiled at me as we finished our conversation. I promised him that I would have a talk with my sister in the very near future, to find out where her head was at about him. I asked him to not be surprised if things didn't change overnight, but if he loved her as much as he claimed to, then he is a great person for her to have in her life, if he is faithful and believes in the best possible outcome for them both. I asked him to stay the course with her and wear her ass down! As I said, "Because you never know, Bo, you might just catch her slipping and whisk her off her feet! And you might find yourself standing before one of her judge friends while he prepares to marry both of you. So, keep your head up: this is not the end of yours and Maxey's life, it's just the beginning!"

"Thank you for giving me some of your time, Ms. Roxanne." As he spun around in the chair and prepared to exit my office, Bo got to my door and looked back at me.

"Oh, by the way, my uncle told me to tell you hello!"

Then he walked out the door without me saying a word. I was lost in all my other thoughts about my life to give Sissell much thought. I pray that his life is just what he wanted and needed it to be, but for me, I had bigger dragons to slay! Sissell and I couldn't play that cruel game with each other anymore, because he put me through hell when he asked me to release him. I still pray for his success, and he was a sponsor for my business; but I am no longer where he left me almost five months ago. I am a new Roxanne with a new purpose, so his subtle intrusions into my life have finally lost their luster.

Once Bo had left my office, I sat still for several minutes because I had no answers for anybody. I knew that I was going to make up with Akheem by the end of next week! I looked at my watch. The time was nearing 8:30 p.m. and my dealership was humming along. I got up, closed my computer and went to the restroom, thereafter heading to the main floor. I noticed that several sales were being finalized by staff while I walked on to the repair shop.

I saw the usual suspects preparing to close the shop. We exchanged pleasantries as I openly joked with some of them. I told them that if they did not have any plans for Thanksgiving dinner, I would love for them to come and dine with me. They were all struck dumb because I had never asked them to come over to my house for anything. Knowing that most of my team had their own families, I just wanted to put it out there, in case any of them found themselves lonely. I then told them that if their plans fell through and they found themselves alone on that special day, they could feel free to come and share a meal with me!

I left the repair shop in a hurry because I did not enjoy the fumes that came out of there! I was thrilled that they heard me ask them to dinner, because sometimes the message can be lost when someone else delivers it. I could read what they were thinking as they looked back at me, but for once I did not care.

I walked back to my office and began to finish up some work on the computer. I became lost in my thoughts again when I began to offer up silent praises to the LORD.

I never thought that my life would come to this. I was tired of some of my life's mistakes! I heard some of the staff leave for the day, and since the time now was 9:00 p.m., the last sale of the day was already closed. The Pastor came in and told me that the cleaning staff was here, and he would be leaving soon. I told him to have a good night plus I asked him to tell Cherokee that I said hello.

The Pastor told me that he would take care of it and would see me in the morning.

He said, "Get some rest Baby Sister and enjoy your early evening night. Keep recognizing God's blessings in your life."

I walked him to the exit and locked the main doors behind him! I turned to see Bo walking around. I guess he was making sure that everything was secure. I heard him talking to Sammi on the other end of the walkie-talkie. I also noticed that the cleaning staff was down the hallway. I went back into my office and closed my computer. I powered my system down and put my security code in place. I then went to the employees' restroom because that was where my two favorite ladies were located.

Both Nova and Ossie were as thrilled to see me as I was to see them. We hugged each other and began to talk at the same time. I stopped talking because I wanted to hear what they were trying to tell me. I only could gather bits and pieces of what they were saying. I just leaned against the sink in the restroom while they both rambled on. My attention was already drifting, but I did not take my eyes off them.

The thing was, it was rather fun to visit with them! It had been several months since we had the chance to talk with each other made our time together precious. We began to laugh heartily at some of their stories. We were almost caught when their supervisor busted into the restroom to check on them! I guess her thunder was stolen when she saw that they were talking with me. We stood around and just laughed for a couple of minutes.

Ossie wanted to know if I ever tried the dance moves, they taught me months before. I smiled as the supervisor exited the restroom! I informed them that I did indeed use the moves that they taught me! But the fact of the matter is that the man that I was involved with at that time was in my past now, we were no longer on speaking terms. I made them aware that he chose to rescue his family which was in crisis, and I had understood why he had to let me go. I admitted to them both that I did miss him sometimes, but both of us have moved on with our own lives.

Then they both allowed me to tell them about the new man in my life. Even though we were not on speaking terms today, I was hopeful that we would find our way back to each other. I laid out several charming stories about our involvement, but they could tell that I was a little sad about my man and how things were working out between us. Nova told me to keep my head up because I had a lot to offer him.

They were a little confused about the rift between us, but Ossie kept telling me to hang on in there and things would get better as time went by. Then she said, "Ms. Roxanne, give him time to find out what it is to be without you. And when you do see him again, don't play fair. Show him what he is missing out on, because there is not a man alive that could resist a hot little number like yourself. You have the total package that most men wish for: you are a very attractive woman and you own this dealership, plus, he would be a fool to allow you to escape from his life!"

We all smiled at each other once she finished talking.

Nova said, "Not trying to be too personal, Ms. Roxanne, but has he sampled your body yet?"

We all knew that she was asking me if we had fucked yet. I shook my head up and down emphatically and began to giggle! I explained that he was a very sexy and dangerous type of man, and that I found him over the top sexy.

"He enjoys practicing tantric sex, and I must say that he is great at it," I enthused.

"Damn, Ms. Roxanne, you hit the jackpot with this new man," they said. "Does he have any brothers to introduce us to?"

I told them that we were still both trying to find our way in the relationship, that we both were dancing around the subject of who was the leader and who was the follower in the relationship.

"Well there is your problem, Ms. Beaumont," observed Ossie. "You have been so used to being the leader, now you've found someone who can lead *you*. Maybe you should try to lead the relationship where you think it should go! But here is a quick question for you—Ms. Roxanne, don't you enjoy being a woman?

"If your answer to my question is yes, then you should allow yourself to be led by this man. That is, if you want to keep him around. If you are not sure if you want him and you need to play the role of the lady when you are with him, you are more than welcome to give him to me, because I will welcome him into my life, and be as helpless as he wishes me to be! So, once you find out if you are going to lead or follow this man, you'll no longer struggle over unnecessary bullshit!"

I gave them both a hug as I thanked them for their advice in this matter. I informed them that this conversation had been quite informative, and I would give what they had both said to me some thought. I would find a way to surrender myself to Akheem, because he did offer my heart shelter, and I don't have to pretend to give myself to him. But maybe there is a power struggle that I am not aware of. So, if I must readjust my train of thinking about being the leader, I was proud to tell them about what was really going on with Akheem.

I knew that I could allow him to be the leader. It was just that no one had ever wanted to lead me; before, men were always happy when I made all the decisions. I found it odd to be told what to do, because I have always overseen everyone and their lives. I wanted to give him what he needed and if letting him lead us will ease some of this pain in my heart, then I would be the follower. I wanted and needed him in my life!

CHAPTER 10

CLARITY DOES NOT UNDERSTAND ITSELF!

It came time for me to leave. Even though I had enjoyed my conversation with Nova and Ossie, I had other things to attend to. They'd given me a different outlook on Akheem, and with the new day right around the corner, I needed to give myself some time to wrap my mind around him being the leader! While I exited the restroom with my two friends, I wished them both happy holidays and a great night. I walked back to my office to gather my things.

I picked up my handbag, travel bag and some papers. Finally, it was my turn to leave at the end of the day. I was tired and glad to be done with the day. I was apologizing to myself for fucking up a great relationship. But I was determined to get it back on track, because I knew that this could not be the end of Akheem and me.

I informed Sammi that I was gone for the evening and I would see him later. He walked me to my car and held the door open for me. I invited him over for Thanksgiving dinner, too. He told me that he already had plans, but would join us if anything changed. He and his family might stop by for dessert. I smiled as he closed my door and I drove off. My cell phone was making beeping noises to let me know that I had missed several phone calls. I had two new voicemails on my phone, but there was so much traffic to navigate, I chose to listen to them once I got home. I sang to myself as I drove. It was a little strange, singing and talking to myself, but I guess I was having a necessary conversation with myself.

When I got home, kicked off my shoes, pulled out my cell phone and sat down at the kitchen table. I listened to my voicemails; both were from my kids. But it was past 11:30 p.m. so I knew they were both in bed. I told myself that I would call them first thing in the morning. I could not wait any longer to get my tired body in my bed.

When the noise from my alarm clock filled my room the next morning, I jumped out of bed to turn it off. I picked up my phone and dialed Franchescia; she answered her phone on the third ring. She knew that it was me calling her first thing in the morning, so she put a smile in her voice. "Good morning, Mom, how are you doing?" she said. "Do you miss us keeping up a lot of noise in the house? Did you get our voice messages?"

I was trying to respond to her questions when her father knocked on her door. He told her that she needed to be ready to leave in 30 minutes! I waited for her to tell him that she would be ready, but she refocused her attention on me.

She asked, "Mom, did you hear my questions?"

I began to swiftly answer them.

"Well, good morning to you too, stranger. I am doing well and yes; I did receive both phone calls. But it was too late to call you back after my day ended. That is why I am calling you before the day gets too busy. How was the rest of your night with your two new brothers?"

She suggested that they'd had a great time, but said she would talk about them later. I told her I was almost becoming lonely in this big-ass house all by my lonesome. I knew that they would be back that weekend, so I'd be just fine until their return.

We both laughed at my comments. Then I asked if her brother was close to her.

"Hold on, Mom and let me summon this knuckle-headed boy to the phone!"

I hung on and listened to her scream his name. I heard him in the background walking into her room. I guessed Anthony just entered without knocking. So, she told him to get out and knock before he entered her room! I heard him sigh as he exited her room, because she was showing him who was the boss! I could hear a crazy knock on her door, at which Franchescia told Anthony not to knock on her door that way! After a short delay, I heard another knock on her door.

Franchescia called out, "Who is it?"

Anthony's voice came, muffled. "It's me, Franny, may I come in?"

She told him that he could enter for now, then I heard a struggle for the phone! I knew that when Michael and I were not present they were more than likely cursing each other out. I could tell that Anthony wanted to tell his sister to go fuck herself, but he knew that I was on the other end of the phone. I still remember telling my sisters to go get fucked on a regular basis when I was younger. And I knew that Fran indeed made him so mad that he could just kill her. I must remind her that Anthony won't always be smaller than she was, that in time his height would change. She just happened to be older than he was and should learn to get along with him. Anthony's voice broke my reverie.

"Hi Mom, I miss you and I can't *stand* your daughter! I can't wait to come home on Saturday because I miss you more than I wanna talk about in mixed company."

I responded to his concerns about his sister. I told him he needed to be nicer to her because he and I both knew that she was crazy! We have been doing a great job of not letting the rest of the family know our little secret and he would not have to put up with her and her nonsense too much longer. Anthony and I laughed. He also told me he had a nice time with his two brothers last night but was ready to come back home and unpack his clothes.

We both laughed again and referred to his sister's ever-changing state of mind. I heard Michael tell them that they both needed to be leaving soon. Anthony told me that he loved and missed me something bad. I told him that I missed him too, and I couldn't wait to see him this weekend. Maybe if they weren't exhausted, they could help me move some furniture around at the dealership, I mused. Anthony told me that if he wasn't too tired, he would love to help me! I ended my conversation with my kids as I walked towards the shower to turn it on.

I made up my bed as I thought of what I was going to wear today. I began to relax as I mentally chose a dress. Once my bed was done, I walked into my closet and pulled out a black and gray sweater dress. I was almost afraid to wear it because it hugs every part of my body, but knowing that I had lost weight, I wanted to see if I could see a difference in my body. Since the dress had a jacket to accompany it, I did not feel too bad about being overexposed. I untangled my hair and pulled myself together.

My face took me the longest to do. I couldn't get the liner straight on my right eye and was becoming pissed. I'd had to remove my eyeliner twice already, but on this last try, I finally got it right. Then once I was secure in how my face and hair turned out, I felt redeemed as I put the dress on. I was no longer puzzled as to how much weight I had lost—I was swimming inside that dress. I walked around the room, virtually walking on air. It had been such a long time since I'd worn that dress. I knew I'd still wear the jacket to cover my ass, even though I did look great. I was still modest about my body.

Knowing that it was past the time that I should have been on the road, I gathered all my belongings and walked out of my house. I knew Isabo would be there before me, so I made a stop to find myself a biscuit or something for breakfast. Once I had gotten breakfast I was on my way to the dealership. I nibbled on my meal as I drove up to my parking spot. I removed my driving shoes and put on these fierce boots that made me feel sexy, but my legs were drowning inside of those boots as I smiled to myself.

I exited my car and grabbed my handbag, cell phone and papers. It was going to be a great day as far as I was concerned. I walked into the dealership with a killer smile on my face. Isabo greeted me because the dealership was not opened yet. We talked as we made our way to my office. I hadn't had the chance to tell her that Akheem and I suspended our romance. I did not wish to bring her down, so I kept changing the subject.

Isabo asked me several times how Akheem was doing, so I finally told her about our misunderstanding. Her face showed immediate concern for me. I told her that he did not wish to speak to me for the rest of the week. I was not going to contact him until next week because I respected his request to be left alone; pretending that his words did not hurt me, but they did.

When Isabo began to exit my office, she began to sing the song that plays in Heaven when I am praying to GOD. The song was "Roxanne" by The Police! Isabo said, "I will pray that you two can work out your problems with one another! But Roxanne, are you sure you wish to let him go?"

"Isabo, the operative word is *suspended*, not dissolved. I am hopeful that we will be able to get back on one accord. I will let you know when we make up with one another! So, do not trouble yourself with the goings-on in my life."

She asked me if I needed her help with this matter. I told her that Mr. Fulwad and I would work this out, but I thanked her as she exited my office. I sat still for a couple of seconds before breaking out into my own version of "Roxanne"! I had a smile on my face because I knew that Akheem and I were going to be

OK. After a 15-minute break, before the dealership opened Isabo called me on the intercom system.

"Roxanne, I know that you have not asked for my help—but are you sure you are willing to let the captain of your heart go? I know that he hurt your pride when he asked you not to call him. I think you should contact him even if you *are* done with one another."

"Isabo, I will respect his wishes and give him what he asked for. He might just need a chance to get over me and my big mouth. This is not your problem; why it is troubling you so?"

Isabo suggested that grass does not grow under a rolling stone, pleading the case for me to call him; but I had turned a deaf ear to her! Then when she called my name twice more, I came back to myself. Before we concluded our exchange, she had one more comment for me.

"Roxanne, I meant to tell you that you look *great* in that dress."

I told her that I really appreciated her compliment; that I didn't plan on becoming a rolling stone, nor would Mr. Fulwad be allowed to escape from me without a struggle! I advised her to wait and watch him and I work through this rough spot. It *was* nice to know that she was willing to help me with him, because there were a million reasons to release him. Then I mentioned to her that things were my fault right now, so I was dealing with it.

"The fact is, Isabo, that I said something out of turn to Akheem, and now I must deal with the consequences that my words caused," I said flatly, "I'm not searching for anyone else, nor am I willing to let him go—since he wants to be left alone, I can give him that, for now ... however, don't count me out of the game with Akheem, yet! I know that being in the doghouse was my own doing, so keep your head up for me! Now, Let's go out there and sell seven new cars today ... we'll let the trouble with Mr. Fulwad and myself float away until it's a better time to deal with it!"

Now it was time for Isabo and I to open shop. I ran to my personal restroom to make sure that everything was in place. Once I made it back inside my office, I heard the main door being unlocked, signaling the start of another day selling cars. I turned on my computer and began to scan the graphs from yesterday's activities.

I still had a personal goal that I wanted to reach for the dealership, and I was thrilled to know that we would end the year with excessive growth. That fact pleased me more than anyone could ever know. I finally found something that I was great at, and I loved my job! Even though it came with several massive failures in my life, I am still glad that this is *my* life.

The time was 10:15 a.m. and activity at the shop was just getting started when Lily buzzed me on the intercom. We exchanged pleasantries, and then she informed me that she had great news about the caterer for Thanksgiving dinner. She asked me if I had a couple of minutes, so we could go over her findings. I asked her to give me 30 minutes, and Lily replied that she'd be there. We ended our conversation with laughter in our voices!

I was going to be at my best with everyone on that special day, but when the intercom rang once more, I had a strange feeling that I was about to be involved in another odd occurrence. When I heard Incomplete Maggie on the other end of the system, I *knew* I was in for a rude awakening. Maybe, just *maybe* my spirits would not be dampened as she spoke to me ...

"High ranking official, phone!" came Maggie's voice.

I knew I was about to suffer the consequences of allowing Incomplete Maggie to answer phones for the dealership. But she was like family, so I had no choice but to put up with her crazy ass! I just remained silent for ten seconds before I asked her to be a little clearer, but I guess I was having a moment, because clarity does not understand itself when it's around Maggie. I asked her to give me another try, to figure out what the *fuck* she was talking about.

"Major Morrison, line one!" said Maggie this time.

Then I understood what she was saying and proudly said,

"Thank you, Maggie! Let's see if we can do this for the rest of the day."

Maggie said, "Was that not ironic?"

I hung up but for a second I thought, she was aware of her shortcomings. She hid behind being hard to understand and I did not wish to waste any more energy on her. I needed to speak with this man from the Lexus Corporation because we had business to tend to! I cleared my throat, putting a smile on my face and in my voice as I pressed the button to accept the call.

"Good morning, this is Roxanne."

"Good morning Roxanne, this is Major Morrison calling you on behalf of the Lexus Corp. I have been placed in charge of the in-house security breach, which has caused us to do our own in-house investigation of your dealership and your employees. I welcome your granting me a slice of your time tomorrow for this little distraction to be put to rest, ASAP! I wanted to make sure that we were still on track to meet at 11:00 a.m."

I heard myself say, "I also welcome our meeting tomorrow, Mr. Morrison, and maybe we can dispel the rumors of an in-house security breach here at my dealership. Because I will not believe that any of my employees would ever steal from me. I have never known this type of deception from someone whom I have hired!"

Mr. Morrison proudly requested that I call him Major, but I kept our conversation on a professional level. I giggled to myself because for some reason, I knew—without ever seeing this man—that he possessed a short man's complex. I could hear it in his voice, and I was mindful of whom I was dealing with. This was someone whom Akheem handed me to! I knew that this man was all about informing me about the breach and how we could protect ourselves in future. Major. Morrison and I ended our conversation by making sure that our time frame was still a good time to meet.

"Have a great day, Major. Morrison. I am eager to see what you have found out for me and my dealership!"

"It's been my pleasure speaking with you as well, Ms. Roxanne. You have yourself a great day too, and I will see you in the morning!"

I felt just fine following our conversation because I was not sure of what was going to be said. I was not afraid about our conversation and I did not expect him to be as pleasant in person as he was on the phone. But somewhere in the back of my mind I still thought he was a short man! I let out a tiny laugh to myself, then pulled out my list of concerns I wanted to address with Lily. My heart was as light as a feather and I felt great as the day went on. It was such a rare occasion to find myself with a break in time, I just sat back in my chair and relaxed! A gentle knock came from my door and I said, "Come in!"

Lily had arrived, with a big smile on her face. She had an older yet small laptop computer with her. It was neatly tucked under her arm. Lily told me she had scoured the yellow pages last night looking for the perfect catering company to help me out.

"Ms. Roxanne, thank you for asking for my help, because I love doing whatever I can to help you and the dealership. You saved my life several times in the past, and if I can do anything more to help you with your family over the holiday season, please do not hesitate to ask! I have narrowed the selection down to the top three caterers in the city. I was not sure how elaborate you would like the menu to be, so I needed to inquire about your preferences before I secured a company to serve you!"

I just sat there, looking at Lily, who really seemed to have found her calling. She would make a great events coordinator, but I hope that she would recognize that soon. Maybe I could ask her to help my sister plan her wedding. But I would put that on the back burner for now. We got down to finding out what each company offered on their menu, then I wanted to make sure that they could adequately supply a modest amount of food for this holiday gathering. Lily informed me that she had already done a background check on all three companies and one of them stood out with the best references. She then mentioned that they specialized in revisiting meals from clients' youth.

"Damn," was all I could say, because I really liked the fact that this company would try and help me recapture the feelings I had in my youth when we dined on meals my grandmother used to prepare. My mom and grandmother used to handle all that stuff for us, but now since the baton was handed to me, I was aware that I could never be as great a cook as either of them. I was very interested in offering up a lovely and nutritious substitute, plus I wanted to enjoy myself without the headache of preparing a meal for the holidays!

"Well, Ms. Lily, what is the name of this company claiming to help me revisit and recapture my youth through their meals?" I queried, intrigued.

"Their name is Deuce and a Quarter!" Roxanne said brightly.

I fell out of my chair laughing, because that was the type of car that my grandfather used to drive before I damaged the interior by cleaning it with bleach! I really fucked that car up when I was a little girl, and it amazed me to remember that I was such a handful when I was younger. To underscore the fact that I am still a handful now, I looked up to see Lily looking at me as

165

if I had just lost my mind! That was the perfect time for me to share a small part of my life, so I told her of some of the things that I encountered when I was a little girl. I told her about the mishaps with my grandfather's car, which was called Deuce and a Quarter. We both shared a couple of laughs while I told my story! I found her smiling back at me so naturally, and she understood why I wanted to use that company, since they made me revisit a happy time from my youth!

"I guess we will go with Deuce and a Quarter, Ms. Roxanne," Lily observed. "I pray that they will inspire your family and friends with joy just like they've already done for you, enabling you to remember some happy times."

CHAPTER 11

LOCK PICKER!

Lily and I planned the menu, and then I asked her if she planned on joining us for dinner. She told me that she would not miss the event to save her life. We both gave a troubled smile at her comment, but I knew that she meant that she was very glad to be invited. Lily told me that she needed to go back to her desk and finalize her plans for this event. I had no fear about whether she knew what she was doing. She almost danced out of my office because she was so happy to have something to do that brought out her talents.

The time was 12:45 p.m. and I still had several more things to address on my personal list. I located my cell phone and dialed Cherokee. I counted seconds until she answered the phone as sometimes Cherokee didn't allow her voicemail to pick up her calls. She would want to do it herself plus her phone could ring up to 25 times before she answered it, but she picked it up on the 9th ring this time!

"Get your monkey ass out of the bed, BITCH." That was my greeting, and we both began to laugh.

"Nigga, I was going to call you today, but you beat me to the punch. How the hell are you doing, Ms. Roxanne? Are you still talking to that non-pork eating motherfucker or what?"

I did not wish to go into detail with her about him, so I told her that we were still involved.

"I did not call to talk about myself, Cherokee, I was checking in with you to find out if our father and brothers are still coming for Thanksgiving dinner, and would you be bringing several dishes? Even though I hate to admit this, you still make the best pecan pie I have ever tasted!"

Cherokee told me that she was going to try her hand at preparing another dish for the family. I began to sweat immediately, because so much could go wrong when she tried to step out of her comfort zone of singing. I was so surprised and shocked at her next words.

"I felt like trying my hand at preparing some mustard and collard greens for the family!" She sounded optimistic.

I knew in my heart that this was not going to turn out well for any of us. If in fact she did try her hand at fixing some greens for dinner, I did not wish to hurt her feelings. I needed to let her know that we would love a pie from her, but please, no greens! We might not get the chance to walk away from another one of her concoctions; she liked to take shortcuts. She could become downright careless with our lives while she tried to cook a dish for us, and I had a life that I wanted to live, and I just did not wish to die from my sister trying to make a new dish.

The last time she tried her hand at bringing greens to a dinner five years ago, everyone in the house got sick. We found out that she washed the greens the night before she cooked them! But she misunderstood the concept of washing the greens, because she soaked the greens in dishwashing liquid overnight, and cooked them the next day! Cherokee cooked those greens for 9 hours. The suds where still in them after she placed them in a fancy bowl for all of us to take a serving from! Once we gathered up the courage to eat them, everyone got sick except for my grandfather.

We have all felt safer when she bakes pies, cakes or cookies! I was trying to be sensitive when I asked her to not strain herself with preparing greens. Considering that we would be having a lot of different guests at my house, I did not wish to hurt her feelings. Knowing that I was having it catered made me smile, and there was less stress for me, so I just shook my head and let go of the crazy thoughts that I was entertaining.

Eventually I just said, "Fuck it, bring whatever you wish to bring!"

Secretly I was praying that no one would die at my house after eating something she had made. I asked her how the wedding plans were coming along, and did she need me to do anything special for her? She could not come up with anything right then, but said she would keep me in mind if she needed anything done. I told her that I would lend her my personal assistant, because she was great at preparing last-minute events. I gave her Lily's cell phone number and told her not to hesitate to call and ask her for help. I did add that she needed to be nice to Lily, because I would not tolerate her being mean to her. Cherokee basically ignored my comments about Lily, so I changed the subject. Next, I wanted to know if she had spoken with Maxey this week.

"Nope, but maybe this is a good time to call her; just because she is pregnant, it doesn't mean she should get out of doing her fair share for the Thanksgiving dinner!"

"Well, before we talk to her, I need to ask you a question."

"Go for it, Roxy!"

"Do you think that Maxey and Bo are good for each other? The reason I am asking is because Bo stopped by my office last night. He was troubled and concerned things are not moving in the direction that he desires. He asked me to have a talk with her because he keeps asking her to marry him, but she will not even give him an answer. He is becoming concerned that she does not wish to marry him; and if she does not, then maybe he should move out of her way."

Cherokee picked up an old habit as she began to mumble her answer to me, but I heard everything that she did not wish for me to hear clearly.

"Bo should count his lucky stars and shut his mouth about marriage to our sister. Correct me if I am wrong, but isn't he a fucking *convict*? He should be happy enough to know that our sister wants to spend time with his ass."

"What was that, Cherokee?"

She cleared her throat and continued speaking.

"Where is it written that they have to get married? Shit, Roxy, Maxey has already been married three times to the wrong motherfuckers. If she is a little gun shy of doing it again, then Bo needs to sit his missing-front-tooth-ass down and shut the fuck up! Men seem to think that marriage is the end all to every woman's life.

"If she keeps that nigger hanging on for another three years, he should count himself lucky; and if that bastard has the balls to ask me for help with her, I will have no problem cursing his black ass all the way out. How dare he try to pressure her in the condition that she is in? If he knows what's good for him, he should fall on his knees every night and tell GOD thank you for blessing his crazy ass with a jewel like Maxey!"

I was going to jump in and defend Bo, but as far as I was concerned, he was on his own with Cherokee. After 12 seconds passed without either one of us saying one word, I began to speak to my sister and ask her to calm herself down. I knew she felt bad for Bo, understood why Maxey was not willing to give herself all the way to him, and why she didn't know if she wanted to marry him at all. I know that Maxey did care for Bo, and he should stop acting like their love is now or never! They both seemed to be the best of friends, and if he is lucky, he will have a lover of his mind for the rest of his life. I will pray that he does not place her under undue pressure.

Cherokee and I called Maxey on her cell phone, but we found out that she'd been in court that day, so we would have to talk with her later. Before we ended our conversation, we agreed on a time for the festivities to begin. Both of us came up with 3:00p.m. so no one would have to rush over to my house. And far as I was concerned, once dinner was over with, it would not be a problem for anyone to exit in a hurry.

I told Cherokee that I had invited some of my employees and a couple of friends. I was not sure if any of them would show up, but I thought that she should be aware of some of my guests. We ended our call by saying that we would see each other next week. I told her to give our father and brothers the time, because my plate was full of so many other things, I did not have time to call and give them the information.

"One more thing before you go … thank you, Cherokee, for your help with the kids last week."

"You are welcome, Roxy!"

I made it to the showroom floor and watched Maggie pretend to be busy! She made me smile as I walked out onto the dealership's parking lot full of cars. There were only three salespeople in the process of showing cars. I guess the time was not right to buy a car from us, but I knew that we had to go through this course. I looked up at the sky. I just knew that someone would buy a car from us today and there was no rush to pressure any of the salespeople. Several of my salespeople came out to check on me, but I told them that I was just enjoying the view!

Isabo came out to join me as I walked around the lot. We got this novel idea of taking a test drive in one of the fancy new sports cars. I called The Pastor on his walkie-talkie and asked him to go and retrieve the keys for me. He was eager to give me what I wanted. I was sort of shocked when I saw the Pastor come out to speak with me because normally chaos follows him, but I knew that his life was changing. I asked him to stick around outside while Isabo and I took a test drive. He told me that he would love to, and maybe he could scare up a sale while we were gone. He was closing tonight, and he was hopeful that we would make our projected goal.

He returned with the keys to this triple black on black two-door sports car. This car had very black tinted windows that you could not see through, and there was a sound system that was out of this world. It was time for us to have a little fun. This car looked like a very hot and expensive woman all framed by an animal look to it, as I grabbed the handle and looked inside! I knew that it was going to be challenging for me to see out of those triple black windows.

My vision seemed a little blurred, and I was unsure if I should drive it right then. Although I wanted to see what this car could do, before the rest of the day got me down and depressed because business was rather slow. I wanted to drive fast on the freeway, but I was having a hard time seeing through the windows because they were so dark. I asked Isabo to give us a tour of what this car could do on the road! She pulled out her sunglasses from her pocket and gave me a killer smile!

We both got into the car and strapped ourselves down. I know that I have been accused of being a little heavy with my foot, but Isabo is *out* of her mind while she drives. I was unsure if I had made the right choice of car, because she seemed like she was going to have an endless amount of fun with me. I knew that it had been a while since I had been in a car with her, and I don't know why I let her drive me around, but it was too late to change my mind! Maybe she had improved her skills behind the wheel, but I did not care at this moment because she did not disappoint me as we pulled out into traffic!

Isabo could have raised the dead with the way she was driving. Meanwhile, I was saying prayers as we entered the freeway, asking for forgiveness for whatever sin that I had committed today! She did not disappoint me with her technique in handling this fancy new car. We drove the freeway like we were being chased to deliver a cure for whatever was troubling your soul or body. I began to laugh as she weaved us in and out of traffic! I was having a nice time while she drove. she asked me if I would answer just one question for her, as she dropped the car into 5th gear and began to open it up more!

"Ask me anything, my friend, just as long as you deliver me back onto the lot once you are done scaring the *shit* out of me!" We both looked at each other and smiled as she was giving that car what for, driving like she was trying to shatter the speed record!

"Roxanne, have you counted how many blessings you have thrown back into God's face? Before you answer my one question, allow me to give you my reasoning behind why I am asking you this rather odd question. You see, Roxanne, I am what some people might refer to as a LOCKPICKER of the SOUL. Know that I have sat back and watched you conquer many of life's obstacles, but for the life of me, I cannot understand how you can keep losing your place in this life.

"It troubles me to know that you can count seconds and you are always aware of how long it takes for people to do most tasks. But I don't think you know how blessed you truly are, and I feel that it is my job as your friend to really find out what you are willing to sacrifice, to keep throwing blessings back to God. These blessings seem to keep knocking at your door, Roxanne, but you keep selectively choosing to dismiss the obvious. If I don't speak my truth to you right, you could consider it a dereliction of my duty as a friend.

"Too many blessings have passed through your hands and I have stood on the sidelines just watching you. I pride myself on being a friend to you, Roxanne. But when do you think that God would have had enough of bestowing enormous amounts of blessings on you, in this lifetime? Today, I find that I have the nerve to ask you what your tally is so far, because from my count, Roxanne, you have had a truly blessed existence, so I cannot resist putting this question to you. I truly understand and appreciate your feelings for the loss of your grandmother from your life, but look at all the other blessings that you seem to keep dismissing.

"You have your health, your children and your very successful dealership. You have been blessed with an abundance of friends, not to mention the love of your life, Mr. Fulwad. But if I was keeping score on you, it seems to me that you have been paid in full several times over! Knowing that you and I are good friends, I truly want to know what in the hell is really going on behind that pretty smile of yours. I need you to take some foolish advice from me, my friend. You better change the way you operate in this world, because you're going to look up one day, Roxanne, and GOD is going to cut you off! And if ever that day shows up for you, will you be able to know how many blessings you threw back into God's face?"

When she finished with her questions and statements, all I could do was be still and quiet! I was at a loss for anything to say as I looked out the window, I could not pretend that I was not hurt by her questions. Telling myself that I would not be crying any more today was all that made me keep my mouth shut. I just stared out the dark window! There were no more words said between the two of us. I was ready to go home and be by myself; maybe in the morning, I would be able to face what she has just said to me.

I am having a hard time trying to conceive why my friend would say those things to me, but I understand what she thinks she sees with me. I knew that I was no saint and my life was shifting, but I was not up to answering any questions about me. I knew that I was at the proverbial fork in the road and about to snap; so, to save my own life, I just remained silent!

We pulled back onto the parking lot and I told her that I would be gathering my things and leaving for the evening. I stepped out of that car and marched my happy-go-lucky ass back into my dealership! I did not speak to anyone nor did I make eye contact with them. I walked back into my office, turned off my computer, grabbed my handbag and turned my lights off. I did not break my stride as I walked out of my building. I walked to my car and pushed the button for it to open for me. I heard Isabo running after me, but still I moved forward and got into my car!

Once I was all the way inside, I locked my doors and turned on the engine! I placed my sunglasses on my face and put my car in gear! I guess Isabo was feeling somewhat fearless because she was gazing at me as if I was a wounded animal. I placed my car in drive and pulled off the lot. If she was feeling somewhat invincible, today was not the day to try out her powers on me. I was feeling like a rhinoceros that was always dressed for battle, plus I had my boots in the trunk of my car, so I could keep my footing!

It was best for me remove myself from doing verbal battle with any one of my best friends today, because all my emotions were tangled up inside the questions, she had put to me. On some level I was truly aware of what she was saying to me; I just did not wish to offer her an interesting answer. That is why I ran away from my friend, because I knew what she was looking for in my answer. The crazy part of the whole conversation was that I already had a number in my head to her question.

I did not wish to introduce my number or answer her question because some things are better left unsaid. I drove rather slowly as I exited the parking lot. I turned on my sound system as I made my way to the freeway. I put on some Alanis Morrissette as I drove home. I was ready for this day to end and I needed to eat a good meal, take a shower and go to bed. My cell phone kept ringing as I drove through traffic. I allowed it to go straight to voice mail because I was in a strange frame of mind and it was best if I stayed away from everybody.

I was not hiding from anyone, so to speak, but I just needed to be moved out of the spotlight for today. Although she kind of hurt my feelings, this too shall pass. Then as I slid into my garage, I picked up my items from my car as God only knew what I was truly thinking! I was wondering what I was going to prepare myself for dinner.

I walked inside my house, placed my belongings on the counter, and got lost inside my own thoughts. I pulled off my shoes and walked to the refrigerator. I had a taste for grilled steak and pasta with broccoli. I set out to prepare myself a delicious meal although my cell phone kept ringing. I glanced over at it to make sure that it was not anything of importance! Once I discovered that it was Isabo dialing me repeatedly, I just allowed her calls to go unanswered until I finished preparing my meal.

I planned on consuming a whole bottle of wine as I turned on the television on and began to watch an old black-and-white movie. I looked down at my watch and saw that the time was 7 p.m. I remembered that I told myself that I wanted to be home by seven o'clock tonight, and here I was, dining in front of the television, enjoying a nice, thick steak and a bottle of wine. I heard my cell phone ringing in the kitchen, but I chose not to retrieve it. I did not wish to experience anyone else's lip service.

CHAPTER 12

Dust The Floor!

I walked into my bedroom and put my wineglass next to the tub. I leaned down and drew myself a hot bath. I walked to my bureau and picked out some pretty pajamas! I removed all my clothes and eased myself into the tub. I was not too far gone from the wine that I was drinking, once I was situated in the tub. I poured myself some more wine and leaned all the way back so I could relax! I closed my eyes and allowed my thoughts to swim around my mind. I began to think about nothing, but my mind decided to revisit the comments Isabo had made earlier. I was becoming mellow as I finished my glass of wine.

Next, I began to cleanse my body and play in the water. I turned the tap back on because my water was cooling down a little, and thoroughly enjoying exceptionally hot baths, I wanted to remind my body of how hot I really liked the water. Once my body temperature had been raised to an outrageous limit, I felt myself falling asleep as I was mentally soaring out of my body. I knew it was time for me to get out of the tub and I almost fell as I missed a step, but I caught myself just in the nick of time!

While I stood in the bathroom drying myself Isabo's comments were replaying themselves repeatedly in my mind. As I got dressed, my cell phone pulled me back from daydreaming. I sat on my bed and checked out who was on the other end of the line. I saw that it was Macy calling me.

"Hello old friend," I said. "How did you know that I needed to talk with you?"

"Hey Doll," Macy said. "Have things slowed down for you so far, or are you still entangled in your own version of chaos?"

I did not wish to speak any more about the misunderstanding between me and Mr. Fulwad, so I kept that part of my life to myself. I felt as if I had been beaten up enough today. I need a different distraction. I told my friend that I did not wish to talk about me, but I was all ears to hear some new and exciting events involving *her* and other aspects of her crazy life!

"Well, before we jump too deep into my life, Roxanne, I just wanted to let you know that I will indeed be there for Thanksgiving dinner, and I am just over the *top* excited to be in your sister's wedding! I will not arrive in town until Thursday afternoon because I must go on military maneuvers with my squadron. But I will be at your home before 2:00 p.m. I hope that I will not be upsetting your scheduled time for dinner?"

Macy made me smile with her onslaught of comments and concerns. I told her that whichever time she arrived at my house would be appropriate, so she shouldn't be concerned with small details. I informed her that dinner started at 3 o'clock, so her making it at 2 o'clock will be perfect. I was so looking forward to spending some time with her, because we hadn't been in each other's presence since my grandmother's funeral almost five months ago.

Macy was quick to add that she had to make a swift departure on Saturday evening, because she was going to save up time to spend a week with me for the wedding. I accepted her excuse for not spending more time with me at Thanksgiving, as I was aware that she was a very busy woman. I sat back in my bed and allowed her to tell me whatever was on her mind. She

185

began to spin a tale involving my new brother, and not only did I find out that she was coming to town to see him also, but she planned on spending two nights with him while she was here!

Several smiles crept across my face as she was letting me know that I was basically her pit stop for her and my brother, Gordon! I guess they both kept in touch with one another and it has developed into a long-distance romance. Even though I was not interested in her dealings with Gordon, I pretended to be captivated by the fun that she was having with him.

Macy said, "Now that all of the preliminaries for our conversation are over with, I can get down to the heart of the matter. I need to talk with you about something, Doll. I need your undivided attention."

I did not recognize the tone she was using with me, and I had no clue what she wanted to talk about, so I climbed up to the head of the bed and got under the covers. Macy had my full and undivided attention then. I could hear her sobbing on the other end of the phone, so I just waited until she gathered herself. I glanced at my alarm clock to take note of the time. I saw that it was 10:15 p.m. and I could stay up if she needed me to. If it meant staying up all night to talk with her, then I would. We both depended upon each other, so if she needed me now, I was there!

I began to pray as she prepared to drag her truth out into the open. I was prepared to carry her problem, but I didn't know what I was up against. I wanted to give her all my attention, so I decided not to count seconds. I just sat there and waited for my best friend to tell me what the problem was and why she was crying.

I could hear that she was wrestling with her thoughts. I loved this crazy-ass woman and would do anything I could to help her. I was about to ask her to talk to me, but her tears began to fade away and her voice returned to her.

"Doll, I had some tests done last month and they found several shadows on my lungs. Now, I am scheduled to have exploratory surgery three weeks before Christmas."

I became sad for my friend. I put my hand over my mouth to hold the sounds inside, while she spoke again.

"Doll, it's going to be all right. You can cry if you need to. I have done my fair share of crying, but it is going to be all right."

I began to laugh on the other end of the phone. Here was my friend, diagnosed with God knew what, and *she* is trying to comfort me. I felt my tears caressing my face. I was in disbelief. Knowing that Macy never smoked a day in her life troubled me; maybe it was a genetic thing going on with her. I was not too scared for her as I felt the heat rise in my body. Her words kept repeating in my head. She was the picture of athletic health; she was active throughout her life. I took three big gulps of wine before I could muster up the strength to say anything to her.

"Macy, I love you, and it's going to be all right. We will weather whatever they believe this is; I am confident that you will pass this test with flying colors. Although I am having a hard time understanding why are they looking at your lungs if you have never smoked a day in your life. I guess I need you to make me understand—does any form of lung cancer run your family? Because it seems that you are healthy as a horse. If you and I had to go in for a physical endurance test, we all know that you would dust the floor with my DBA (Damn Black Ass)!"

I laughed out loud on the phone, trying to be silly with my friend to help lighten the mood. I could tell that she was trying to be lighthearted, too. I knew that this was not going to be like any other adventure that my friend had undertaken. How I was hopeful that things would work out for her, because I love her crazy ass more than I can say. She began to cough. Once she regained her composure, she started talking with me once more after I'd asked if she was all right.

"Well, Doll, cancer does run in my family, but I guess we have to just wait and see what my results are. I need you to listen close to me because I have a lot of information to tell you. But first, I need a promise from you, Roxanne! I need you to keep this information about me to yourself. You cannot tell *anyone*; that means not even Mr. Fulwad should know my secret; and for God's sake, *don't* tell your family about anything that we are discussing tonight. Do I have your promise, Roxanne? Remember, I will know if you are lying to me, plus I will know if you have broken your promise when I see you. I need you to keep my secret until I tell you that you are free to talk about me! Are we clear, Roxanne? I don't want you to tell no earthly soul! If you break your word to me, I will know that you have betrayed and slighted me!"

All this information that my friend was placing at my feet was totally uninvited for me. But if this is what she wanted; wild horses could not get me to betray my friend! I cleared my throat because I was about to answer her, but she spoke instead.

"Doll, there are aspects of my life that you are not aware of—but let me be the first to tell you my truth. I have been smoking without your knowledge for the past 23 years! The reason I never told you, nor did I ever smoke around you, was because are asthmatic and I did not wish to be thoughtless and smoke in your presence. I chose not to smoke around you, and I decided that it was in your best interest not to know that I smoked. I have been smoke-free for the past two years, so when I went in for my annual checkup that is when they discovered a patch on my left lung."

I was at a loss for words—not a sound would exit my mouth. I was trying to figure out which topic I should rejoin our conversation with, because I was becoming pissed off with my best friend. I didn't know she was a smoker and I felt like a fool. Shit, Macy and I had shared every detail of each other's lives! I remembered most of the guys that she had had sex with, and I couldn't believe that she kept such an enormous secret from me. All these years in our lives spent together, and she was lying to me. It gave me pause because I remember us vowing to tell one another everything in our lives.

I remember us becoming blood sisters and how we would spend hours together. I was tempted to curse her the fuck out, but I remained silent. I decided that I would give up being mad at her right now, because I knew things were out of her hands and it was inappropriate for me to be pointing fingers. We both sat there and cried.

"Macy, I understand that you are afraid right now, but God has kept you these all years and it is not for us to understand why. We both need to keep our heads up. I need to make room in my brain for all this news you've just given me. What you have told me has not sunk into my head yet! I am sure that everything is going to be all right."

I could hear her on the other end of the phone, swallowing and crying! I reminded her that she is loved, and she didn't have to go through this all by herself. Then I wanted to know the exact date that her procedure was going to be as I listened to her breathe. I was concerned that she was crying once more, so I waited for her to speak again.

"The procedure will be done on December 5th, but why are you asking me for a timeline, Roxanne? I do not wish to interfere with the goings-on in your life, and I did not ask you to come and be with me."

"Bitch, after all that you and I have been through, don't you know that I will be there when they knock your black ass out and when they wake you up? If by chance you are unclear about my intentions, Ms. Pissy Waters, I am coming to be with you! The sooner you wrap your fucking mind around me standing with you while you find out what is going on with your health, the less stress you will encounter. But if you wish to pretend that you do not have me in your corner, then you do not know me at all.

"I will fly to wherever they send you, because you are my best friend and I value having you in my life. Plus Ms. Macy Priscilla Rivers, you are a keeper, so you can't get rid of me no matter how hard you try. I need you in my life, too! What type of friend would I be if I did not stand with you while this line of chaos is going on in your life?"

Both of us began to cry once more on the phone as I made mental notes to have Lily redo my schedule for the first part of

December. Macy was my oldest friend in this world, and I would move Heaven and Earth to make sure that she was happy! I desired to be with her when the procedure was being done and I was hopeful that this little detour would turn out successfully for her. If I had my way, we would not even be walking down this road; but since I am just an observer in this situation, all I can do is sit back and let GOD delight in the details while he makes her body well!

Once we had reached an understanding about me coming out to be with her, Macy told me that she would be flying to another base or military hospital to have the procedure done, but she would make sure that I knew her location! She was glad I was coming to be with her because it has eased some of her worry. I asked her what type of friend would I be if I did not show up for her, but it was getting late and I needed to be going to sleep.

We traded pleasantries as we hung up the phone. I reminded her that I would see her next week for dinner and we would talk before Thanksgiving weekend was over. We told each other that we loved one another, following one of the most enlightening conversations we'd had in years.

I looked at the clock and saw that it was 3 in the morning. I knew that I was going to be operating on fumes that day, but I was optimistic that I could make it through. I thought I would have gotten more sleep, but knowing that I had a very important meeting in the morning, I knew that all I could do was catnap. I did not wish to be late for that meeting, plus I already had questions that I wanted to ask about the security breach.

I was eager to hear Major Morrison's findings because I wanted this chapter in my life closed all the way up, or at least switched off. I got out of bed and got on my knees while I offered up 13 prayers of thanksgiving to the Lord for my friend! Then I thanked Him for my family and friends. Next, I said a prayer for my lover and friend Akheem. I got back into bed, drifted into a light sleep, singing Amazing Grace in my head! My Angels did not appear at all as my mind entertained this secret Macy had told me.

I welcomed my alarm going off because I could not stay asleep to save my life. All the information shared with my mind active all night long. Despite it all, though, I was not worried for my friend, I was just tired and sleepy. I would have to place that part of my life on hold this morning since I had other business to attend to. I collected my thoughts as I made up my bed. I wanted to make a memorable impression on Major Morrison and his team. I needed to show a somewhat softer side of me, considering I did possess dominant tendencies.

I wanted to be on middle ground with Major Morrison, so I gave plenty of thought to what I was going to wear. I went into the bathroom to prepare myself for the day. I brushed my teeth three times before I finished with my face and hair. I put my hair up and pulled out a couple of strands to frame my face. I told myself that I needed a large cup of coffee. I was feeling in my bones that I was exhausted before the day had even started. I wanted this day to be magical, so I said several prayers as I chose the perfect outfit to wear. I decided to dress businesslike with a fraction of femininity showing—when all was said and done, the boss was still a lady!

I put a dark blue pinstripe suit on because this smashing outfit had seven buttons down the front, plus the pants made my ass look like a gift. I put a white shell under the jacket along with a 13-strand pearl necklace. I saw my Angels smiling at me as I checked out myself in the mirror. I was mentally rehearsing the questions I had for Major Morrison as I applied a small spray of Chanel No. 5 perfume to my wrist and hair. Although, I was trying to hide behind my looks, I was pleased at the image that I projected. I placed my cell phone in my pocket and picked out the shoes that I would sport today!

I walked downstairs and ate a cup of yogurt, thinking about how I was going to handle Isabo today! But for the life of me, I could not remember why I was pissed off with her! I asked God to guard my mouth today and keep my heart open to my friend. Then it came back to me why she troubled me so yesterday! She thought I heedlessly threw away untold numbers of blessings, but little did she know that I never did.

I have kept count all my life, but it was none of her business about the number of blessings. All she needed to know was that *she* was a blessing that I did not dismiss, and if she played her cards right, I would continue to keep her in my life; but her comments did hurt me a little yesterday. I guess that was the price you paid for some people being so familiar with aspects of your life!

I ran back upstairs to re-brush my teeth once more before I left for my long and hectic day. I gathered all my things and made my exit. I was so secure about how the day was going to turn out. I pulled out of my garage as I left a message on my kids' voicemail. I told them both to have a great day and would talk later.

I drove through traffic in total silence because I wanted my mind right for the meeting. I was telling myself to have an unbreakable spirit today and be on my best behavior with this stranger, plus I wanted to be the first to apologize to Isabo whenever we encountered each other. I need her in my life, and I knew that I was being an ass with her yesterday, so it was my job to ask her to forgive me for my poor manners yesterday.

I put a smile on my face as I exited my car. Once I made it to the dealership, I changed shoes and took hold of my handbag. I moved toward the main door, but Isabo was already walking towards me. We both opened our arms as we merged in a hug! She had tears in her eyes as she looked at me. I told her I was sorry for being rude to her. She wanted to apologize to me also for her behavior to me. I did not let her take the blame for my bad attitude. We just called it a draw as we walked into the building holding hands. Then I looked over at her and told her that if I should mess up my makeup because of her, I was going to beat her ass! We both laughed as we went inside my office.

The time was 9:45 a.m. and we had time for a mini-meeting. I asked Eric to come into my office, but while he was on his way, I called Lily and told her to clear my schedule for December 4th,5th and 6th. I told her that I had some family business to tend to and would be out of town until the 7th, so she should work her magic and reschedule those days for me.

Eric walked into the room looking as if he was going to be a hero for the dealership for the day. I smiled as he sat down in a chair. I told them that I had a couple of issues that I wanted to address with them early. When Major Morrison and his team showed up, we would show a unified front.

CHAPTER 13

75 STEPS FROM MY OFFICE!

I asked Eric and Isabo whether they believed that we were still in jeopardy at the dealership. They both agreed that we were.

"Well, before Major Morrison gets here, we should agree on our next game plan," I said. "These are some options we should put in motion to protect this dealership more. First, I believe we should weed out all employees with pass codes to the computers, because you must be at a certain level in the organization to have accessibility to some files.

"Next, we should cut off computer entrance into certain levels of the dealership, plus we need to change all computer pass codes, so that way we will not be accusing anyone of leaking pertinent information from now on. We will just be watching their digital fingerprints, so maybe they will be able to lead us to our own weakness! We should block all unrelated correspondence between employees because it could be some type of code that they are using. Then we should change the levels on the database, so we can track which divisions of the organization that each employee visits daily!"

Isabo put in, "It looks as if you have given this plenty of thought, Roxanne. I can't think of anything else to add to your analysis, plus it looks like we will no longer be playing Scrabble with the security of this dealership and our livelihood!"

"I feel that we will no longer be bullied by someone trying to harm this organization from the outside," assented Eric. "Also, they won't be able to attack us with our pants down, so to speak! Removing all fields of entry offers all of us a sense of seen and unseen security. Your comments and concerns have relieved me, because I do not like feeling as if someone could snatch the rug from under us at a moment's notice!"

It looked like all of us agreed on our next move, but just in case the meeting with Major Morrison did not go well, I felt like all of us were in sync as we came together for the betterment of the dealership, and it felt pretty good. The dealership had already opened during our mini-meeting while our sales staff was already prepared for the day, we did not have to hold anyone's hand.

I already knew that Lily had the boardroom prepared for our meeting and I was going to step to the restroom before Major Morrison arrived. I asked Isabo and Eric to give me a couple of minutes to gather myself. They exited my office as I went to the restroom. I checked my face and hair and washed my hands. I applied lotion on both hands and reapplied some more lip-gloss. I popped a couple of mints in my mouth; I walked out the restroom and grabbed my laptop and cell phone.

My boardroom was seventy-five steps from my office, and I counted all of them as I walked down the hallway. I could not explain how I was feeling, but I was walking on air. No matter what this man was going to say to me my team, I already had a game plan for our next move. Once I was in the boardroom, I walked to my chair. The room looked great as I was feeling fucking special. I was proud of the work that Lily had done for all of us. She had placed a large bouquet of roses and calla lilies right behind my chair! As soon as you walked into the room the flowers caught your eye. She also had a bowl of ice, bottles of water, an assortment of juice, soda and snacks.

Isabo and Eric walked into the boardroom and sat next to me, because Major. Morrison and his team hadn't arrived yet. We were all laughing at some stupid joke that Eric was telling us. I had to turn my back to them because it was a sorry-ass joke. I reached inside my pocket to turn off my cell because this meeting was very important to me and this dealership. I did not wish to experience any unnecessary distractions. At exactly 11:00 a.m. on the nose, in walked Lily and four other men.

The one who was the shortest of them was the one I focused all my attention on, as I sensed that he was the boss. It was almost like he was the focus of my own personal tracking beam. He seemed like the leader, even though he was the shortest white boy I had seen in a long while, plus he sounded like he had on the phone—short!

God was about to play a real cruel trick on all of us. Because this real slim white boy walked in after his crew made their entrance. He walked in and jumped his ass to front of the line and told us a very clever tale. Drama was beating the shit out of this boy. When he introduced his crafty ass to us, I ignored everybody else in the room. It seemed like he was traveling with his own theme music, as I smiled back at him. I saw some sort of pleasure all over Isabo's face as she looked at him. Everyone could tell that this motherfucker was HIGH! His mind was still out in the parking lot as he looked at me and all I could do was laugh with my eyes!

Isabo became as mellow as a weeping willow tree. She let out a breath as she began to speak to him. I thought that I was the only one to hear it in her voice, but I could tell that Eric also heard something in her speech. Although Eric noted that he'd heard her because this man looked good to her. She did not lower her eyes as she took the newcomer. Lily was waiting until he got inside the room before she spoke.

"Ms. Sagar, this is Major Morrison and company! They are your 11:00 o'clock appointment."

I extended my hand to shake his and said, "Please call me Roxanne. It is a pleasure to meet you, Mr. Morrison! These are my two captains. First allow me to introduce Eric Rich and secondly to Isabelle Meltova. Together with our support staff, we are Rox Sagar Lexus!"

Once everyone had been introduced Lily offered everyone a beverage. Then she exited the room as smoothly as she had entered. I looked up at this motherfucker, who looked like he was singing some song in his head! He looked like he was humming, singing or mentally dancing to "Bad Boy/Having a Party" by Luther Vandross. All I could do was smile, because whatever he was on, in his mind, it had his ass locked down! Next, we invited him and his associates to take a seat but the one who was the shortest in the group kept staring at me. I placed my rear end in my chair as I watched him watch me

I did not catch his name as he was being introduced because my eyes were fixed upon the black lace blouse which hung from under his shirt around the neckline. I thought that my eyes were playing tricks on me. But upon further observation, this man had so much hair hanging out of his suit, I had to look away because all the hair was hypnotizing me. I thought maybe he was a cross-dresser, and even though I did not mean to stare at him, he did not guard his flaw to me. Since I love looking at strange people, I had found myself a new part-time plaything for my eyes. I began to count the strands of hair on his chest. Major Morrison was the first to speak after all the pleasantries were done.

"Ms. Roxanne, you have a lovely establishment here. I have never seen so many pretty women under one roof in my life. I thank you for all the pretty people to look at for now."

While he was delivering his rehearsed bullshit of an opening speech to us, he placed all his attention on Isabo! I was happy for her because my plate was full, and I did not need another admirer. Eric was sitting at my right hand and Isabo was sitting at my left. Eric kicked my feet under the table and I in turn kicked Isabo. All the while Major. Morrison's associate had not taken his eyes off me. But that short, hairy man was of little concern to me at this moment. Major Morrison asked one of his associates to pull out their laptop and show us a PowerPoint presentation. The un-named player from his team at the back of the room got up to deliver our presentation.

The man with the hairy lace blouse stood up to inform us of their findings concerning the security breach. But my eyes could not look away from the hair protruding from his shirt, while a tiny smile showed on my face. I sat up in my chair because I wanted to hear what he had to say, plus maybe some of his hair would carry the conversation for him. I shook my head to try and remove those crazy thoughts! I knew that I was being bad, but I did not care while I continued to look back at him!

The hairy caterpillar of a man set up the visual display and then he walked over to the wall to point at certain parts. His voice was strong and firm but his boss, Mr. Morrison kept jumping into his presentation. Before he could finish his findings, Major Morrison stood up to tell us how the company plans on rewarding this dealership with state-of-the-art computers along with all the high-tech accessories to give our business the edge over our competitors. Then he advised that our corporate office wanted to handle the security breach on our own terms. He told us that he wanted this dealership to grant him and the corporate team total authorization to turn over their findings to the Feds!

Major Morrison said, "We have been tracking this one individual that works for your dealership for several years. But now, since he slipped up here at this dealership, we want to follow how embedded he really is inside of his organization. Therefore, we are considering offering him a job with our company, and maybe he can teach all the dealerships what to look for when they experience a security breach like the one that you encountered.

We know that you are aware, Ms. Roxanne, that this breach has caused a disaster inside your dealership and our corporate offices, too. We hope that you and your team are willing to stay on board while we handle the situation at a higher security level. At the end of the day, it is all about making the most of the money that we have, and how we can make it grow for all of us at the Lexus Corporation."

Mentally, I took notes of everything that he had said, as I glanced over at Eric, who was also taking notes. I looked at Isabo, whose face showed nothing but displeasure as she played with her fingers. My mind was wandering for a couple of seconds, because I was troubled by his statements.

I could feel the displeasure coming from my two co-captains, in fact. But I was determined not to get too pissed off with this man from Lexus Corporation. I moved my head from side to side as I let my eyes fall upon Major Morrison. I knew that I was about to venture into uncharted territory with my words to him. I was becoming pissed smooth the fuck off more and more as time was rolling past!

I sat still for 48 seconds, as I replayed his statements in my head. I moved my eyes back to Major Morrison, licked my teeth and put a smile in my voice, because I did not wish what I was about to say to seem harsh or dominant. I was going to ensure that before Major Morrison and his team exited our boardroom, he would be taking back a different answer from what he had expected to return with today. I stood up and asked whether he was finished with the presentation. If he had anything else to say, my team and I would welcome hearing it.

Major Morrison and his hairy friend sat down, informing us that there was nothing left to say about the situation as far as they were concerned. I felt privileged to know that *he* felt sure the deal he had just offered my dealership was done! He had another think coming for his ass, as I asked his friend to remove the display from my wall. I stood there and watched him turn off all his equipment. Then when the room was still, and the lights back on, I began to present my outlook for my company. I knew that by the time this was over, we were not going to be on the same page.

CHAPTER 14

MY BRAINWAVES WERE RAINING CATS AND DOGS!

"Well, let me begin by reminding you that this dealership is called Rox Sagar Lexus! It is apparent to me that your team must have missed the memo that spoke about me and my dealership when you were gathering information for this presentation. I don't take fault with you for thinking that your presentation was satisfactory. But so that all of us are aware, what you have just said to me makes no sense under the sun.

"For you and your company to think that I would grant you total authority and accessibility to the goings-on here is one of the most ludicrous ideas I have heard in a long time. Therefore, I believe that you are all under some illusion that us joining together and working as one is going to happen without a fight.

You and your entourage are sadly mistaken about my intentions to guard my dealership.

"Another thing, Major Morrison, what makes you think that your request would be welcome here at Rox Sagar LEXUS? You have not answered any of my major questions and concerns. You are not fixing my problem of the security breach! But let me get this right also, you wish for me to allow known criminal activities to continue here under my roof, so you can find out how deep this employee is embedded inside of his criminal organization? Major Morrison, before I relinquish total control of this dealership and help you out with the destruction of my thriving dealership. I would liquidate everything and return the cars on this lot to the factory, then I would jump ship and go work for another company, or start up my own Jaguar dealership, before I give this dealership away to the likes of you and the Lexus Corporation!

"Believe me when I tell you that I gain no pleasure from my statements to you. The truth of the matter is, Major Morrison, I am committed to staying an independent dealership. If I must sell everything here on the premises to hold onto my freedom, then so be it! I will end this dealership on my own terms before

210

I allow you and your team to systematically destroy what we have worked on for years. All my years to become a very successful dealership will not be in vain as far as I am concerned.

"The stakes are too high for me to grant you authority over me and my workers. How could you ask me to allow such thievery to go on under my roof, only so you can find out how they are moving all this criminal information? Your words sound outlandish to me, and they remind of something that a true outlaw would say. So, thank you for your help, but *no* thank you!"

"Ms. Roxanne, let me be the first to apologize to you and your team for our assumption that you would even consider my offer," ventured Major Morrison. "My offer of help to your dealership was made in bad taste. Please forgive me for trying to become more familiar with how you and your team operate. It is apparent that if you disband this dealership because of my careless words to you, it would be a poor outcome for the Lexus Corporation. I meant you no harm, and I am aware that I might have stepped out of bounds. I was trying to make a great impression on you.

"We will remove our offer to partner up with you and your dealership, because it looks like you have everything well taken care of. Please forget the conversation about including the Feds to help catch this crook! Put the thought of your dealership being left vulnerable without our guidance or direction out of your head, since I understand that the last thing that you want is to be left to fend for yourself. We are not outlaws, and we value you and your organization. We only wanted to help."

I stood there, glancing all around the boardroom and becoming more and more pissed. Maybe Major Morrison was under some illusion that I was a fallible fool and would allow him to do whatever he wanted to do to me and my dealership. But little did he know that I would die and go to hell before I allow him and the Lexus Corporation to dishonor my dealership. I knew that it was my turn to give him a few words of wisdom because he was speaking rubbish to me! Mentally, my mind was sending up an SOS as I licked my teeth once more and began to count seconds in my head! I tried to get my heart rate to calm down, then I cleared my throat before I spoke once more.

"Mr. Morrison, I do not wish for my dealership to be left alone to fend for itself. I will not be bullied into accepting an offer that will not be in my best interest. And make no mistake about it, I welcome any type of assistance from the Feds, but I will not allow this dealership to be used as some sort of proving ground for the Lexus Corporation. And if you do not have another plan, then maybe we should consider another line of defense because it is my understanding, Major Morrison, that ROX SAGAR LEXUS has been quite a successful venture for all of us who are involved. I know that the company has earned some nice year-end bonus packages off this dealership.

"To my understanding, this dealership has never experienced any type of economic turmoil. So, if I must shelter all my employees under my umbrella until things become resolved about the security breach, then I don't have a problem with that at all. And knowing that I am very sensitive about my dealership, I will go to great lengths to ensure that when things start to go wrong here, I will make our corporate office aware that this unnecessary trouble that could have been avoided because you chose to be careless with my dealership! You are asking us to be host to an infection so you can track it back to its origins, but suck luck. My dealership is not diseased, and I thought that you had a remedy for me, but I was wrong."

I watched as my threats danced around the room, because I did not take kindly to his threats. His ideas of how he sees us moving forward with this security breach as he lets us be taken over, so he can plot a course to track down the real origins of this illegal team and how they steal from all of us. I wanted to show him what it was like to be talked down to! I looked him dead in his face as if it was raining cats and dogs in the room, while Major Morrison stood up from his chair.

I do believe that his high was gone for a minute as I had just placed some new ideas in his head. He probably thought that he was going to come down here and tell me what they were going to do for me and my dealership, but when I did not roll over and play dead, I guess his manhood was challenged for a moment. My thoughts were, why did Akheem assign this man to my case? Did he not know that I was a force to be reckoned with on all levels because I did not like his plan?

Then the man who looked like a hairy caterpillar smiled strangely as he stood up and spoke.

"Please forgive my minor deceit, Ms. Sagar, but *I* am Major Morrison. Before this meeting spins all the way out of control, allow me to extend my sincere apology. Forgive me, and I do understand your uneasiness over this shameful travesty I was willing to be a part of. Whether or not you believe me, I am truly sorry for this display of poor taste. I wanted to be an observer and experience you for myself. I asked my co-worker to pretend to be me, for me to see you and your dealership in action. Believe me you rose to the occasion with flying colors, and I am in awe!"

The fake Mr. Morrison sat down and the man who looked like his hair was crocheted together extended his right hand to me! I just stood there eyeing this man, unsure whether he was still lying! I was unimpressed with his excuse, too. I thought I must be inside of a tripped-out version of Truth or Consequences game show, or I was being punked. I was trying to figure out what type of clown or demon I was in the process of entertaining. There were several moments of silence from me as Eric stood up and shook that man's hand, as did Isabo.

"Wow Mr. Morrison," Eric observed, "you have a strange sense of humor. I am not offended by your trickery, but I cannot speak for my boss or co-captain. I want to know how long you and your team were willing to ride this little joke of yours?"

I still did not have anything to say as I kept my eye on this short and hairy motherfucker! But before he could answer Eric's question Lily stormed into the boardroom and moved towards me like lightning. She whispered in my ear

"Ms. Roxanne, your mom is on line 1, and it's an emergency."

I knew this phone call was that short motherfucker's saving grace, because I was about to get knee-deep into his ass! I could not imagine *ever* playing such a trick on a dealership. I had to replay Lily's words in my head. What type of fool must he really be to play such a childish game on this dealership? I'm nobody's fool nor did I wish to be made a fool of for any reason. Although this dealership is experiencing a crisis, we are still big fish in a little pond here in the auto world in Sacramento, CA! As far as I was concerned, all roads and rivers led to Rox Sagar Lexus, because we are a company to be reckoned with, as Lily's word to me brought me back to my right mind!

Well, needless to say, I walked to the phone and picked it up. I pressed the button and waited to hear my mother's voice, in prayer-mode right away.

"Mom, what's wrong?"

"Roxanne, I need you and your sisters at the hospital right now. My daddy's brainwaves have come back, and his mind is becoming active."

I began to shake, because my grandfather had been in a coma for nearly six months. We thought we had lost him, and he didn't know that his wife was dead. I allowed tears to fall while my heart was refilling itself full of hope. I told her that I would be right there. She told me that both of my sisters were on their way. I hung up the phone and asked Eric to carry on in my place while he and Isabo stood close to me, wanting to know what the news was. I told them that my grandfather's brainwaves are coming back, and I was going to leave so I could be with my family. I walked over to Mr. Morrison, shook his hand and said, "Eric has my authority to act on behalf of this dealership!"

More tears rolled down my face even though I wore a smile while I told Mr. Morrison that I didn't understand why he would choose led us astray. To me, his action towards me and my dealership was viciously unkind. I decided to give his action thought, and maybe it would cast away all my doubts in dealing with him. I turned to walk out of the boardroom with Isabo heavy on my heels. Mr. Morrison asked if there anything that he could do. As I walked out, I told him that his offer to help was very sweet, but I would have to decline the offer. Isabo was right by my side as I walked into my office.

CHAPTER 15

A SHOT IN THE DARK!

I pulled into the parking lot of the hospital as I began to sing my own theme song. I wanted to make sure that GOD heard me. I sang several verses from "Roxanne" by The Police. I sent up far too many prayers to keep count of, but I knew that GOD was with me. I turned off my car, got out, walked to the main desk and found out which room he was in. I knew that my dreams for my family were not dead as I knew that more positive changes were about to happen in our lives. I was in the elevator on my way to be with my family when my Angels showed up! They all told me I had nothing to fear.

"You don't understand," I protested. "He is all that I know, and the three of you don't know what I fear."

"We know all too well what you fear, Ms. Beaumont," they replied, "but it is your job to keep the faith. We will do the rest for you."

Here I was standing in an elevator with three heavenly beings surrounding me, telling them that they didn't know what I feared. I was hopeful that the Lord would not call my grandfather home right now, because our family was already hanging on for dear life by God's grace. I'm not sure if we could continue if he left us too. Then it occurred to me as I looked at my Angels that I wanted to know where they'd been, and why they were dressed as they were. I glanced at Danielle as she adjusted her outfit, a costume resembling The Statue of Liberty. Samantha-Ann was dressed as a Stop sign and Earnestine looked the weirdest of all of them. She did not have on an outfit that I recognized. I asked her whom she was pretending to be, or what she was.

She smiled at me and said, "I'm just an angel right now, Ms. Beaumont but don't worry yourself about your grandfather, or as we refer to him, Speak. He is more than a handful for any soul to do battle with, but he will be just fine. Forgive me for being so tired; I wrestled with your grandfather all night long. I am glad that he has been prevented from leaving you and your family right."

I looked at her with a twinkle in my eye. "What do you mean, he was prevented from leaving?"

Samantha-Ann, dressed as a big-ass STOP sign, answered.

"Ms. Beaumont, your grandfather, AKA Speak is attending a party inside his own brain. It's almost like he is having his own Mardi Gras party. He kept trying to leave last night but we would not allow him to exit this world. That is why I am dressed as a STOP sign, because he thinks that what he wants is his own liberty, but he is not ready for it yet. So, we had to do battle with him last night and since Earnestine watches over him always, she had to physically do battle with him.

"She is the only one of us who could touch him on your behalf, and that is why she is dressed as you would be. He was trying to run from us, and his body is still trying to heal itself, so he must be gentle with himself and give himself more time to make his appearance to you. He is not ready to come out of his slumber yet, but when he does return to you and your family, he might ask you why you did not walk with him as he was trying

221

to exit this world. You will tell him that it was not time for him to go, so you had to block all the exits out of his room!"

"We are aware that you do not have a clue of what we are talking about, Ms. Beaumont," Danielle added, "but when it is time for you to understand, you will have all the clarity you need. Believe us when we tell you that we are aware of what you fear. Now go on and be with your family, and just know that we kept the wolf away from your grandfather's door last night!"

Next thing I knew, my Angels broke out into their own version of the song "Dream On" by Aerosmith as I exited the elevator. I had a big smile on my face as I walked to my grandfather's room and pushed the door to enter. My mom and sisters were all there. We started to do our family prayer circle for our grandfather to gather his strength to return to us, for over 99 seconds.

The doctors came in shortly after I made it to the room. They updated us that Grandfather's brainwaves are somewhat scattered right now, but with constant stimulation from us, they believed that he would be back with us soon. If we wanted him to be the person he used to be, we all needed to re-establish our relationships with him by coming to his room daily and sharing our lives with him so he could mentally catch up. Then we were informed that their lead brain specialist would check in on our grandfather tomorrow, to assess him.

I could not wait to tell him of the events that had gone on in my life recently, because we used to talk all the time. I was ready to get started, knowing that he'd been involved in a wrestling match last night with my Angel Earnestine, so he would not check out. I was eager to talk with him; understanding that his soul was restless and ready to be free only made me desire to talk with him more. I had to ensure to be on my best behavior and not cause a fight with my family about anything, because he had everything to gain if we all played our cards right.

I started a conversation with our mother first, then once all the pleasantries were done with, I began to inquire how he ended up at this hospital, because he'd been in a senior citizens' rehabilitation home. I wanted to know what had happened to bring him to this hospital. Our mother told us to take a seat, so while we all gathered chairs to rest our bodies, mom began to tell us how she and her father ended up here.

"As you all know, girls, I go and visit with my father every day, unlike you three ungrateful heifers who can only fit him into your schedule once a week. When I saw him yesterday his face looked troubled, almost like he was ready to die, and I became so upset looking at my father, I could not rest any last night. When I made it to the rehab center today, he looked like he had been up all night fighting. I questioned the staff about how his night was, but they didn't report anything out of the ordinary. My heart stayed troubled by the way he was looking.

"That is when I asked for the specialist at the rehab center to come in and check him, and of course they thought I was mad. I could tell something was wrong with him, and after all my complaints and threats, they ran several tests on his brain and saw that he was regaining some of his thought patterns. The doctors had him picked up and transferred to this hospital. Once we got here, the doctors thought that he will be coming out of his coma soon, and they had no reason to lie to me. That is why I called my girls to be with me, because he is going to have a ton of questions for all of us. But until he reclaims his own life, I need the three of you to help me with pieces of your lives. I need one of you to come and visit with him every day, because I know this one thing: he will be at a loss without his wife."

I told her that she didn't have to rush to the hospital, because I would visit with him in the morning, and that way, I could tell him what had been going on in my life.

We all decided to go grab a meal together. The day was over with for all of us except Cherokee; she had to work later that night. We all got up and gave our mother group hugs, then each of us kissed her on the cheek as we exited the room. I looked down at my watch and saw that it was 7:00 p.m.; we had been here for over six hours. Dinner did not sound good to me at that moment, but if my sisters wanted to go somewhere to eat, I would go with them.

Maxey told us that she had trial in the morning and had asked for a continuance for her to be with us today. Then Cherokee wanted to go home and get a couple of hours rest, so we all decided not to go for dinner after all. We scheduled a different time next week. Once I pulled in my garage I sat still, prayed and cried because I was happy.

CHAPTER 16

SAILON MY FRIEND!

Since it was just Thursday night, I ate only a small salad, then went upstairs. I took a very long bath and got in the bed, not in the mood to speak with anyone. I needed to process all the past couple of days had placed before me. I was tired to the bone and sleepy. I began to sing myself to sleep. I don't know why the song "Sail On" by The Commodores came to my mind, but I sang that song in its entirety as my body replayed scenes from my day. I was in bed by 10:00p.m., glad to be done with this day.

I was not sure if I had any dreams or not, but the fact of the matter was, I did not care. I was so eager to get out of this week because it had really been trying for me. I prayed that I had no more battles to face before the rest of this week was over. I woke up at 8:00 a.m. feeling great. I really had needed the rest and it had been too long since I'd had a good night's sleep. I was moving rather slowly because I had a long day ahead of me. I jumped to my feet when I heard a noise from downstairs. I could not remember where the fuck I had left my handbag. Then it came to me that I threw it on the counter as usual, so I pulled out my reserve gun and went to investigate the noise!

I owed it to myself to take care of my family and me ... then it came to me that maybe Gloria was checking in early, as I walked to the railing of the stairs and called down.

"Identify yourself, or there will be hell to pay!"

A man's voice came back from the kitchen. It was Diaz. He was bringing his wife's belongings back into the house!

"It's just us chickens, Ms. Roxanne!" he called back.

Then I laughed and said, "Touché, touché, Diaz! How have you been, and did you have a great time with your wife and kids?"

He walked to the bottom of the steps and looked up at me, asking if I would put my gun away before he answered me. I told him that I was sorry; I would put my gun down and be right there to greet them both. I went back into my room and put on a pair of sweats and a top. I went downstairs to greet Gloria and her husband, tears in my eyes as I looked at her.

Gloria said, "You look like you have lost more weight since the last time I saw you."

"Well, if I look smaller since the last time you saw me, it is entirely *your* fault for being gone so long," I replied, laughing.

As Diaz went to gather all her things from the car and take them up to her room, Gloria and I continued to talk. I sat down at the kitchen table as she prepared breakfast for me. Once Diaz was done unpacking Gloria, he told us that he needed to get to the donut shop, and he would see her later tonight. She walked him outside, so they could say their good-byes.

Gloria came back in and said, "How have you been, Ms. Roxanne? And why are you allowing your voluptuous body to dwindle down to nothing? Have you been eating while I was gone? How are the kids and did you enjoy your impromptu trip to Texas?"

I asked her to allow me the chance to answer her questions, because she put five questions to me, before I could begin answering the first of them. Gloria told me that I had until she finished making my breakfast, because that would give me plenty of time. I set out to give her answers to all her questions. I told her I'd been fine since she left, and not allowing my body to dwindle down to nothing. As hard as I tried over the years, I would never be a small person. I am still a big girl; it's just that I am a little more compact than the last time that she saw me.

I assured Gloria that I had been eating while she was gone. I assured her that the kids were great, with their father for now, but they would be back tomorrow afternoon. I gave her all the sordid details of what happened with Franchescia and Anthony while they were with my mother, while I was at the LA auto show. Gloria's face began to change as she listened to the details that involved the kids. She began to shake her head as I gave my explanation. I informed her of the trouble with the state and Anthony, and how I'd had to ask Cherokee to retrieve my children from my mom. Next, I told her that I'd had to purchase my mom a dog for her to drop the charges against my son.

As for my answer about my trip with Mr. Fulwad to Texas, all I could say was that it was better than I could have ever expected—but for now we weren't speaking to one another. I gave Gloria the good news about my granddad, and she smiled when I informed her that he might be pulling out of his coma soon! She did not say anything to me for 27 more seconds, when she finally spoke.

"Are you acting like you are wounded duck and not taking care of yourself because of Mr. Fulwad and your grandfather? Because I need to let you know, Ms. Roxanne, you have your two kids to look after. If anything should happen to you, who would take care of your children? I recommend that you take better care of yourself and never give in to anyone who does not wish to be in your company. So, if Mr. Fulwad wishes to deal with you from a distance, then allow him to make all the steps to you. Never let him know that you miss him; go on with your life, Ms. Roxanne, and if you want to deal with any man, it should be on your terms. You have done your time begging for love, and if Mr. Fulwad wishes to deal with you, *he* will come to you!"

I heard what Gloria was saying to me as I looked away. She said I was acting like a wounded duck. I smiled at her words, because I'd never been told that before. It did not hurt my feelings because somewhere in the back of my mind, I knew that she was telling me the truth. I ate the breakfast that she had prepared for me, and we talked about her trip with Diaz. We spent an hour at the kitchen table until I looked at my watch and saw that it was time for me to go. I told Gloria that I was glad that she was home, but I had a busy day to get started on, so I needed to end our conversation. I sailed upstairs and prepared myself for my very long day.

I was running slightly behind schedule, but my first stop was going to be visiting with my grandfather. I dressed in a semi-casual manner because I did not know how I would find the shooting range. If things were not as tidy as I wanted them to be, then I knew that I would not be to upset. I put on a gray pantsuit and black and gray boots to match as I pulled my hair up in a twist, because I did not want it to get in my way while I was shooting a gun. I applied a small amount of makeup to my face and put a pair of diamonds earrings in my ears—they looked as if a ray of sun was shining off of my earlobes, they were so pretty.

I brushed my teeth 3 more times, then I walked downstairs and told Gloria, welcome home. We hugged once more as I grabbed a bottle of water and walked out the door. I felt like my life was pulling itself together. I got in my car and plugged in my cell phone. I backed out of my garage and called the dealership. I spoke with Isabo and Eric and told them of the progress that my grandfather was making. I told them that I would be in later today, and we could revisit everything that happened after I left the day before. I was on my way to the hospital to check in on my granddad, then I was off to the firing range to make sure that I passed the requirements to carry a gun for the dealership.

CHAPTER 17

BE THE PIG!

Once I was done speaking with Isabo and Eric, I asked them to transfer me to Lily's phone, adding for God's sake, they should *not* make the mistake of allowing Incomplete Maggie to answer the phone. Isabo transferred me over to Lily just as I told her that I would see her later today. I exchanged pleasantries with Lily, then asked whether she had secured me a caterer. She told me that the company named Deuce and a Quarter would be happy to prepare a meal for me and my family.

I asked her if she was still planning to attend my gathering. Lily laughed, thrilled to be invited to my home, then I told her of the news about my grandfather. I asked her to inform Maggie of where things stood with him. I ended my phone call with her as I pulled into the parking lot of the hospital.

I was glad to be the first one to visit with my grandfather today. I made one small wish as I got out of my car. I asked the LORD to prevent me becoming upset with anything or anyone today, and let me bring some type of joy to my granddad. I walked to his room and found that it was just the two of us there. I removed my jacket and pulled up a chair on his left side. I wanted to be on his left, because that was the side on which his heart is located. I did not wish for my words to travel too far, and since I was going to be talking from my heart, we would be on an even keel with each other.

I repeated the Lord's prayer before I got started, then I placed my hand inside of his, and began to retrace the past 6 months of my life. I did not censor my conversation with him. I found that I was using graphic language while I talked to him but the conversations that we were having felt great to me. I cried for several minutes as I retold him of the death of his wife. "I miss *both* of you, daddy," was what I said to him after I finished informing him of her untimely death.

I squeezed his hand 12 times while we were having our conversation. I smiled as I told him about how great the funeral was and how he would have been so proud to see how lovely his wife looked. I told him that Michael and I were now divorced, but the kids were doing a great job of adjusting to the changes in our household, but with time to comfort all of us, I was sure that things would all work out for the best. I sat still in his room for several minutes as I kept my hand inside of his. I even found myself telling him a couple of jokes along, with a lovely analysis of a story that I found intriguing; plus, I knew that he could appreciate it.

I was not sure if someone had told it to me or if I had read it in a magazine, but I keep this story close to my heart because it reminds me of him and me on so many levels. I had even apologized to my grandfather if I did not repeat it the right way, but I wanted to give credit to whomever said it, and I could not for the life of me remember who it was or where I had heard this story, as I continued to speak.

Although I did remind him that I am just a girl with big eye and a killer smile, I told him that I was going to do my best and retell this little story. The story goes something like this, as I said to him: "In the egg and bacon breakfast story of life: The chicken is somewhat involved, but the pig is committed." I said to him, "I am the pig who is committed but with one change to the little story for me. I am the pig who walks around in high fashion CFMs (Come Fuck Me shoes)! I know that I have given my all to my family and friends, so I guess I am the pig!

I kept saying out loud, "Be the pig, be the pig" over and over as I continued to talk with him. After I finished with my story to him, I got up to use the restroom. I smiled as I walked into the restroom because I was enjoying keeping my word to my mother. It felt great to spend some alone time with my grandfather, even though he still being held in his dreamlike state in a coma. It did me some good to just sit down and talk with him as we used to during old times together.

I relieved myself, washed my hands and checked out my face and my hair. o

Once I was done, I exited the restroom. When I walked back into his room there was a good-looking man standing at the foot of my grandfather's bed, looking over his chart. He was not as tall as Sissell but around the same height as Akheem. He had a nice face for a white boy, but he looked as if he was lonely, for some strange reason. I asked him who he was and asked what was he doing in here.

He smiled at me then said, "I'm not just your average anybody standing here, I am Mr. Beaumont's doctor. My name is Doctor Russell Henely, and whom might *you* be, since you are asking so many questions?"

"I am Mr. Beaumont's first granddaughter, Dr. Henely. My name is Roxanne Beaumont-Sagar and I have a quick question for you, doctor, if you don't mind. I would like to know when do you think he might come out of his coma, or am I asking for too much information too soon? Because our family really misses him, and we need him back with us to run our family."

"Well Ms. Beaumont-Sagar, it might be anybody's guess, because when you are dealing with the brain, anything is possible. We just must sit back and wait for your grandfather to rejoin us. There is no given timeline for him returning to you and your family. You just must show some patience, but I can tell that you are a very patient person, because you have watched every word that has jumped out of my mouth thus far. It is almost like you were counting them one by one as my words leave my mouth!"

I smiled at his observation about me because I was counting his words. His comments to me made me realize that he is just as observant as I am about certain things to do with people, but he is a trained professional and I am just a selective spectator of a counter through this life with subtle tendencies. I guess he was secretly decoding one of my many flaws as he looked at me. I smiled back at him as I informed the doctor that 81 words sprang from his mouth during this now recent exchange between the two of us.

I did not count his first sentences to me but if it would entertain him, I am sure that if I put my mind to it, I could revisit his past sentences and count them for him also, because I normally do not count words. I find it more soothing to count seconds, but it is sort of funny how he noticed one of my subtle but small flaws. Since I do not move my mouth as I am counting, I found it charming that he noticed what I was doing … but I was not here to quibble about my OCD and me. I needed him to focus his trained eyes on my grandfather and not pay any attention to me.

"Ms. Beaumont-Sagar, your slight OCD (Obsessive-Compulsive Disorder) does not concern me. But it's thoughtful and quaint that you noticed me noticing you. Although all my attention is on your grandfather for the moment, I can examine you later if you wish, to have my professional opinion about your OCD. I need you to allow me to finish with my diagnosis of your grandfather. I can carve out some time for you later today, but know that I will be out of your way as soon as possible."

I backed away from the doctor and his slight smile, allowing him to finish his visit with my grandfather. I stood in the corner and watched him perform several tests. I did not know what he was checking for during the examination. I kept still as he went about his work, then I asked him if he wished for me to leave. We both looked at each other as I tilted my head to the right side and smiled once more, but Dr. Henely told me that he would be done in just a moment. I informed the doctor that I was not going to stay.

I removed my jacket from the back of the chair and picked up my handbag. I walked up to the doctor and shook his hand while we both smiled at one another. I tilted my head to the side as I looked at him up and down for three seconds. I let out a little giggle as I moved past him. I mentioned to the doctor that I would see him later as I exited the room and moved towards the elevator. I looked at my watch as I pressed the button to call the elevator. The time was 1:15 in the afternoon and I started thinking about my appointment at the shooting range. I was thinking that the doctor had a kind face with strange eyes, but once the elevator made it to me, my attentions had refocused on my next adventure of the day.

Once I made it downstairs, I stepped off the elevator and put my sunglasses on. The strangest feeling came over me as I walked towards my car. I noticed a couple moving in my direction. I was grateful that I had my sunglasses on, because they were Sissell and his wife Judy—or Joanne. I just could not remember her name at that moment. They were a good distance away from me, but I knew it was he as I kept my eyes trained upon them. Sissell looked over at me and graced me with a smile. I nodded my head in acknowledgement.

I knew that I would always have a special place in my heart for him. Mentally, all I could think of was that song that Cherokee sang to me when he broke my heart by asking me to release him, "Love TKO" by Teddy Pendergrass.

I reminded myself that he was the one who requested to end our affair. I respected him enough to give him what he asked for, because I honored his wishes. I forced myself not to waste more thought on him, since he had pulled the plug on us. I would always remember the fun that we had, I thought to myself, as I sat still for 53 more seconds then got the rest of my day moving.

I then began wondering if his daughter was at this hospital or if the two of them out doing their charitable duty to the church. I started up my car. Eventually I pulled up to the shooting range and secured my handbag and jacket in the trunk of my car. I took my ID and a charge card with me and walked in at my appointed time. I took my place with all the other people who were in the process of securing a license to carry a concealed weapon.

I passed that stupid test and was instantly recertified, even though I had to spend two hours to secure my license once more; still, it was worth the hassle. I wouldn't have to re-qualify for three more years, for which I was truly glad. My day was slowly winding down and I knew I needed to appear at the dealership, so I suffered through the beginning of rush-hour traffic. I pulled up on to the lot at 5:15 p.m. because the shooting range was on the east side of town and my dealership was on the south side.

I gathered all my things from the trunk of my car as I watched Lily hold the door open for me. We greeted each other and she informed me that I had an impromptu meeting with Major Morrison. I asked her what the purpose of the meeting was. As far as I was concerned, we discussed everything yesterday, and any other decisions that were needed were settled Eric and Isabo.

"I understand what you're saying, Ms. Roxanne," Lily said, "but Mr. Morrison expressed his concern for you and your grandfather, so he mentioned that he would drop by the dealership on his way out of town today."

I had to remind myself of the vow I took first thing this morning. I asked her what time he said that he would be gracing us with his presence.

"He mentioned that he will be here at six o'clock, but if you would like me to try and reach him, I will hunt them down and ask him to reschedule, because I see that the last thing you need is to make time for someone forcing a meeting with you."

I smiled as I looked over at Lily. She was developing a Roxanne Beaumont-Sagar mindset, and I liked that. I told Lily that there was no need to reschedule. I welcomed another conversation with his short-ass, and if he chose to become unruly, I would have Bo toss him out on his rear end! Both Lily and I began to laugh at the idea.

I then wanted to know if Eric and Isabo were available. Lily told me that both were in their offices. I asked her to have them meet me in my office in 15 minutes. I also requested that she go to the deli and grab me an iced tea and a banana. She asked me if I needed anything else. I told her that I didn't, as I placed my coat on the back of my chair. I stepped into the bathroom to freshen up. I wanted to pull myself out of the gloomy thoughts that were hanging around. I checked my face and my hair and reapplied a spot of lip-gloss and perfume while I popped a mint in my mouth.

Isabo and Eric had arrived in my office with looks of excitement. I was eager to hear about the conclusion of yesterday's meeting. I wanted to see how Major Morrison and his team offered up their best analogy on the security breach and what the plans were for us moving forward. I told them that Major Morrison would be here in less than 45 minutes, and I needed a summation. Eric spoke first.

"Once Major Morrison was finished apologizing for his stunt, we got down to business. He told us that upon further investigation, it looked as if all roads led to William AKA Trigger, and other accomplice here at the dealership. He was unsure who the other person is. He was proud to inform us that Incomplete Maggie was eliminated as a suspect. She was only guilty by association, and the fact that a young man showed her some attention made her behavior understandable. The Lexus Corporation has a special investigator assigned to actively hunt down the ring of thieves that William works for.

"To show you how sorry he is for misleading the meeting yesterday, he will be supplying the dealership with new computers and all new high-tech hardware. The company will also have the dealership rewired with the latest tech and they will assume all costs for us signing up our customers into a credit-monitoring agency. Major Morrison assured us that when we become a fully functional operation with high tech everything onsite, it is highly unlikely that a situation like this should ever present itself again.

"To make sure that we stay on board with the Lexus Corporation, he is willing to authorize the company absorbing the cost of the furniture purchased on Monday. He wants to make sure that you are aware that we have a promising career ahead with them, and that would be unfortunate if you should feel the need to liquidate your holdings in the company. He will also write off the remodeling of the dealership as part of the restructuring he and his team are implementing for us."

I felt like a well-fed cat sitting behind my desk. All I could do was smile at Eric's magic words I felt a twinge of excitement run down my spine when he said that he would authorize the company to absorb the cost of the remodel! Plus, they were going to equip us with state of the art everything!

My energy level shot through the roof, once Eric finished laying out the elaborate plans in store for my dealership. I was no longer jaded by his actions yesterday, and if Major Morrison saw it fit to show up unannounced at this dealership in the future, I wouldn't have a problem! He proved himself more than worthy of my appreciation, and I planned to tell him just how pleased I was with his actions.

Isabo jumped in, adding, "We also found out that Major Morrison would prefer that we keep his secret from yesterday. The corporate office would not be pleased to find out that he allows different members from his team to pretend to be him while he hangs out in the background! We assured him that his secret is safe with us just if he writes off all the expenses for the dealership. It was a win-win situation for all of us, and he was truly concerned about you and your family, Roxanne! That is why he is stopping by before he heads off to his next destination. He wanted to come back to make sure that all of us are in one accord. Once you give him your seal of approval, he will be drifting on to another unsuspecting dealership!"

All three of us began to laugh hysterically because all I was thinking of was rectifying the security breach here at the dealership. I was thrilled about all the money that we'd be able to be credit back to our accounts and re-invest. Because of Major Morrison's generosity, the yearly bonuses would increase. When I got the chance to speak with Major Morrison, I could promise him that my lips were sealed! Once we tied up all the business about the dealership, I shared with Isabo and Eric a glimpse of what happened yesterday at the hospital. I told them of the situation pertaining to my grandfather, that it was all just a waiting game now.

Isabo and Eric offered to make themselves available to work an extra shift at a moment's notice, both being aware of how trying the situation with my granddad had been on my family.

I thanked them both sincerely for handling the dealership with such care. We continued to talk about my family when Lily informed me that Major Morrison was here for our meeting. I mentioned to Eric and Isabo that he was outside waiting for me, as I stood up and put my jacket back on. I asked them whether I looked presentable.

Eric said, "You look as lovely as ever, but I can tell you're somewhat understated today because normally your beauty caresses the room more."

Isabo and I both looked at each other and smiled.

"That is one of the best compliments you have ever given, me Eric! On top of all the other good news that I've heard today, now I *officially* feel like a million bucks!"

I walked them both to the door and met Major Morrison in the main showroom. I shook his hand with such conviction while we walked back to my office. I asked him to take a seat and offered him something to drink, but he told me he could only stay a moment. Major Morrison went right to the point regarding the understanding reached yesterday. I assured him that the offer he'd made to this dealership was more than welcome to my staff and me.

Major Morrison said, "Ms. Sagar, I am so glad that you find my offer comforting because we at the Lexus Corporation wish to keep you on board. Whatever we need to do to facilitate you in staying employed with us, will not be too much to offer such a prosperous dealership as the one you are running here. I invite you to take advantage of anything that I could possibly offer you and your team. I hope that certain stipulations attending our deal meet with your approval. I would hate for anyone on the corporate level to ever find out that I routinely allow my teammates to pretend to be in charge, while I watch!"

"Major Morrison, I assure you that your secret is safe with me. You do not have to worry about my staff or me speaking out of turn. I am quite aware of the work that goes into securing a haven for yourself and your co-workers. I commend you on offering to absorb the purchase price of furniture for this dealership. Before we finish, I need to have our understanding in writing. I do not wish for there to be any misunderstanding or miscommunication. And if by chance I can ever be of any assistance to you in the future, please do not hesitate to contact me."

Once I had concluded my remarks, I smiled and tilted my head to the right. Both of us sat there for 15 seconds looking at one another. I guess he was trying to figure out if he could trust me. I was not interested in going on some sort of power trip with this hairy little man. The thing was, I didn't know this man to trust him, so without written agreement, he could change his mind and cancel his offer.

That was why I was asking for a legal document of our verbal transaction. I didn't mean to be unkind to him or his team, but I need to make sure that he would have just as much to lose if he backed out of our arrangement. I wasn't about to allow him to dismiss or discount his dealings with us. A smile crept onto his face and I knew we had a solid deal. I stood up and extended my hand to shake his! I wanted to know when I should expect my new equipment and when the money would be credited back to my business account.

"I will have the contract sent to your dealership by the end of the day," Major Morrison assured me.

He went on to promise me that I would receive the new state of the art equipment before the end of the year (considering that we were already kicking the door in on Thanksgiving), and the credit would be returned to my corporate charge account before the end of next week. I knew that I would have everything that I needed, soon. Major Morrison told me that it was time for him to go and he did not wish to take up any more of my time. He said he knew I was very busy. He started clearing his throat, seeming as if he had some words tangled up in it.

"No wonder you fascinate Mr. Akheem; he would be a fool to let you slip through his fingers," Major Morrison observed. "We will see what develops between you, because he would be sorry for his misstep with you. If he is as smart as they claim he is, I hope he won't self-sabotage himself with you. You are the only woman he has ever spoken of during our time together at the company! If you are in ever need of anything or you wish to contact me, simply send me an e-mail and I will get back with you real soon. Thank you for your help and attention with this matter, Roxanne, and you take care of yourself."

I walked him to the main showroom door and watched him get into a company car. I saw the employee who was pretending to be him yesterday wave goodbye to me as they exited the parking lot. I asked Isabo what his real name was, and she told me it was Reggie Coleman. He enjoyed impersonating Mr.

Morrison because they had a special type of relationship. I did not care what she meant by her statement because my head was so crammed full of other people's shit.

Isabo walked back into my office and reminded me that she was off tomorrow, but she would see me early Sunday morning. Then she wanted to know how things had gone at the shooting range. I told her that my concealed-carry permit was re-certified and it took me two hours to hit all the marks, but I persevered and finished the procedure. So here I was, ready, willing and able to shoot someone if I had to protect my dealership or myself. We both smiled as she exited my office. I finished what I was doing and prepared to leave. It had been such a long and prosperous day, and I looked forward to going home, at peace with everyone.

CHAPTER 18

15 WAYS AROUND SUNDAY!

I ended my day at the dealership around 8:00 p.m. I told Eric that I would see him in the morning as I mentioned that were still on schedule for Sunday. Then I wanted to know if we would have some participation from employees to help us out with the semi-remodel. He assured me that the remodel of the dealership would go on without a hitch.

"Hey, Eric, tell me how things are going for you and your wife," I inquired.

He looked at me rather strangely for a couple of seconds. I smiled as I exited the building.

"I was just teasing you, Eric; I wanted to tell you that you looked lovely today."

He had on a red dress with red shoes and a red wig. I guess he knew that he had conformed to my wishes yesterday and wore a business suit to represent the dealership. He looked great yesterday, but today, he almost looked authentic, which was scary; but since I was on my way home, I did not care. He was the man that I needed him to be for us at the dealership yesterday, and that was more than enough for me. I walked out of the dealership and drove myself home. I was so tired. I got home, and Gloria had prepared me a healthy meal.

I guess she was trying to fatten me back up, since when I walked into the kitchen, she had my meal already waiting on me. She must have missed me as well, since while I ate my meal we continued with our conversation from this morning. I sat and ate, feeling weak and wanting to lie in bed to rest. I sat there listening to her list the virtues I brought into people's lives. I was in total agreement with her observation about me, but I was only of a mind to listen. I was quite aware of some of the seen and unseen flaws that I possessed.

I allowed her to speak her mind about me, and when I felt as if she was done, I got up, kissed her on the cheek and excused myself to go to bed. I was halfway up the stairs when Gloria asked me if it was OK for Diaz to spend the night with her. I told her that I did not have a problem with it, that she should just lock up the house before they retired upstairs. A gleaming smile came over her face.

"Welcome back home, Gloria, and good night."

"It's good to be back home, Ms. Roxanne, I will see you in the morning. What would you like for breakfast?"

"Gloria, sleep late with your husband, as I need to be at the dealership early. I will see you tomorrow afternoon, then we can come up with a menu for dinner because the kids will be back later that evening. I don't think I will be through digesting this meal in the morning, so sleep late and enjoy your day!"

I made it all the way upstairs to my room where Gloria had put fresh linens on my bed and refreshed my room. I was eager to get some rest while I removed my clothes and plugged up my cell phone. I was glad to be home and could not *imagine* being anywhere else right now. I stepped into my bathroom and started myself a bath. I was ready to relax in preparation for sleep. By the time I got in the tub, it was 10:00 p.m. and my thoughts were becoming fuzzy.

I did enjoy my bath, but needed to get in bed, so after 30 minutes of soaking in the water, I exited and dried off my body. I put on a pretty gown and got on my knees to say my prayers. All three of my Angels walked into my room and formed a circle with me as I prayed. They never spoke one word to me, and I was unoffended by their silence. I was respectful of them, but I was sleepy. Maybe they could tell that I was exhausted beyond compare. All of us got into the bed as I mentally placed all my cares at the feet of the LORD!

I let out several sighs as I smiled. I set the timer on my alarm clock and began to fall fast into a restful slumber. I was humming unfamiliar songs as I went to sleep. I was replaying the events of the day. The statements that Mr. Morrison had spoken about Akheem and myself particularly kept resurfacing. I told myself that I would deal with Mr. Akheem next week because I did love and need him. Since he was the guy that I had been looking for, I felt pretty damn special.

My alarm went off and I dragged myself out of bed. I had only gotten nine hours of sleep, and was tired already, before the day even began. I knew that I had to be there to open things up because Isabo was off work today. Although I did enjoy a longer sleep this time, I was still uneasy with the day, but I put some happy thoughts into my head. I knew that when I returned home today my children would be there, and that gave me hope. I whispered several words of encouragement to myself because I was aware that some days, you must minister to yourself. Once I did so, I was ready to face the day.

I put on a lavender and black pinstripe suit on as well as a white shirt with a matching necktie. I put tons of curls in my hair and chose a pair of soft lavender-colored earrings. I applied a thick black line over my eyes. Then I traced it with lavender-colored eyeliner. I was praying that nothing showed up today that the Lord and I couldn't handle. I picked a pair of black pumps that virtually serenaded my feet, while I grabbed my cell phone and my travel bag.

I forgot to put on some perfume, so I put all my items down and walked back into my dressing closet. I did not know which fragrance to wear. I closed my eyes, picked up a bottle and began to spray myself. I closed my closet, picked my items back up and walked out the door. I heard Gloria and Diaz struggling in bed while they were having sex, and smiled as I walked downstairs! I picked up my handbag and grabbed a bottle of water. I pressed the buttons to open my garage. I placed all my items into my car. I pulled out of my driveway and began to head to my dealership towards the freeway.

My cell phone rang, and I answered, "Good morning, this is Roxanne."

The voice on the other end said, "Good morning, Rox, this is Sissell."

I thought that I was hearing things as he said his name once more, but I could hear the love that he still had for me hiding in his voice.

"Rox, don't tell me that you have gotten over me that quickly. Why are you not saying anything? I know you saw me yesterday in the parking lot. Seeing you opened a tear in my heart and caught me off guard. I still remember how beautiful you truly are; that is why I am calling you today. I just needed to hear your voice once more and to make sure that you are OK."

I paused for what seemed like a long time because I did not expect to hear Mr. Linwood's voice so soon. Even though I did see him yesterday I had previously removed his number from my phone, as I didn't want to be tempted to call him and ask him to come back to me. I put our chance encounter out of my mind from yesterday, because he'd opted to leave my life and, I assumed, had moved on. Sissell was like a ghost to me but when I saw him yesterday, I sort of envied his wife because he looked so good. However, today was a new day, and I had nothing to offer him except common courtesy, which one might bestow upon a mere acquaintance!

"Good morning Mr. Linwood, how is your daughter doing?" I eventually responded. I knew that he must have been at the hospital yesterday to visit someone close to him, so I just assumed that it was his daughter. My guess was correct.

"We had her moved back to the local hospital because she has made such a vast improvement. We thought it would be better if she were closer to home. Even though I did not call you to talk about my daughter, thank you for your concern. How are you *doing*, Rox? It looked like you have lost some weight and it did my heart well to see you in the parking garage. I wanted to make a move over to where you were because a small part of me cried when I saw you. I cannot tell you how much I have missed you."

"Well, Mr. Linwood, I released you over five months ago, so there is nothing else for us to say. Take great care of yourself because it is unfair for you to call this late in the game. You *left* me, Sissell, and I wish you and your family the best that life can hold. I can't give you the authorization to steal my heart any more … so have a good day, *sir*."

I disconnected our phone call because I do not need any more fog in my life. I knew that he was only giving me thought because he just happened to see me. He already stole my heart once and I wasn't interested in him trying to do it again!

I made my way to my dealership with 17 different thoughts of Sissell running through my head. I know that it was time for me to move on, so I changed my mindset to the new life that I had now. Even though I was at odds with my guy for now, I still valued and wanted only Akheem. I placed my mind on Mr. Fulwad and how would I re-establish our relationship.

A warm feeling of love came over me as I pulled into my parking space. I made it to work on time, but GOD knows that I was tired. I removed my things from the car and made my way inside. I felt as if I was guest starring in my own life, but once I walked inside of the dealership, I was brought back to reality. Bo was holding my door open as I came inside.

"Good morning Ms. Roxanne, my uncle would like for you to call him," said Bo.

I looked up at Bo. "Good morning Bo, was it a mistake to hire you? Are you my employee or your uncle's errand boy?"

Bo looked a little puzzled by my statement, but I was serious as a heart attack. I did not wish Bo to run interference between Sissell and myself. I was going to make my point utterly clear to him. He could not work here if he was going to keep an eye on me, and petition on behalf of his uncle. I asked Bo to walk with me. I had him close my door behind him. What I was about to say was for his ears only. I did like and respect Bo, so I did not wish to shame him. Once we were alone, I asked him to take a seat. I placed all my things inside my closet, while I walked around to my chair and sat down.

I began by saying, "Bo, you know I have the utmost respect for you, and I am thrilled that you have found a connection to my sister—but if you and I are going to stay friends, you need to help me get some closure with your uncle. I do still love him more than I could ever tell anyone. Your uncle rescued me when

260

I had lost all hope in my life, but then we moved away emotionally from one another. Know this, Bo, your uncle asked me to let him go, I did not wish to have him out of my life; I had no control over that. I am asking you to help me release the hold that he has on me. Please do not offer me any excuses or pleas from him. I am in love with someone new. I gave Sissell just what he asked me for, and I think it is unfair for him to ask you to deliver a message to me.

"So, as the both of us move forward in our lives, keep whatever thoughts or concerns he has expressed to you about me, Bo, to yourself, please. I have just learned how to live without your uncle. I do not wish to go back and wait for him to dismiss me once more. If Sissell has anything that he needs to tell me, he knows how to get in touch with me. Make no mistake, Bo, I still love him, but it is a different type of love now. Maybe one day we can learn to be friends once more, but I only did what *he* asked. Sissell is free of me and can now focus on his family."

"I understand Ms. Roxanne," Bo said. "You do not have to worry about me saying another word to you about my uncle."

We both smiled at each other as he stood up to leave my office. I asked him how my sister was doing that morning. Bo

261

told me that she was great as he smiled back at me. He added that he would tell her that I said hello.

I watched as he left my office and closed the door behind him. I reached over and turned on my computer. I pulled out my reading glasses and read the figures on the computer. We had a slow day yesterday but if we played our cards right, we could do well today, plus it had been several months since we had not closed ahead of schedule. I was still feeling sort of lethargic and decided to order myself a nice strong coffee. I passed by Eric's office as I went to the deli. I stuck my head inside his office and he wished me a good morning.

I was aware that the Pastor and Allen would be the ones to close tonight. I walked into his office and told him that I would be right back, so we could talk. He stood up and said that he would go with me. I kept that smile on my face as we walked to the deli. I asked Eric how everything was going for him. I was praying that he would tell me that all was well with him; I did not wish for any more pressure to be put on me. I held my breath as he told me things were good for him and his wife. I laughed as I heard his reply.

"Roxanne, I don't understand why you came to work today anyway, because you are more than welcome to leave right now. I will take care of everything for you, so if leaving is what you have on your mind, you are more than welcome to, now!"

We both laughed as we had our coffee. I told Eric that I had tons of paperwork to do. I needed to remove all my things from my desk so when we received the new furniture tomorrow, I would already be packed and ready to move.

"I thought Lily was going to take care of that stuff for you, Roxanne. You need to learn to delegate more of your responsibilities to your support staff. Knowing that Lily is always eager to help you, I think you should allow her to earn her keep and pack up your office, so you can leave early."

I replied that I would indeed utilize some of Lily's organizational skills.

"I think I will be leaving around 3 o'clock today, to have more time with my kids," I said thoughtfully.

I thanked him for looking out for me and my family as I stood up and walked back to my office. I knew that I had a lot of invoices to go through. I sat down behind my desk and replaced my glasses on my face. I went to my computer screen to check all the confirmed deliveries to the dealership. I noticed an e-mail from Major Morrison and opened it up! He made good on his promise, providing reference numbers to purchases of the new equipment for the dealership, plus he included a draft of the refund that would be credited back to my corporate account.

I was glad that he kept his word to me, since I intended to honor my promise to him. I read almost all the e-mail sent to the dealership or, if they held no interest for me, I forwarded it to Isabo and Eric. Knowing that I needed to learn to delegate more authority to them, I had no trouble forwarding some of the dealership's mail. I looked down at my watch and noticed that it was 12:04 p.m. I got up to go to the restroom, and once I was done relieving myself, I washed my hands 3 times and then reapplied my lip-gloss before I exited the room.

I saw Maggie sitting at the main desk and I kept moving. I did so with a big smile on my face. I could tell that Maggie stood up because she thought that she would make me upset with her today. I put a song in my heart as I walked away from her and the chaos that she thrived on. I walked on outside to the parking lot as I called Lily and asked her to meet me outside. Until she made it to where I was, I walked around and greeted several customers, making sure that they were being helped and inquired if they needed any assistance with a car.

Lily appeared in 300 seconds while I was walking up and down each aisle. I heard her coming before I saw her. She had her pad and pen in hand, and I was impressed by her eagerness to see what I needed. Sometimes Lily reminded me of a cheerleader, because she often repeated things I said. Then she adds an "OK" at the end of what she just repeated!

I liked the girl, as I'd said before, so I would help her as much as I possibly could. I began to inform her of the things that needed to be addressed. I informed her of the new invoice from Mr. Morrison. Then I addressed how I wanted all the excess funds to be distributed among all the employees in their bonus checks. Lily smiled as I told her of my plans. I then moved onto asking her to pack up my office. I did not want her to do any heavy moving or lifting, however. I just wanted her to empty out all my drawers and relocate my files into the storage closet until the new furniture had been delivered. I then asked Lily if she was ready to have her own office, or was she happy working alongside Incomplete Maggie all day long? Before Lily could answer my question, I heard my name being called by an unfamiliar voice.

I turned around to find out who was calling my name. I kept hearing someone say, "Beaumont-Sagar" repeatedly. I looked up and found the face that was calling my name. It was my grandfather's doctor, Dr. Russell Henely, moving in my direction, the brain specialist I'd met yesterday. I smiled at him standing in front of me.

The doctor said, "Your mother told me where I could find you. I did not know that you were the Rox of Rox Sagar Lexus."

I placed a charmed smile on my face and made a mental note to tell my mother to stop sending men my way. My cup was overflowing in the men department. Now it seems as if I have a new admirer or fan or whatever in this new man. I extended my hand to shake his, thinking to myself that it is truly was rough at the top. I was trying to figure out what in the world he could possibly want with me.

"Why, Dr. Henely, is everything fine with my grandfather, or are you here to purchase a car?"

He was holding my hand just a little longer than normal!

Dr. Henely said, "Ms. Beaumont-Sagar, I was thinking of 15 ways around Sunday for me to ask you out for dinner. I thought you would prefer the straight approach, so here I am, asking you out for dinner … or coffee, at least?"

Lily told me that she would check back with me in a couple of minutes. She turned around and left us standing in the parking lot. I was experiencing another indomitable silence. I looked over and saw that the good doctor had driven up on my lot in a grayish/blue Phantom Rolls Royce. I could tell that he was not in the market for a new car, considering his outstanding Phantom. I made him aware that the type of cars we sold could be used for him to allow his maid to go to the grocery store in style.

Maybe he was here to waste some more of my time because if he drove that style of car, it could be that he was just being kind to me, for some reason. I did not expect to see him here today. I thought that his request was rather nice, a brain surgeon wishing to have a meal with me. My thoughts dancing around in my head went like this: my, my, my things are changing for me.

Then a wicked thought showed up in my mind. His being here reminded me of something from my past. I have never encountered many white men who considered me attractive, not even in my younger years. It could be that they knew that I could be their Kryptonite; which would be why they never made attempts to pursue me or made me aware that they found me attractive. It could be that they were unsure if I would even give them the time of day, so they just stayed clear. I guess the doctor was in a league all by himself. I could have him destroyed just for wasting my time, but there *was* something sweet about him. And for that trait, I could be a little nicer than I normally choose to be.

CHAPTER 19

THE EAGLES' NEST!

I took my time taking in Dr. Russell Henely because there was a change going on with both of us as he kept his eyes on me. Although I did see him yesterday, I did not pay much attention to him. But now that I am standing in front of this white man, I am at a loss for words as he tried his best to present his cool side to me. I could tell that he was a nerd, and I was not in the mood to experience another crazy-ass white boy today. Since my encounter with Trevor in Los Angeles, I had been somewhat leery of making idle conversations with strangers.

I took my time responding to his request to join him for a meal or a drink. The more I gave it thought, the more Dr. Henely reminded me of an eagle. He seemed cool to the touch, but he had the most intense green-blue eyes I had ever encountered. They could have almost put me in a trance if I wanted him to.

But since my eyes are larger than his, his gaze did not have the effect he probably wished on me. He was a tall man with a big head, maybe because he holds a lot of information about the workings of the human brain and body.

His hair was what you would call dirty blonde and stopped on his collar. It looked thick to the touch, but it was a nice grade of hair. He reminded me of the actor Jeff Goldblum in a strange type of way, but he was a little thicker in the middle. They shared the same type of projection and tone of voice. He was tall and leggy just like the actor. Dr. Henely would not let go of my hand and I found that odd. Out of the corner of my eye, I saw Bo moving towards me! I held up my other hand, to let Bo know that everything was fine.

I looked at Dr. Henely and said, "If you do not let go of my hand, my enforcer is ready to toss you up into a nest! An eagle's nest, if you will. It would be to your advantage to let go of me, please!"

I had a smile in my voice and on my face as I talked to him. The good doctor did not recognize the true danger that he was placing himself in by standing so close to me. Something crazy was going on between us! Maybe it was a gravitational pull on us as I felt heat come off his hand. Dr. Henely let go of my hand quickly when Bo stopped in his tracks and asked if I was all right. I nodded my head to him that I was fine. We watched as Bo turned around to walk back into the dealership, but stood at the main door with his eyes on me!

Both of us began to laugh as the Doctor asked me whether my enforcer would really do any harm to him, or was he just for show. I looked the good Doctor deep in his eyes, his sharp and piercing eagle eyes, as I prepared myself to give him my answer. He had a certain old-world charm about him. I did not wish to place him in harm's way, because I am always protected no matter where I go! I saw a desire in his eyes for the truth, and that was what I was going to give him.

"He would have crushed you like a bug if you would have tried to harm me or made me feel uneasy in the least. Those are always his orders, to protect the queen! I am the queen here at this dealership, and if he did not defend me with in an inch of his life, then there is no need for him to be here with me. I know that you do not wish for him to lose his job, do you? So, while you are here, you need to be on your best behavior, Doctor."

The Doctor took three steps back from me and made a bow! I tossed my hand in the air and told him that he could rise at any time! The doctor with his eagle eyes stood up and smiled at me once more. I asked him what he was really doing here.

"Well Ms. Beaumont-Sagar, you had so much good energy about yourself yesterday. I was truly fascinated by your charm and beauty so when I saw your mother, I could not help but mention to her that I found you and your presence over the top in the beauty arena. I then informed her that your smile made me soar. She had no problem telling me where I could locate you. Then she told me that you are a newly divorced lady with two lovely children. She also mentioned that you are the most modest of her girls. Next, she told me that for a white boy, I was kind of cute."

We both laughed at his comments. They sounded true and his words seemed like something that would fall from my mom's mouth. I smiled at his comments because I felt odd standing there looking back at him. Maybe some parts of the truth were creeping inside of my mind as he finished speaking.

"So, let me get this right, Doctor Henely," I said skeptically. "You got *all* that information about me from my mother? You felt compelled to come down and check me out, because you thought that you had made some type of connection with me?"

"I believe that between the two of us, Ms. Beaumont-Sagar, there was a connection," he explained. "There was so much chemistry between us yesterday, I felt obligated to come and seek you out to make sure that you felt it too! I wanted the feeling that I shared with you yesterday to be explored a little deeper, plus the scent that you had on yesterday lingered in my nose all day. You smelled so damn wonderful, I didn't want to lose that feeling—so I came to see if you were real or if I dreamed it all."

I began to bat my eyes because I could not believe that line of shit that he was trying to use on me. Although I could see that he was indeed smooth with his delivery and oozed confidence. I began to tilt my head to the right side as a smile ran across my face. I did not know what I had done to this man yesterday because I was just being my old charming self. I had to tell Doctor Henely that I was already involved in a torrid love affair. I did not wish to be a total asshole as I was talking to this man.

I waited for 30 more seconds for him to get the real Roxanne experience locked in his mindset. I told him that I was dating a man of mystery that my mother didn't know about. Even though my mother did speak to him out of turn about me, I can only tell him that I am over the top flattered by his coming by. Right now, I was not in the market for a new relationship; I was working on the one that I had right now. After I was done bringing him up to speed about me, Dr. Henely offered me one of his business cards. I took it and placed it in my pocket for safekeeping.

"Hold onto my card, Ms. Beaumont-Sagar. My personal home and cell numbers are on the back! I might be a needed feather in your cap one day soon, because you never know when you might need the comfort of another great friend."

He then reached down to take hold of my hand once more! Bo began walking out the door again. I threw my other hand up and told him to go back!

Dr. Henely kissed my hand and said, "You still smell good, Ms. Beaumont-Sagar."

I thanked him for the best compliment I'd had had all day.

"If you were mine Ms. Beaumont-Sagar, you could survive on all the compliments I would give you freely. I do look forward to seeing you at the hospital one day next week if possible, and maybe you will trust yourself enough to go and have coffee with me."

He released my hand as we both said our goodbyes. I watched the good doctor walk away from me as I was trying to figure out what chemistry he was speaking about. Maybe it could be that now that I am a fully mature woman something else is going on with my body chemistry, or maybe he was speaking about the pheromones that I was putting out. Here I am a 43-year-old woman, and I get more offers of sex than the average girl half my age.

I was unsure of this little-known fact, but maybe men can tell that I am in my sexual prime, because I have often heard that pheromones are your nonverbal communication with the opposite sex, letting them know that you are ready to be engaged with them in sexual activity. Pheromones are the chemicals secreted by animals in order to attract the opposite sex, but I doubted that aspect of myself with him.

Maybe that is why the good doctor flung himself in my direction. I don't remember setting out to attract the opposite sex. It could be that my receptors gave him false hope about me.

I was unsure of what was going with the both of us, but I was glad that he was gone. I walked back into the dealership and straight to my office. Bo was coming back up the hallway as I passed by. He wanted to know if everything was alright. I told Bo to keep up the good work, and no matter what was going on at this dealership, his main goal was *always* to protect the queen! We both smiled as I walked into my office. Eric appeared shortly thereafter.

"What is this that I hear about a new man making advances toward you? Incomplete Maggie is telling the whole dealership about your encounter on the parking lot."

I smiled at Eric as I put my reading glasses back on. I mentioned to him as he sat down that the man was my grandfather's brain specialist that I met yesterday. He wanted to come down to check out where I worked. Even though we only met each other yesterday, he gave me his business card and told me to keep it because one day he might be a feather in my cap. I added that one of these days, Incomplete Maggie's mouth was going to get her old and crazy ass in trouble. You never know, I might be able to use his services one day soon to help me dispose of her and her incomplete-talking ass."

I then told Eric that I was under a severe time constraint, so I had to bypass these small conversations for a minute. I then set out to inform Eric of The Pastor's request regarding his new business venture. I told him how I felt about his offer, but I wanted to know what he thought. Eric smiled widely and told me that he was aware of The Pastor's offer to me. The Pastor had mentioned it to Eric first, and he had given him pointers on how to present his offer to me.

From his expression, I could tell that Eric thought it would be a solid business offer. I asked Eric to do some research about this sort of business because I wanted to make an informed decision about it. He mentioned that he believed it would be a great move on our part, and it would take little capital to store the mobile car cleaners here at this dealership. I was happy that he believed it a smart move on our part. But I needed a little more information before I committed this dealership to sponsoring another business venture. The last business that we had agreed to sponsor was the in-house deli. Even though it has paid for itself over and over again, we need to be cautious about our business affairs.

"I will find out everything I can about this new business venture with The Pastor," Eric stated. "We want to make sure that we continue to add to the successes of this dealership. I want him to be successful for him and his new wife. I know The Pastor has a very colorful past, but I do not believe that it would hinder us in any way. Nonetheless, I can understand why you are so apprehensive with your dealership. It's like you have always told us: CYA (Cover Your Ass), because we cannot afford to drop the ball this late in the game."

I waited 35 seconds after he finished making his point, before I added my two cents to his concerns

"What kind of fool would I be, if I allowed his business venture to place all of us in harm's way?" I asked rhetorically. "I want to help him be a better person and thrive with this new venture. I'm glad you understand that I need to be as wise as a serpent and as harmless as a dove, to guide this dealership to total success. I have no problem playing the villain because I have my own sack full of dreams for this company. If I need to walk with caution on this business deal, then so be it!"

Eric told me that he would take care of it before we moved on this venture. All of us would be aware of what we were in for. Eric stood up to leave my office, and asked me whether I was still leaving early today. I told him that I planned to leave by 3 o'clock. He told me that it was 1:45 p.m. right now, so he was off to go get himself something to eat.

"Your lovely wife did not prepare a meal for you?" I asked.

"She is out of town to visit with her family, so it is just me to cook for now; but I do enjoy going out to eat occasionally! I will be back before you leave, plus The Pastor is here if I am not back before you go."

I told Eric to enjoy his lunch as he walked out of my office. I was not hungry yet. I would eat when I got home. I finished up some reports and then called Lily on the intercom system. I asked her to come to my office, so we could finish our conversation. Before I had disconnected from her, she was knocking on my door. I asked her to come in and take a seat. Lily placed herself in a chair with a broad smile on her face, all ears and eager to hear what I had to say.

I started up once more with our previous conversation.

"Lily, I am aware that you need your own space for you to continue to flourish at this dealership, because we all need the skills that you have to offer. I need you to stay around here to help us; that is why I would like to offer you your own office. Even though I know that it is rather small space, I believe that you will be happy in your own surroundings."

"I accept your offer, Ms. Roxanne. I would love to have my own office!" Lily gushed. "It has been a learning experience to work alongside Ms. Maggie, but I know that both of us would do better if we had our own spaces. I know that Ms. Maggie really enjoys seeing everything that goes on here at the dealership, and she has the perfect vantage point where she is located. I believe that I need a more soothing environment, so I gladly accept your offer."

I was becoming involved in her excitement with the prospect of Lily having her own tiny office. I had to tell her that there was no window in there, but she did not care about a window because she was happy just having her own office.

"I'm glad that you are happy," I went on, "because I ordered you some furniture also, and it will be here tomorrow with the rest of the order."

Lily jumped up out of her chair and ran around to where I was sitting! She gave me a hug that almost cut off my supply of air, but I was thrilled to make her happy.

Since I'd already told Eric and Isabo about the offer that I was making to her for a new job position, Lily's reaction only made the end of my day more pleasant. She wanted to know if she could tell Incomplete Maggie about her news, or did she have to remain silent about it?

"Lily, keep the news to yourself; *I* want to be the one to tell Maggie. I want to tell her that the new desk will not have enough space for the both of you, so that is why I am moving you into a tiny office with no windows. I believe that Maggie will believe that she got the better end of the deal, plus she can come and visit you anytime she wants to."

Lily was fine with my reasoning. She prepared to leave my office with a big smile on her face. When she turned around, she looked at me and said warmly, "*Thank* you, Ms. Roxanne."

"You're welcome, Lily!" I said, beaming.

I asked her to send Maggie into my office as soon as she returned to the main desk. Lily reminded me that she would see me at 9 o'clock in the morning, plus she would have my office packed up before she left at the end of the day. I looked at the time on my computer and saw that it was 2:30 in the afternoon. I just had two more chores to attend to before I left for the evening. I wanted to talk with Incomplete Maggie and The Pastor. I was going to give the Pastor a small office also, but I had not had the time to talk with him about it yet.

I thought I might have to have Eric give him the good news, because I really needed to leave for home at 3:00 p.m. Incomplete Maggie showed up at my door while I told her to come in and take a seat, but before I could give her the good news about her having the desk all to herself, she jumped right in and asked the strangest question.

"Roxanne … am I fired?"

I just sat there and looked at that crazy-ass woman. Then a soft spot for her showed up in my heart.

"No, Maggie, I am not firing you today," I said, masking a sigh. "I just wanted to let you know that since we are getting new furniture in the morning, your surroundings will be changing. There will not be enough room for you and Lily to sit at that desk. I chose to allow you to stay at the main desk, so you can keep an eye out on everything and everyone. I will have to relocate Lily to a small room with no windows in it because, you have been here the longest and you deserve to be seen. That is the news that I have for you, Ms. Maggie, so remove those unsure thoughts about being fired. You are part of the team and we need you. Where would you get such a crazy idea about me firing you?"

"No talk to me," said Incomplete Maggie.

I guess in her head, if I do not speak to her, I was about to fire her for some unknown reason. Once I told her that I just did not have the time to speak with her at that moment. I am free to talk with her about anything her little head wants to talk about.

"No more share desk?" asked Maggie.

I repeated that it would be just her sitting at the main desk from now on, but if it was going to cause her any problems, I would make Lily come back and sit there with her. I just wanted to let her know that the desk was going to be smaller than normal.

"Glad to be alone." Maggie said.

"Good for you, Maggie. Oh, do you plan on coming to help us out tomorrow?"

"I've got church tomorrow," she replied.

I looked at her and asked, "Does that mean that you will be here, or will we just see you on Monday morning?"

"See you Monday morning and I'm there for dinner."

I told her that it would be good to share a meal with her, and added that that was all I wanted to tell her for now. She wanted to know if she should tell Lily about the move. I told her that I would break the news to Lily tomorrow, so she should keep the news to herself.

"My lips are sealed," Maggie agreed, as she got up to exit my office.

I sat still for a couple of seconds because I was proud that I did not lose my cool with her. Besides, it was time for me to be leaving. I put all my things away then I grabbed my handbag and my duffle bag as I turned off the lights in my office. I walked to Eric's office and asked him to tell The Pastor about his new office. I cautioned him to tell him when no one was around, because I did not want any more hurt feelings from anyone. I told Eric that I would see him in the morning. I waved goodbye and was on my way.

I walked into my house and removed my shoes. I had three hours before my kids made it home. Gloria was in the kitchen cooking dinner for all of us. I asked her if she'd heard from the children today. Gloria told me that they had called home around 12:00 noon and put in a request for a special meal. I grabbed a bottle of water from my pantry. I then told her of my plan for tomorrow. I told her that since I have a couple of hours before they made it home, I wanted to take a nap to ensure that I would be able to keep up with them both. I asked Gloria to wake me up at 6:30, which would give me at least a couple of hours to rest.

She told me that she would see me in a couple of hours. I walked up the stairs to my bedroom. Gloria had changed my bed linen, cleaned my room and unpacked my bags for me. I removed my suit and put on a pretty caftan that I had purchased in Texas. I pulled my cover back and slid inside. I just needed a couple of minutes to myself; rest was the cure that I looked for now.

CHAPTER 20

PLEASE PARDON ME!

I placed my head on that fresh pillow and began to count seconds. I closed my eyes and began to sing myself to sleep. I don't know how long it took me to drift off towards, but I was not in a rush to wake up. When I heard Gloria call my name several times, I knew that the hour was fast approaching for my kids to come home. I told her that I was up, and I would be down in just a minute. I lay there until I heard my kids come in the door. I jumped up, checked my face and rinsed my mouth out with some mouthwash. I made sure that everything was in place before I made my way down. I had a smile in my heart and one on my face as I walked down the stairs to greet my kids!

Anthony and Franchescia were in the process of telling Gloria everything that had happened to them while Michael was sitting at the kitchen table with a plate of food in front of him.

He looked up at me as I walked into the kitchen. He got up and gave me a kiss on the cheek.

"Roxanne, it is good to see you and time has been kind to you," said Michael. "But as for me, I think I have aged several years on my face since our divorce. You still have the prettiest smile under the sun!"

I smiled at him as the kids came over to give me a kiss on the cheek. They gave me tight hugs, told me that they missed me, and how much they missed their own rooms also. Most of all they told me how badly they missed Gloria's cooking! We all laughed as I took a seat at the table. Michael sat back down and continued to eat. Gloria prepared plates for Anthony and Franchescia and soon we all were seated at the table, enjoying our meal.

Gloria had cooked fish and broccoli for Franchescia, and her famous chicken nachos for Anthony. The kids and Michael were in their own version of Heaven because all the fast food that they had consumed over the past week made them long for a home-cooked meal. I allowed Gloria to fix me a small plate of both dishes while all of us were revisiting our recent doings for each other. I could see that we were all reminiscing over days gone by, but we must make room for the future, for us to make it through the rest of our lives.

I looked over at all of them as I consumed my food. I could see that we all were happy. Gloria excused herself so we could be alone. Michael got up to get something to drink, and I looked over at him, accepting of all that I had done to contribute to our new existence. I heard his soul ask me a question. His soul wanted to find some type of shelter with us. It was just for a moment, so I was unsure of what I thought I heard his soul ask me, so I just sat there and looked at him. Once Michael made it back to his seat, he looked over at me.

"Roxanne, I need to ask you a very important question," Michael said. "The kids and I have already discussed it, but we need to know if it is alright with you."

I already knew the question that he wanted to ask me because his soul already broke the silence. I sat there and waited for him to ask to join us for Thanksgiving dinner.

"Ask what you wish to know, Michael, and I will try to give you the best answer that I can. I do know this one thing; you need to understand that we are still working through our own feelings for this new chapter in our lives, so please ... be ever gentle with your question."

"Roxanne, will it be all right for me to share Thanksgiving dinner with you and the kids, even though we are no longer married? I hope that you will grant me this favor. I will not stay all day; it's just I need to have a place to go that is just for me."

I stared at him because I already expected his question, but I would make him work for an answer from me. I gazed at him for 45 seconds, locking my eyes on him and not releasing him until I was ready. Michael was becoming uncomfortable as I stared. I sat up in my chair and began to look at my nails; then I tilted my head to the side and smiled! I looked back at him as my children were becoming uneasy at my silence. They began to shift their bodies in their chairs but their uneasy posturing was of no concern to me. I had several questions of my own for him, so I began to speak.

"Please pardon me for staring at you, Michael, but I have several questions for you myself. So, if you would indulge me with a couple of answers to my questions, we can move on from this strange place that both of us are visiting."

"Ask what you will, Roxanne," Michael said equably. "I do not have anything left to be discovered. I have changed my way of dealing with my new life so, knock yourself out and ask!"

"Michael, I was under the impression that you had a new love in your life. So, I find it odd that you do not wish to enjoy a meal with her and your sons."

"She does not cook, Roxanne, and she will be spending that day with her family."

I was trying to forgive his answer, but I guess this is what you call Instant Karma. I chuckled to myself because when we first got married, he made sure that I knew how to cook. I was wondering how he could spend his time with someone who could not cook for him, but times had changed for all of us. I let that excuse slide away. I then asked him why he did not wish to spend time with his mother and siblings on that day. All the time we were married, he always wanted to go over and have a meal with them. Now that he has the time to spend with them, why does he wish to be with us?

"I will stop by and see my family, but I need to know that there is still a place here for me," said Michael. "I shiver to think that this is the first Thanksgiving that we will not all be together.

I know it sounds crazy to you, Roxanne, but I did enjoy my life with you and the kids. You still have me under your grasp, and I want to see you and the kids. I wanted to secure a place for me at your table. You need to remember, Roxanne, we were together for over 20 years, so you and the kids are all that I truly know for sure. I am aware that it is asking a lot of you to allow me to drift through your lives, but I still love all of you. Nobody knows me like all of you do. If it is going to be a problem for you and the new man in your life, I will stay in my place, pass right by your home, and make my way over to my mother's house for dinner."

"Michael, it would be our pleasure to have you join our family and friends for dinner on Thursday. But you need to be mindful that my father and brothers are coming over that day too. I invited some of my employees to come by and share a meal with me as well. You are more than welcome to join us!"

Then I added, "Oh, by the way, Macy is coming home that day also, so if you could help me entertain all of those wandering souls in my home, I would welcome it and be so appreciative of your help. And forgive me for being such an asshole to you, because I am unsure of what the day has in store for all of us.

291

We need to pull together as a team and make that day a blissful success. I don't need you wondering if there is still a place in our lives for you. We will still be a family no matter what; and I promise to not spill a drop of your blood on that special holiday!"

My kids began the clap their hands at my response to their father, while I placed a big smile on my face as I looked over at him! Now that all of us were on the same page, we would be able to help each other out. I was feeling like a million bucks as we finished our meals. That was, until Michael asked me would there be anyone there special for me, because he wanted to be prepared for my new suitor. I looked over at him and smiled and said, of course—our children!

"Roxanne. You know what I am asking you. Why are you being so evasive?" queried Michael.

"Michael, my new love interest will be out of town for that special holiday. But I will let you know when I wish to let you know anything about him, and when the time is right for the both of you to meet each other, I am sure you and he will have a lovely conversation about me and my special talents and desires!"

Michael sat there and looked like an un-stuffed rabbit. My kids did not know what to say because they had made peace with their father having an assortment of women in his life. But it somewhat troubled them to know that their mother who was no longer a married woman could have all the privileges that were afforded to their father. My children did not smile following my comments to Michael, but it was not my concern that they troubled. When the timing was right, I would make sure that everyone got an opportunity to meet my new love.

I couldn't imagine what else I could possibly say to them. I remained silent for several minutes because I had always been the open book of the family; but this time, I had nothing else to say! I guess my children were in the process of pretending not to hear me, so they turned their attention to another subject so as to alleviate the silence in the room. Michael and Anthony both inquired at the same time about my grandfather. They both wanted to know how he was doing, and was there any progress with his health?

I began to share with them the new information about my grandfather. I told everyone about the transferring of my grandfather to the hospital and the new activity that his brainwaves were displaying. I mentioned to them the possibility of him returning to us one day soon. The hope of him returning to us was little more than I could handle, because a tear fell from my eye as I was speaking about my grandfather. Franchescia picked up her soda and made a toast to my grandfather! The rest of us joined in on her lovely toast. Everyone raised their beverages and touched one another's glass!

Once our meal was done the children and I began to discuss their adventures from the past two weeks. Michael told us that he needed to be leaving but he would be here early Thursday morning. I told Michael that his presence was not required until 12 noon, because I did not expect anyone to be here until after then. The game had changed with all of us now, but if he could just respect my wishes. We were going to have several misunderstandings before the holiday was over. Michael smiled at me, as he stood up to leave.

"Roxy, I'll see you around 12 noon on Thanksgiving Day. I will see the kids next week, because I plan on picking them up from school. Thank you once again for allowing me to join you all for dinner. Tell Gloria to take care of herself, and you lovely people have yourself a great evening."

Both kids stood up to walk their father to the door.

"Good night, Roxanne!" Michael called.

I in turn said good night to him too. The children walked their father to the door and he gave them a kiss before he left. I was glad that this adventure with Michael was over for now. The kids and I moved into the den as we caught up with each other's lives. Once Michael was gone, Gloria materialized in the kitchen and began to clean up our mess. I was thrilled that my ex-husband had not defeated me and had not enraged me by his comments. I was truly proud of myself for maintaining my composure. While my children and I sat in the den for a couple of minutes, we all had our own stories to tell.

Anthony was the first one to mention that he was glad to be home. Then Franchescia eased my mind by informing me that she thought it all right for me to have a new love interest. She told me that she didn't want me to be lonely. I did not wish to talk about my new relationship, so I steered the children in a different direction. I informed them that I needed to be leaving early tomorrow because I had something to do. I told them of the purchase of new furniture for the dealership and how tomorrow would be the perfect day to have it delivered. I talked with them about their grandmother. I asked my children to be on their best behavior with their grandmother, because she had a difficult time demonstrating her love for all of us.

I apologized for their misadventures with her, but I put a different spin on it for them both. I told them of several misunderstandings that had developed between my mother and myself when I was a child. So, in my eyes they only had a brief detour of some of the drama that my sisters and I lived daily. All three of us begin to laugh at the past two weeks. Both my kids promised to be gentle with my mother when they saw her next. I was glad that they understood that my mother is operating in a different gear, because we all needed to be mindful that she just lost her mother.

I made mention to them that her mind was not at ease due to her mother's absence, and so it seemed like she was running at 1,000,000 miles per second. I had a difficult time explaining that she had a hard time exposing her heart, plus she liked to pretend as if she was always in control of everything. But the truth of the matter was, she was afraid to be alone, so the next time they approached her, would they please remember that she is still in the process of grieving the loss of her mother.

Also, I asked that they remember that she still must deal with her father being in a coma. I told them if anyone had been dealt the short end of the stick, it was truly my mother. She had not been offered any form of consolation prize for the whole situation, and they thought she was acting out, they should just think about *they* would react. If you had been dealt the same set of circumstances that she'd had to deal with on a regular basis, all of us might act just a little more differently.

Nobody really knows her true troubles, I went on, but God and I would appreciate them treating my mother with the respect she so richly deserves. Both of my kids promised to be on their best behavior with their grandmother. Then they both wanted to retire to their rooms as well, because they had been held hostage for the past two weeks, missing their rooms and their belongings. I excused them both, after I received my goodnight kisses!

I stopped them to ask if they would like to join me at the dealership tomorrow.

They responded, "Thank you, but *no* thank you, mom. We want to sleep late and enjoy a delicious breakfast from Gloria."

Anthony added, "I hope it's not going to hurt your feelings if we don't join you tomorrow. I want to reestablish a relationship with my bed. I would enjoy sleeping late and being alone; and it has been two weeks since I have had delicious omelets!"

I listened to my little man talk, because Anthony had never requested alone time before. I guess he had been living out of a suitcase for the past two weeks, not having anything that truly belonged to him around. I could understand how he wanted to get back in sync with his own life. Knowing that my feelings were not hurt because my children chose not to go with me did not lessen the fact that I was glad that they were home.

They both went to retrieve their luggage and head up the stairs. I sat there and listened to both of my kids argue with each other as they made their way to their rooms. I gazed around the den for several minutes. I told myself that it was time for me to retire for the night, because I had so much information floating around my head and I needed to rest my body and soul.

I turned the TV off and dimmed the lights in the den. I walked back into the kitchen and told Gloria that we all thoroughly enjoyed our dinner, and how much I appreciated her exiting the room for us to speak freely with one another! I then poured myself a glass of wine and gave Gloria a gentle reminder that I would be leaving early in the morning. I did not know how long it was going to take us to address the rearranging of the new furniture for the dealership. If things were going to extend over into the late afternoon, I would give her and the children a call.

"Good night, Ms. Roxy, get some rest and we will talk some time tomorrow. I just want to say that it feels good to be back home with you and the kids. I did miss all of you, too."

I smiled as I walked up the stairs. I looked at my watch, which said 10:15 p.m. I knew that I needed to be getting into bed ASAP. Once I made it upstairs, I said good night once again to my children, before I closed my door. I felt in my body that I was exhausted. I took couple sips of wine and plugged up my cell phone as one last thought occurred to me. I walked over and pressed the intercom button.

I asked Gloria what time her husband's doughnut shop opened. Gloria pressed the button and told me that Diaz's shop opened at six o'clock in the morning. I asked Gloria if it were possible to place an order for three dozen assorted donuts, one dozen muffins and one dozen bagels; I could be there to pick them up around 8:30 in the morning. Gloria told me that my order would not be a problem and if I liked, Diaz would deliver the donuts to the dealership!

I told Gloria that I would welcome him delivering the order to the dealership in the morning, if it weren't too much trouble. Gloria asked whether I would like an assortment of juices and beverages to go with the order, or would plain coffee and decaf do? I mentioned to her that an assortment of beverages and coffee would be nice. I then thanked her for placing the order for me.

I apologized for the lateness of my order, which almost slipped my mind with all the crazy things that I was involved in today. We said our good nights once more. My body was starting to go into shutdown mode as I took one last sip of wine and stepped into the shower. I allowed my body to stay under the running water for several minutes before I moved. I began to go over my plans for the upcoming day. I began to lather my body up and found myself singing in the shower; for the life of me, I do not know why I began to sing, "Anyone Who Had A Heart" by Luther Vandross!

I was in the process of calming myself down while singing. I concluded my shower and put my pajamas on. I sat down on my bed and put lotion on my hands and feet. I was making a mental note of what I was going to wear tomorrow, even though I do not enjoy working on Sundays. This was a necessary adventure for the whole dealership, and I knew that it was going to be a challenge, but it was going to get done. I was tired as I got on my knees and said my prayers, wondering if God was keeping an eye on me.

I sent my prayers up to Heaven, then crawled into the bed and set my clock for 6 a.m. in the morning. The time was 11 o'clock and I was past exhausted. I boarded the sleep train and felt as if I was floating! I felt all three of my Angels give me a group hug. I was encouraged that they found their way back to me. I was reluctant to engage them in a conversation because my mind had already retired for the evening. All I could muster aloud before I went to sleep was, "I want to be a marvel, not a monster!"

I was tired of being the monster in all my family's life. I would try a little harder to be a better person because I did not enjoy being out of season in my own life. I did want this love affair with Akheem, but every time I opened my big mouth, I always messed things up. No one must ever tell me to shut the fuck up! I feel that I kept doing him harm with my big mouth! One day I will learn to be quiet, so everything could turn out good.

If I could pause for several more seconds before I spoke, I could save myself from doing harm to myself! Maybe I should have my mouth sewn shut for a couple of days, but it would just be my luck that someone would have something to remove whatever it was that was blocking my mouth from moving! It would just be my luck that while my mouth is blocked shut, I would run across someone who happened to have a spare axe with them ... that's the last thing I remember thinking to myself as I received the gift of sleep.

CHAPTER 21

I KNOW MY MIND HAS TRULY LEFT ME!

The next morning, I did not have the luxury of dissecting that crazy dream, so I stood up and walked to my closet. I did not know exactly what to wear but I knew that today would require me to be a little more casual than normal. My mind was caught up inside itself and I could not understand what the fuck I was doing, dreaming of red lollipops, axes and paper cuts! I know that my mind had truly left me because I kept looking down at my fingers as I picked out an outfit to wear. I settled on a red and white jogging suit that had a sort of fancy tee shirt to go with it. It showed that I was sporty but still in control.

I found some matching sneakers or kicks to wear with this outfit because I needed to be comfortable. I stepped out of my walk-in closet and grabbed some pretty undergarments to match my outfit. I got dressed and stood there looking at myself in the mirror. I placed a small amount of make-up on my face because I did not wish to look totally plain. I made sure that my eyebrows were on properly, then I put my hair in two ponytails with matching rubber bands. I could not believe that I looked so much like Franchescia today because when I was a little girl, I did not look like I do now. But the older I get, the more I revisit days from my youth.

I could even hear Macy inside my head, telling me that I looked like a black Pippi Longstocking. I smiled as I put some diamond earrings on! I remembered what I used to call Macy when we were both young girls: Puss-N-Boots, because she would always wear these hot-ass boots when we were little girls. She was committed to whatever outfit she had on at that moment, but she always gave me the choice of which color boots she would wear with her outfit for the day. I was daydreaming that I was having a lovely conversation with her as I walked from my vanity set from doing my make-up and hair!

I guess Pippi Longstocking was going to make her debut at the dealership today. I liked the way I was looking so I knew that I was going to have a beautiful day. I picked up my cell phone and my travel bag. I stopped by the kids' rooms to check on them. They were still locked inside their own slumbers. I just gave them each a kiss on the cheek. I made my way downstairs and ate a fresh banana while I finished off a bottle of water. The house was still quiet as I walked outside into the garage. I placed all my items inside my car, but the thoughts of me and my friend still lingered inside my head as I drove myself to the dealership!

I pulled up into the parking lot; there were five cars there ahead of me. Lily, Erica, Isabo, Bo and The Pastor had pulled in before I did. I was truly pleased to see that my team was all ready to get started. It was great to know that my team was ready to advance the dealership and eager to assist in getting it done. Bo came out to meet me at my car, offering to take my travel bag as I exited it. But just as he was walking towards me, two big 18-wheeler trucks pulled in front of the dealership. Bo began to inform me that the doughnuts and juice had already been delivered and the rest of the team was on their way. I could feel the emotion of the excitement dancing in my stomach and knowing that I was ready to get this over with made me more energized for this adventure. Bo held the door open as I walked into the dealership to get the day started.

Lily was in my office preparing for the arrival of the new furniture. We said our good mornings to each other. I was so thrilled to see her because I remembered what my Angels had said about her! I wanted to show my appreciation to her for not taking her life, so as the rest of the team made it to the dealership, I asked The Pastor to pray a prayer of blessings over this new furniture. I asked him to offer up a prayer of economic growth along with years of continued success for all of us. The Pastor revealed a shy smile as he told us all to join hands long enough for him to petition God's assistance with today's venture. His prayer blew through the room as he asked for protection. The prayer fell effortlessly from his mouth with such grace and elegance.

So exactly at 9:00 a.m., those two big 18-wheeler trucks began to back up to the main entrance of the dealership. Peter was the first one to exit the truck. He moved swiftly towards me with a serious look on his face as he said,

"Good morning Ms. Roxanne, and how is today going for you so far?"

I kept my eyes fixed on him and said, "Well, Peter it all depends upon what you are going to tell me, because you and I have an understanding. I am aware that you fully understood the stipulations of the contract that I signed with you. So, for your sake, Peter, let's hope that you and I have a great day!"

I was hopeful that we were about to get off to a positive start because the look on Peter's face concerned me. I wanted him to be the first one to present his side of the situation. There was a sense of restless silence between the two of us. I began to count seconds until he found the courage to tell me what was really going on. My team stood behind me in total silence. They were waiting for me to give them a signal to move forward. I was waiting on Peter to tell me anything. I guess it took a couple of moments for his voice to catch up to him as Peter moved a little bit closer to me.

"Please pardon my staring, Ms. Roxanne. You do not look like yourself, you look like a very young girl. I was unsure of whom I was really dealing with for a moment; I thought you had younger sister and she was pretending to be you for the day."

My heart skipped a couple of beats because I thought he was about to give me some type of bad news. I knew that he truly understood that I meant exactly what I said to him the other night. If he did not have all the items that I had ordered, then he and his crew could turn around and remove those trucks off my property because I wanted *everything* that I ordered. If he could not deliver my request it would be to his advantage to not have shown up. But since he was standing before me, I just assumed that he had exactly what I requested. All the funds have already been debited from my charge accounts, so I was just thrilled that he understood the ramifications of his actions.

Peter offered me a clipboard to double-check my order. I stood there as he asked me to read over the manifest order form. Smiles began to surface on both our faces because he had everything I had asked for. I gave the signal for my team to jump into gear. It was all orchestrated chaos because the doors from the trucks swung open as his team began to remove all the old furniture. They placed it on the dealership parking lot. The male members of my team ushered all the new furniture to the main entrance of the dealership. Once the dealership was empty, the delivery team went to remove the new furniture from the 18-wheeler truck.

Peter's and my team continued to work at the restoration of the dealership, and I was pleased to see all the men from the repair shop show up to help with this enormous undertaking. I was happy to know that money is still a great motivator, because I was thinking that only half of them would show up. Erica, Bo and Lily were running things without me. Isabo was telling all the deliverymen where we wanted everything. Isabo had a clipboard tucked under her arm and she seemed to be enjoying issuing orders. For a brief moment I felt like I was in the way. I asked Peter if he would like to go get some coffee with me.

"I would rather enjoy a delicious cup of coffee, Ms. Roxanne!"

Peter and I moved towards the deli and prepared ourselves a nice cup of coffee. The Pastor came rushing in, excited about a new occurrence.

"Baby Sister—is it true that you are giving me my own office?"

In all the excitement of the past couple of days, I hadn't informed the Pastor of his new office, but Eric must have told him of my decision.

"Pastor, please forgive me for not telling you the news," I said apologetically. "I became somewhat distracted by events at the dealership. It was my intention to give you the good news because we all feel that you are doing a great job here. We would like to offer you your own compartment here at this dealership. Although I am rather sorry that the space could not be more pleasing, it is just a step towards your greatness to come."

A tear dripped from his eye as he gave me a hug!

"Baby Sister, I recognize that this is just a small step towards my greatness, but to allow me to say thank you. You almost knocked me off my feet when I found out that I had my own furniture. God knows what he is doing with you, so you just continue to be a blessing to everyone you meet."

I felt as if I had just delivered a blessing upon the Pastor, because he was doing the best he could, and I felt his spirit dance in the deli as Peter began to smile. We watched the Pastor catch the spirit and begin to move his feet. Peter began to clap his hands as the Pastor danced all through the room!

Peter opined, "It must be a joy working here with you and your team, Ms. Roxanne. I have never seen precision teamwork like I have encountered here today. The Pastor is correct in telling you that you have been a blessing in many people's lives. Your husband must realize what a joy you bring to others and if he does not see what a jewel you are, he is as worthless as a penny with a hole in it!"

310

I was quite pleased at the compliment that Peter had just given me, and I neglected to tell him I am no longer married. I just accepted his compliment as I excused myself. I wanted to check on the status of the furniture. I walked to Eric's office only to find him enjoying the new furniture. I noticed the look on his face as the statue of the two girls was delivered to her. I stood in the door and watched as he unwrapped it! I had almost forgotten how simply elegant that small statue was. I could tell that he was really enjoying his gift.

"Roxanne, it's hard to make me an emotional wreck but you are almost about to make me lose my composure," Eric admitted. "You know, I pride myself in always being in control. I find it unprofessional to show your feelings at work, so I will have to schedule a time to say my own personal thank you. Everything that you have given me has allowed me to be the person that I wish to be. You have bent over backwards to be accommodating to a fool like myself. I am aware of the talk that goes on behind my back, but I recognize that you truly value just me. You allow me to shine, and one day I will repay the favor!"

I moved close to Eric and watched him take steps towards me. This day has not been so crazy that I forgot to check out what

Eric had on, so as we hugged one another I noticed that he wore a black jogging suit matched with a hot pink tube top. I am aware that the other deliverymen could misunderstand what she had on, but Eric wasn't an ordinary salesperson. He was a part of a team who really needed and understood him.

It didn't trouble us when he showed up in female attire because we think we know the story behind the story about him. He is family, and, in every family, there is bound to be a member who takes your love to the limit by their actions. But Eric was such a perfect fit here at the dealership. I would not wish for him to be any other way than what he brought to us daily.

Once our hug was over with, I was amazed to see that he had on both male and female clothing at once. Maybe he got a little confused with whom he wanted to be today, or it could be that he wanted to give us both sides of him. Either way, I did not care what he had on, I was just glad that he showed up to help. I stepped back from him and offered to help him with his office.

He turned me down and told me to go help someone else, because she needed to get familiar with her new office. She would check in on me later today. I left her office and walked towards Isabo's. But before I could walk all the way through her

312

door, I heard the strangest sound coming from down the hallway. I bypassed Isabo's office and kept moving towards the end of the hallway. I found myself standing at Lily's new office. It was her crying that summoned me to her; I knocked on her door as I opened it very slowly. Lily was sitting at her new desk with tears streaming down her face!

"Why are you crying?" I asked, concerned. "I thought that you would rather enjoy your new office, but if it is not to your liking, I will see if we can find you something else to your satisfaction!"

Lily wiped her tears away as I sat down in front of her. Even though her office was rather small, it belonged to her exclusively. There would be no more sharing of things between her and Incomplete Maggie. Her tears almost made me worry that I had done something wrong. I waited for her to speak to me after she regained her composure. Lily cleared her voice before she spoke to me!

"I am so happy that you value and trust me, Ms. Roxanne. I have never been needed by so many people as I am here at your dealership. But know that these are tears of joy; it makes my heart so happy to know that you want me here. You have

313

included me in your life, plus you have offered me a lifeline. Now here I am with my own office located inside this building. You can't tell me that God does not listen to my prayers.

"I have wanted to be a part of your team for a long time, but it just seems like that everything has changed. When you asked me to work with you today, well—I just don't know how to tell you thank you enough. I will be the best assistant that you could ever hope for and I promise you Ms. Roxanne, I will not let you down because you have offered me a new life ... and the possibilities are endless."

I sat there in her chair just looking and smiling at her. She just gave me the best compliment that another soul could offer me. I was almost speechless as she stood up to come close to me. She placed her arms around my neck and whispered in my ear.

"Thank you for saving my life, Ms. Roxanne. I will make you proud of me."

I began to cry then, because I remembered what my Angel's had said to me about her. Her comments were somewhat haunting to me as my tears faded away. I pulled away from her and told my Lily,

"If I mess up my make-up while crying with you in this small-ass office, I will have to beat your ass for that and then dock your pay! So, dry your eyes and get your office together!"

We both laughed as I excused myself from her office. I told her that I would check in with her later that day. Lily waved at me as I exited her office. I was somewhat emotional as well, but I wanted to be the grown-up and shield myself from such emotional outbursts. I was happy that she was happy; my spirit soared around my dealership! I care for all my employees and there is nothing that I would not do to help them to be better people.

CHAPTER 22

ANYONE WHO HAD A HEART!

I walked away from Lily's new office even though I did not wish to seem heartless. I did not wish to cry anymore because God knows that I had tons of things to cry about; but now was not the proper time. My life had been somewhat overwhelming also and I was glad that Lily felt wanted and needed here at the dealership, because everyone here was aware that I really did have a big heart. But sometimes it could get in the way of the task at hand. I wanted to stay on track with all the things that needed to be done, that is why I removed myself from her office. There were still a lot of things that needed to be addressed, therefore I put my game face back on as I walked to the main entrance of the dealership. All the people were working at their appointed tasks while I just stood still and watched everyone move by me.

I watched as they used the utmost care to install that artwork. Once they were done, I felt good down in my soul. The time now was 12:00 noon and most of the items had already been installed. The only room left to be done was my office and the conference room. I was not concerned by that time that everything had to be reinstalled all over again. I was hopeful that we would be up and running in the morning. If it took us all night to get things up and running, then so be it. I had nothing else to do anyway, but I did find myself getting just a little hungry as I stayed out of the way.

I began to clap my hands as Peter and his team brought in my new state of the art conference set. I looked on as they carried in each piece of the table and chair ensemble into the room. I could already see me sitting at the head of the table while I offered up solutions for whatever problem should arise daily. I knew that we were almost done by now and all I had to do was to allow them to deliver my new office furniture and we would all be done. I moved out of their way while they finished with that room. I walked into Isabo's office for a minute. All her new furniture had been delivered and she was placing items back into their compartments. I asked her if it was ok for me to sit in here for a couple of seconds.

"Roxanne, you can sit anywhere you wish to. Oh, by the way, I ordered some sandwiches and a vegetable and fruit tray from a local shop, and they are on their way here. Maybe they will be done with the furniture soon so all of us could take a break, because we have all been working non-stop since first thing this morning."

I sat down at her new desk and watched her work. I was going over a running list in my head while she went about preparing her office. Isabo walked past Lily's office, stuck her head in and began to talk with me as I got up and walked with her to her office. Isabo had already placed her 3-foot tall statue on top of its own display table because she had it in a corner across from her desk. I kept looking at it because it looked so much like her; but maybe that was just another coincidence. I heard my cell phone go off in my pocket. I asked Isabo to excuse me. I put my phone to my ear.

"This is Roxanne, and what can I do for you?"

Cherokee was on the line and she seemed somewhat prissy towards me.

"Roxy, what do you mean by having my soon-to-be husband working on the Lord's day?"

"Well hello to you too, Ms. Cherokee, and how are you doing today?"

I knew that I was going to get a smart-ass answer back from her, so I braced myself for her reply.

"I'm doing better than your crazy-ass could possibly be doing, but I want to know how long you think you will have a hold on my man because there are some things that I want him to do to me."

I was ashamed by what she was implying about the Pastor, so I acted as if I did not hear her. she continued with her insults towards me, but I knew that my sister was being playful with me, even though I knew that she wanted her man at home with her.

"Cherokee, your man could leave anytime he wants to. I am not forcing him to stay here and fix his new office, but I will make sure that he is aware that his mother wants him home."

Cherokee was silent for a couple of seconds. Then she mentioned that she had met Dr. Henely.

"I saw your new love interest yesterday while I visited our grandfather. Now you are jumping over the racial lines to get a

319

hot piece of tail, or is he just another high-yellow brother that found you and your wide ass intriguing? It seems to me that you always draw out the nerdish men. but what have you done with Mr. Akheem Fulwad? Has he got lost inside of that orbit that you call an ass? You can pretend as if you do not need anybody else in your life, but I know that you are lonely. That is no reason for you to empty other people's lives. You need to find yourself a pastime, Roxy, and remove your hold over all of the people who work for you."

I was becoming unglued as I listened to my sister because there was only so much of her bullshit that I was willing to take. I already had a visual dancing inside of my head of what I would be doing to her if she were standing before me. I would have her black ass inside a headlock. I began to smile as I fixed my mouth to answer some of her questions.

"Cherokee, you are more that welcome to go to West Hell or some other hot place, but do not call my job with your stupid bullshit! If your man wants to come to work rather than to stay at home and fuck you, well then, I commend him on his excellent taste. How dare you bring up Akheem and that doctor in the same breath? If you just take care of your *own* life, you wouldn't have the chance to point out how empty you think my life is! Now that we have exchanged pleasantries, what the *fuck* do you want, or did you just wish to hear my lovely voice?"

Isabo was laughing her ass off as I traded insults with my sister. Maybe we were running out of things to say to each other; I just did not wish to be caught up with her today because it was taking all my might not to go over to her house and kick her ass. I was truly tapped out of insults to offer her so I asked, was there anything else I could do for her?

"Roxy, I just called to check up on you, but I guess I will see you at the hospital sometime next week. Are we still on for Thanksgiving? I spoke with your father and your brothers this weekend, and they said that they will be over to your house with bells on their feet and an appetite in their stomachs. If I was you Ms. Roxanne, I would pull out the hero's cape that you love to wear and make sure that you have addressed all of the wants and needs of your guests!"

It was at that moment my dream made sense to me—the crazy dream that I'd had last night. I was preparing to cut off my sister's head with the axe but instead of cutting off her head I gave her tons of paper cuts on her lips. Plus, in the dream I forced 39 red lollipops inside of her mouth to make her shut the fuck up! I began to laugh at her as I hung up in her face! I was hungry at this point, so I told Isabo that I would be right back once I got myself something to eat.

I'd mentioned to Isabo that I would have to tell her about this crazy dream that I had last night. My soul got happy as I walked out of her office. I walked to the deli and found myself a sandwich to munch on, a small turkey and bacon. Most of my staff was in the deli eating as well. I sat down at a table by myself as everyone watched me; I did not care because I was ready to eat. We had been there for about 25 minutes before Peter came in looking for me. He walked up to my table while I was refueling myself.

"Well, it looks like we are done with our delivery to your dealership, Ms. Roxanne. Let me be the first to tell you that it has been a pleasure working with you. You have such a great team here which has impressed all of us, plus your purchase saved us from being overloaded with more bills. The possibility of mine and my company's success showed up before you walked into my place of business, so allow me to say thank you once more."

I was feeling no pain as he told me his truth.

"Peter would you and your staff members like to join us for lunch?" I inquired. "We have more than enough to share with all of you, and it would be our pleasure for you to join us."

Peter extended his hand to me as I stood up.

"Ms. Roxanne, you and your team have been more than to kind to us, but it is time for us to be leaving now. Even though your offer is most gracious, we all have friends and family that we wish to be with; but if you are ever in need of anything else new for your dealership, please do not hesitate to call on me."

He wanted to go over the invoice sheet one more time to make sure that everything was in its place. I got up and walked with him through the dealership as the first room I stepped inside of was my conference room. I was undone at how beautiful my conference room looked, and that picture with the three eagles on it made me smile even wider. That picture spoke to me on so many levels and to see that all three of the eagles had their heads tilted in the same direction that I place mine most days made me smile.

The new table that I had in here was larger and longer than my previous one and the legs on the table looked like they had clawed feet on it like the eagles on the picture. I did not need to step into Eric's and Isabo's office anymore, because I had already seen their office. I looked in on Lily, who was overjoyed with her new office space. It pleased me to see her so happy. I walked with Peter to my office, so we could check it out and make sure that the queen in me was happy.

This queen was speechless as I walked into my new office. All my new pieces were in their proper places. I was glad that I had updated my office because I had had my old furniture for several years. But the thing that caught my eye was the great picture of the Samurai Warrior and the Geisha girl sitting on the bench! I knew from the start that this picture needed to be in my office. I was happy with what I had done but when I walked towards the main entrance of the dealership, I was blown away by how pretty everything looked. I could not find the words to express the joy that I was feeling as Isabo moved towards us. She spoke for the dealership on my behalf.

"Peter, thank you and your company once more for all of your help with this venture and we will be sure to tell all of our business friends and family where you are located, because you and your company have helped us convey how we feel here at this dealership."

With those last words we all shook hands once more as he walked out of the building. I was eager to get into my office, so I could place my things in their new home. Isabo reminded to me go and check in on the Pastor. I walked down the hallway to check in on him. He was sitting at his desk with a big smile on his face. I tapped on the door before stepping into his office. He looked up at me with a light in his eye and I could see that he was pleased to have a place of his own.

"Baby Sister, you have made me almost as happy as your sister had when she said yes to my marriage proposal. I pray that you are not teasing me with this new office because I am still waiting on an answer from you about the mobile business. I will not pressure your answer, but I will tell you what I will do for you in the meantime. I will keep your sister and mother away from you until Thanksgiving; that way, you will be able to see that I am a needed part of the family, too!"

The Pastor and I began to laugh at his offer because we knew that my mother and my sister could not be kept away from me, no matter how hard he tried. I knew that he was only having fun with me. I just hung out with him in his office for a couple of minutes. I was proud of him as we just sat there and basked in his glory until I exited at 1:30 p.m.

My main goal for the rest of the evening was to work on my office but when I got there, Lily was 85% done with putting everything back in its place. She did not have the empty look in her eyes that seemed to walk with her. She looked overjoyed and that made me happy. Although I had offered to help her with my office, Lily would not hear of me doing anything for myself. I grabbed my laptop and some invoice papers and walked to my conference room!

Lily told me that she would be out of my way in 45 minutes or less, while I encouraged her to take her time putting my office back in operating mode. I wanted her to find her way around my world inside my office. I just looked at her for a couple of seconds before I left. I tucked my laptop under my arm and held onto all my papers. I moved toward the conference room as I passed by the deli. Isabo wanted to know did I need anything else to be done by my team, because I could work them like a group of Hebrew slaves if I chose to.

CHAPTER 23

ANYTHING BY STEVE WONDER IS FINE WITH ME!

I walked into my new conference room and looked around the office for anything that was out of place. Everything was in its proper place and there was nothing for me to do. There were no scraps of paper left on the floor and all the plastic had been removed from all the furniture. I was glad that I did not have to do anything to fix that room as I walked to the very head of the table and put my laptop and papers down. I was amazed at how lovely everything looked and how that picture just kissed the room with success.

I began to smile once more as I looked at it again. I was just about to sit down in my chair when most of my staff came by to let me know that they were gone for the evening. I thanked each and every one of them and I told them that I would see them in the morning. I was informed that the deli was clean, and all the sandwiches and vegetables placed in the refrigerator. I watched as most of my team left the building. There were only Eric, Isabo, Lily, Bo and I left in the building. I walked to the main door to see who was on duty tonight. I saw that Sammi was on guard for the dealership. I stuck my head out the door to say hello to him.

"Hello Sammi, it has been several weeks since I have seen you! I hope that all has been going well for you and your family?"

"Wells, hellos tos yous toos, Ms. Roxannes, ands yes, it's has beens severals weeks sinces I've seens yous, toos. Everythings is goings wells withs mes ands mys familys. I haves beens prayings fors yous and yours familys alsos. I ams prayings fors yours grandfathers, alsos."

I blew Sammi a kiss as I said, "Thank you for your prayers."

I stepped back into the dealership and saw Eric coming towards me. He mentioned that he had done all that he is willing to do for now. He was tired and wanted to get home to rest before his wife returned from out of town. He did mention that he was missing her rather badly. I told Eric that I would see him in the morning for our Monday morning meeting. I watched Eric leave the building, then I saw Bo move in my direction. He and his team did almost all the heavy lifting of the furniture. He had been out of sight most of the day, or maybe it was me who had been out of sight. I looked at him as he walked up next to me.

"Hey, Ms. Roxanne, did you want me and the security team to hang around any longer?"

I hit him on his shoulder and told him to get out of here. I did not anticipate any problems that Sammi and I could not handle.

"You need to go home and be with my sister before she comes looking for you. We know that she needs to remain calm, so she probably needs to lay her eyes on you, Bo. Just get out of here and go take care of her."

Next, I stopped at Lily's door.

"Lily, tomorrow we can go purchase supplies for you and your office, plus I am going to need you to have your own laptop and company cell phone. You need to think about what piece of artwork you would like to have on your wall, even though there is only a small area of wall for you to display your taste. All you must do is tell me what you like, and we will get it for you. There will be no more allowing Maggie to bully you, Ms. Lily, because you have officially been promoted to my personal assistant and you answer to me, only. Everyone else will have to take a number to see you and for you to help or assist them with whatever it is that needs to be addressed. I hope that I have made myself clear to you?"

"Yes, Ms. Roxanne, you have made yourself clear. Allow me to say thank you once more, but I do plan on being respectful of your team, yet I will not be bullied by anyone ever again. If there is anything that you would like me to do for you, please do not hesitate to just ask. I am at your disposal."

I left Lily to finish up with my office as I walked back into the conference room. I took my seat on my new chair and gazed up at the ceiling for a couple of minutes. I twirled around in my chair and found that it was a perfect fit for me and my wide ass! I put my glasses on and opened my laptop. The time was now 3:00p.m. and we were done with most of the work.

I set out planning our sales goals for next year, then I needed to calculate all the yearly bonuses for the employees. I prided myself on being overly fair with my employees, and I knew that they welcomed my willingness to offer them all a great living.

Since I had the time to devote to doing paperwork, I was going to take advantage of it. I knew that I needed to take into consideration each employee and their status at the dealership.

I set out on doing my own in-house evaluations. Since I was the boss, I did not have to ask anybody anything. I just wanted to make sure that I was fair. Forty-five minutes had passed before an interruption came. It was Lily asking me to come and check out my office. I got up to see what she had done for me. I couldn't believe it was my office, because Lily had moved the couch and coffee table to another wall. I called Isabo and asked her to join me because it had a hint of sparkle.

She made it down to my office and expressed her appreciation of the new look. That is when Isabo began to act a little strange towards Lily, as she asked Lily when she planned on leaving because we still had work to do and matters to discuss. I did not understand what in the hell she was talking about because most of the work was already done. Lily, however, got the message that Isabo was trying to convey.

Lily turned to me and said, "I will see you in the morning, Ms. Roxanne."

She then turned to leave us standing in my office as she went in her office and gathered her things. Lily grabbed her handbag and walked to the door as Isabo walked behind her and locked the door! I told Isabo that I thought that she was being rude to Lily, and that I thought she should run out there and apologize to her before she drove off!

"Roxanne, I was not being rude to her. She just needs to get on with her life; she has been here all day long, and I know that you are good and tired. I know that you do not see everything that goes on here at this dealership, but I think Lily might have a stalker tendency. You need to be careful of those stalkers, because you attract the strangest people into your life ... I just want you to be mindful of her."

I dismissed everything that Isabo just said because I did not see Lily the way she did. I know some of the stories behind parts of her life. I shook my head as I walked away from her. I walked back into my office to use the restroom. Once I came out, I sat down at my new desk and put my hands on everything, blessing my new furniture, then I got up and walked into the deli.

I was after an afternoon snack because I did not finish my sandwich and I was still a little hungry. Isabo told me that she was going to put some music on, and did I have a request for any artist. I kept walking to the door of the in-house deli, stopped as I was about to go inside, and turned around to inform her of my request.

"Anything by Stevie Wonder is fine with me!" I chirped.

"I guess I will put on his box set for you, Ms. Roxanne—your royal highness!"

"Thank you, nice lady, and why you are still here with me? I know that you do indeed have a life, plus you never told me about your day off. What did you get into?"

Isabo told me to go and get myself something to eat first and she would meet me in the conference room. I walked into the deli as she went to put on some music for us. I found myself standing in front of a stack of sandwiches. I knew that I would be eating a big meal later tonight. I just grabbed some water and baby carrots to nibble on. I did not wish to lose control and eat all those sandwiches. I just needed a nice snack to wrap my mouth around. I liked the way I was looking in my jogging suit as I laughed to myself.

I thought that Isabo was going to sit down and talk with me, but I was sadly mistaken because she moved towards me and requested my cell phone. She told me that there were a couple of numbers that she needed to store in her file, but she would be right back to talk with me. I reached into my pants pocket and handed her my phone. I could not deny that I didn't miss all the noise and chaos. I was thrilled to be alone because in my mind, I still had lots of paperwork to address, and if Isabo did not wish to talk with me I was truly not offended by her absence.

I turned around in my chair and began to gaze up at that interesting picture that had just been installed. I heard the music begin to play in the background as I munched on several carrots. I heard Isabo moving back down the hallway towards me. I turned my chair back around to face her as she walked back into the conference room. She surprised me as she had her handbag tucked under her arm plus she had her jacket on to leave.

I asked her, "What is all of this? I thought that you and I were going to play catch-up with one another's lives. Why do you have your handbag and your jacket on?"

She is a woman of knowledge and I knew that she would use precise words. I was eager to hear what she had to say, so I sat back in my chair and folded my hands across my chest. I was waiting for a lie to come out, but she has such a kind face and I am one of her biggest fans, so I just stared at her.

"Roxanne, something has come up and I have to leave. We will play the catch-up game tomorrow. I need to be leaving for an important adventure. Believe me, Roxanne, I will give you all the sordid details tomorrow. There is no need for you to walk me to the door. I will let myself out and lock up behind me. Remember Sammi is here, and you can go and work on all of that paperwork that you need to address!"

With her last words, she turned to walk out the door. Isabo stopped right at the door and told me that she had left my cell phone in my office, adding that she believed that she accidentally turned it off. I could not think of a reason why she did not return it to me or why she would turn it off. Mentally I was searching for an excuse from her on why she did not return my phone to me. I did not say another word as she exited the conference room. I decided to get more comfortable as I removed my jacket and shoes.

I noticed that the picture of the three Eagles was slightly misaligned, so I got up and straightened it, then sat back down in my chair. I put my glasses back on and continued to nibble on the carrots. I was enjoying the peace and quiet and the comfort that the music was also offering me. Most people would be afraid to be in such a big building alone at night, but since this was my building and I knew that Sammi was outside and I did not fear one thing. I sat alone in this conference room with my head down and my eyes focusing on the computer screen.

The songs that Stevie was singing to me calmed the despair that I was feeling deep inside, plus I did not allow my mind to dwell with sorrow too long. I was content with my life today, so I distracted myself with the numbers on the screen. I was writing down items for me to address in the next two weeks on a pad and inputting information about bonuses on the computer screen for each employee. I still planned on going to wherever Macy was going to have her procedure done and knowing that I was clinging to a positive outcome for her situation placed me in prayer mode once again.

I thought it was a shame that my friend had to go through this situation with no one standing by her side, which was why I was going to be there with her. I began to play with my ponytail on the left side of my head when the Stevie Wonder CD started

336

playing this song titled, "Superwoman (Where Were You When I Needed You)". I began to sing along, because I loved that song and because to me, it explained aspects of my life. Numerous subjects were dancing around in my head. I began to rub the balls of my feet and continued singing to myself!

I needed my mind to focus on the positive side of life. Macy had been my rock for so many years and I could not get over that this type of trouble was visiting her. I know that I did not wish to lose my friend. She was my one true friend, and we had charted out our lives with each other in them. I smiled to myself as I recalled some of our plans from the past. We had even planned that if she ever got married, I was to be her only matron of honor. Macy has always stood up for me and she was not shy about telling people that I did not know how to fight in my youth, even though I had more than made up for it in my adult life! Macy and I would never run from a fight, no matter what, but sometimes we would welcome a misunderstanding with people … I smiled as I thought about me and my friend!

I also thought about removing Sissell's hand from my dealership because he asked me to release him, something I planned on doing. I wanted total control of this business and I was proud that he thought enough of me to continue sponsoring me; but now it was time for him to take his hands off. I knew that this was going to be a big task to address, but I was sure that it could be done. I was going to enlist the help of my team to see what we could come up with, but until we had a plan to allow us to escape his hold over this dealership, I was not going to make any false moves.

I had been working on my paperwork for an hour; it was way past 5:00 p.m. and I had not talked to my kids. I told myself that I would grab my cell phone as I went to the restroom. I told myself to take a little break because I wanted some more pineapples and carrots, and I needed to go pee! I stood up and laughed as I looked at my picture of those off-center eagles as I walked to the restroom and relieved myself. I washed my hands three times, I checked my face and put some more lip-gloss on. I was becoming hungry and distracted so I thought that it would be a great time to wrap up all my loose ends.

I went into the deli and grabbed some more carrots, then made my way back to the conference room. I decided not to call the kids because I was about to finish up all my paperwork and go home to be with them. Once I was back in the conference room and powering down my laptop, I began to smile at the song playing on the sound system. It was Stevie Wonder's song called "Blame It on the Sun". I loved that song with all my heart, so I sat back down to let that song massage my soul.

I was caught up in the moment as the song filled the conference room. I was daydreaming my cares away as I let that song touch my heartache! As it played, I heard Sammi come back into the building. I put my head down and turned my chair towards the wall. I had tears in my eyes and I did not wish to explain what I was feeling to Sammi, if he passed by and glanced through the big glass window at me. I knew that he was coming in to check on me because I had been in here without making any noise for far too long. I had been too still and I knew that he might be a little concerned about me. I sat back in my chair and waited on him to finish his walk by. When I turned around and looked up at the door opening into the conference room, there stood the new captain of my heart!

The captain with the anchor-shaped dick that could keep me still was looking back at me like he had lost something. Mr. Akheem Fulwad was standing in the doorway and I did not know what he was doing here. I wiped the tears from my eyes and began to stand, but Akheem motioned for me to stay put. He walked to the other end of the table and placed his briefcase on it. There was no emotion on his face as he looked at me as if I was crazy! Little did he know how insane I really was at this moment. He just stood there and removed his jacket. He was dressed in a taupe and burgundy pinstripe suit.

He did not have on a necktie. He was all business as he removed his gun from the waist of his pants, then he placed it on the table and took a seat. He motioned for me to stay away from him and have a seat, too! I felt sad because he looked as if he was about to blame me once more for something. I guess the right song was playing because I felt a dismissive feeling coming off him as we looked at each other!

I wanted to rush into his arms and tell him that I had missed him so. I wanted to feel as if this was a special daybreak encounter, because the sun was shining and I wanted to sing aloud. I loved this man; he'd helped me to be strong when no one else would; but now he was treating me like a stranger. My words just stayed tucked away in my mouth as Mr. Akheem Fulwad spoke.

"There is no need for you to get up and come to me Roxanne; I am only here for some unfinished business between us. This is more than a personal matter right now, and I need you to keep your seat. We will be done with this in a couple of minutes."

Once he had opened his briefcase and retrieved a yellow notepad from it, he placed his gun inside it, not looking at me! He sat there and finally looked at me as if he had something to prove to me. I dropped my head for a minute as I was replaying our last conversation. He cleared his throat and looked in my general direction … not directly at me.

CHAPTER 24

WITH YOUR LOVE!

Akheem started to speak firmly to me. I was on some type of autopilot, because I knew that he was about to get into my ass!

"Roxanne, I guess I was fundamentally wrong to think that you and I were both locked inside a pleasing love affair together. For the life of me, I cannot understand how in the fuck you would allow three people to call me about you. They all expressed their concerns about some rather funny and odd things going on in your life. Like your grandfather gradually working his way out of his coma and returning to you and your family. Oh, I got that tidbit of information from my co-worker. How in the hell did you manage to get Major Morrison, who happens to be a good friend of mine and works for me, to purchase new furniture and computer equipment for your dealership?

"Now to find out that they believe that they might have found an end to your security breach here. That fact made me pause. I thought that you and I were involved in each other's lives, but I guess I must have been wrong. Knowing that you are sharing things with strangers is sort of troubling to me. You are treating me like I'm some random stranger on the street as we try to start this romance. I guess I was wrong about that bit of information too.

"Let me ask you a question, Roxanne, what makes you keep such important information like that from me? *I* was the one who let you know that you had an in-house problem. Although, I am happy to know that there could be an end to this small dilemma for you and the dealership. I find myself wondering about you and if you value me at all. Then to have Sullivan call me and ask me to come down and see about you. Why did Isabo ask me to come out and visit you, afraid that you are on the verge of a nervous breakdown? Are you following my train of thought?

"It is apparent to me, Ms. Roxanne that you do not wish to include me in your life like I thought you did. Maybe you have been too busy to make me aware of the important things going on in your life. I am trying to figure out if this the end or the crazy beginning of this relationship. Trust me, Roxanne, when I tell you that I have given you several chances to call and talk to me. But you keep knocking me down with your actions or your lack of actions towards me. Make me understand, why in the *fuck* did you not call me?"

Several seconds passed as he just looked at me! I kept my eyes on him as he continued to stare. Then he started verbally abusing me one more in his well-thought-out rant!

"Once we are done with this meeting, Ms. Roxanne Camille Beaumont-Sagar, both you and I will have total clarity about these troubling matters, do you understand me?"

I just sat there because I was unsure which question to answer first. It was *Akheem* who'd asked me to give him a break for a couple of days, and I gave him what he wanted. I knew that I was going to give Isabo a piece of my mind when I encountered that *bitch* in the morning. Now, I fully understood why she left here so hastily. She knew that Akheem was on his way to see me. Then this crazy thought crossed my mind as I was looking at him.

He had a choice in asking me to give him a couple of days to gather his thoughts. I was mentally revisiting our conversation as I recalled him asking me not to call. I respected and honored his wishes and did just what he'd asked. Now he did not like the fact that I had delayed calling him for help. I felt as if I had overstayed my welcome with him for now. I needed this man and I wanted him to need me, too, but I just never begged anyone for his attention, ever. I appreciated him and was aware that he is not a possession for me: that was one of the reasons I didn't beg, and I appreciated his knowing his own mind!

I did no more or less than he requested of me. I was the one who spoke out of turn while we were talking this past Monday. Seeing that he was so pissed off with me made me know that I made the right decision to leave him the fuck alone. There is something in him that seems uneasy with me. Although I was thrilled that he had his handgun in his briefcase, it made me think twice about being a smart-mouth woman today. I smiled to myself because I was going to be sweet to him no matter what he said. I knew that I was at a total disadvantage as I watched him. He continued to talk at me, my mind doing flips as his words passed my ears!

345

I guess he was calculating what to say to me next, while I hoped we could move past this misunderstanding. Then, the only sound was the music from the sound system. Stevie's music was filling the space in the room. The song called "Ordinary Pain" was playing. I lacked the words to say to him because we are still in the early stages of this relationship. That is when he picked up his legal pad and looked over at me! His gaze was the most intense that I had ever experienced from him. Akheem and never had a cross word between us, but after ninety seconds passed, he spoke again.

"Well, since you are a very clever woman, I have a little game that we are about to play, Ms. Roxanne. You are not the only one who likes numbers and games, so be a good girl and follow my directions. I came up with five pivotal questions for you, and you can only answer each question by saying yes, Akheem or no, Akheem. If you do not have an answer, then all I want to hear is total silence, Ms. Roxanne. I hope that I have made myself more than clear with you. Because your disobedience will not be tolerated under any circumstances. There will be no questions from you whatsoever. Now that you understand the ground rules, we can begin! You do understand what I am saying to you?"

Several seconds passed before he told me that I could answer his question. He told me that he was so angry with me. That I sometimes make him want to holler and throw up both his hands! Maybe, he was listening to his own personal soundtrack in his mind; it could be that he had Marvin Gaye on in his car as he made his way over to see me. Because that line was out of a Marvin song as I looked down at my hands then back at him. I guess I must have hit a nerve with him, and now he was seeing that I am a warrior myself. He has never encountered me being a bitch to him. I believe that he will have his own personal testimony about me, by the time we are done.

I realized that I did not go to him for help with understanding parts of my life. I just allowed all manner of bullshit to build up. If it had not been for Isabo, I probably would have called him this coming Wednesday, maybe. I was thinking that this relationship had somehow turned into a complicated disaster, as I shifted my neck then looked back at him. All I really wanted to do was to reach my arms out to him and give him a hug. I guess that ship had already sailed away and I ought to let the chips fall where they may. I knew that I was going to be cautious with him and not let my mouth run away with me. I did not wish to leave him in doubt about anything about me.

"Yes, Akheem", was all that I would allow out of my mouth! I knew that I had missed hearing his voice and looking at him, too. It would not have surprised me if I found out that he could sell anything to anybody if he put his mind to it, because he was *such* a salesperson. Akheem was the type of person that could sell ice to Eskimos and be *very* smooth about it. He looked so delicious to me and I was hungry for anything he had to say. I told myself to pay attention to everything that he was saying.

He must think that I was in danger of losing my mind, for him to come all the way out here. I was going to be a good girl and pay attention to him … I could not afford to lose him once more. I was trying to get rid of the stress that I was carrying around in my back as I settle back in the chair. I became somewhat afraid of what he was going to say to me, then I sat on the edge of my chair and waited for the game to begin!

I looked up at him and tried to smile, but he did not return it. He just started in with his questions for me. I sat up straight up in my chair, pushed my glasses up on my face, and prepared myself for his line of questions. He cleared his throat, looked up at me, then back at his pad.

"Question 1. Ms. Roxanne, do you love me?"

Three seconds passed before I gave him my answer.

"Yes, Akheem!"

He showed no response to my answer.

"Question 2. Are you exclusively mine, Ms. Roxanne?"

"Yes, Akheem!"

He glanced at me, and continued.

"Question 3. If you claim to be mine and all mine, and you can tell me that you are in love with me as I am with you, then why in the FUCK would you speak to me so carelessly the other day? Do you wish to carry on with this relationship, Ms. Roxanne, or are you just FUCKING with me because you can? It seems to me that you have nothing better to do, or that you are just toying with me to fill your asshole quota for the year. Do you wish to carry on in this relationship, Ms. Roxanne? Before you give me your response, I want you to really give my question your undivided attention and not just give me another FUCKED up answer!"

Twelve seconds passed by before I answered his question because he had already asked me Question 3 or more questions in one, and I answered them all as truthfully as I could. But it seemed as if Akheem had asked me five or six different questions wrapped up inside a vast statement. I just decided to answer his last question.

"Yes, Akheem!"

Those words flowed from my mouth and my answer made Akheem angrier than normal. He began to shake his head because he was not enjoying this little exchange between the both of us any longer.

"'Yes, Akheem' to which of the five questions, Roxanne? Shit, you do not even know which question you are answering. Correct me if I am wrong, but am I to understand that you *meant* to be careless with me, or are you answering "yes, Akheem" because you are toying and FUCKING with me?"

I chose not to say anything to him because he was whipping himself into a frenzy. I did not know what he wanted me to say, so I just sat there and shut the FUCK up! I removed my glasses as he rubbed his eyes because he looked sort of confused. He picked up his pad once more and looked at it, breathing hard as he looked up at me while I sat up in my chair. I could tell that he was troubled. I was not playing the game the way he wanted it played! I believe that he could beat my ass right now. More than likely, he could, because he was so mad at me. Maybe my words were throwing salt on a wound as far as he was concerned. I was feeling in a giving mood, *if* he asked me the right question.

"Question 4. After all that we had both been through in our lives, do you know that you pierced my spirit with your FUCKED-up words the other day? I am concerned that you find yourself afraid of me. Here is my question to you Roxanne: do you fear me?"

"No, Akheem!" I answered, then retreated back into my mind. He picked up his pad once more, looked down at me and told me that I had FUCKED up his whole week up so far. He then reached into his briefcase and pulled out a big yellow envelope as I sat there. I looked in his direction as he glanced at whatever it was, he was looking at. I was praying that I answered all the questions to his liking. I did not wish to mishandle the beginning of this week any more than I might his days in the near future.

I had no idea that he was so sensitive. He has been suffering after me speaking rubbish to him about being afraid of him. I never knew that he really paid that much attention to all the things that I say. I guess I have finally run across a man who thinks that my words are divine. Maybe this could be what Heaven is like this time for me. He is speaking to me as if my words have mentally had him on his knees this week.

Akheem tried to soften his stare at me. He cleared his throat and resumed speaking to me again in a rather plain and ordinary type of way!

"Final Comments and Question 5, Roxanne! It has amazed me that you have become a habit to me. I was so looking forward to our dreams combining with one another. I have not regretted meeting you, because so far you have been sweet to me. I enjoyed being with you, until you allowed your mouth to slip and made horrible comments. Well, I was unable to rest on what you said to me. I found myself at the doctor's office this past Friday. I wanted to know, where in my heart do you think that the monster in me resides? I asked my doctor to run a new test on my heart and scan it! I wanted to see what you think you see in my heart. Because for the life of me, Roxanne, I could not find where that monster lives.

I brought you a scan of my heart. I want you to come down here and show me where the bastard who scares you lives in me! Show me which chamber of my heart you believe the monster lurks. Do me a favor, Roxanne, come down here and show me on this x-ray just where you think I plan to do you some harm. Please don't get me wrong; you might know more about me than I do. I have been trying with all my might to be a marvel to you. But if you believe me to be a monster, please show me that part of myself because I am blind to it!"

Silence was the only thing in this room after Akheem asked me to come to him! I knew in my heart that *I* was, indeed, the monster that he spoke about. I began to weep uncontrollably, looking down at the floor! I closed my eyes and turned my chair away from him. There was no sound or answer I could make for him to understand that I was the monster and not him. I kept my eyes closed because I knew that he was going to get up and leave me now. I did not wish to see him walk away from me, because the real monster was already in this room before he got here.

I heard him close his briefcase as I stayed turned to the wall while I put my head in my lap and began to really sob. I could not hold back my anger for myself as something went off inside me and I began to scream for several seconds. I kicked the shit out of my wall and ended up hurting my big toe! I had forgotten that I did not have on my shoes. I began to scream once more, because I HAD A BAD TASTE IN MY MOUTH FOR MYSELF. My thought was, what in the FUCK have you done, Roxanne? I wanted to kick my own ass but all I could say was, "DAMN YOU ROXANNE, damn you straight to hell!"

I reached back on the table for a napkin to blow my nose! I must have dropped them on the floor. Moisture was coming out of my eyes and I needed to blow my nose rather badly. I picked my head up from my lap as Akheem, who was now standing next to me, handed me his handkerchief to blow my nose! I blew my nose and totally sullied his handkerchief! He was looking at me as he stood next to me with sorrow in his eyes, looking lonely. His words had eclipsed my heart as I saw the sadness in his eyes, as tears rolled down his face, too. I asked if I could speak, or did he still want me to be quiet?

"Don't speak, Roxanne! All I want to do is kiss you, because I need you to keep what you have to say to yourself for now."

Akheem reached down to lift me out of the chair! His eyes became softer as he looked me up and down then he leaned close to my mouth!

"I have missed you more than you could ever know. I have been lonely without speaking to you!"

With his last statement, Akheem reached around my waist and pulled me close to him! He pushed me against the wall and began to devour my mouth. He placed his hands inside of my jogging pants and began to manhandle me. Akheem brutally aroused me with his fingers because his touch sort of felt out of place to me, almost like he was making another debut with me! His hands were inside of my panties as he manipulated my little glory, his tongue overwhelming my mouth. His fingers were pressing out some type of Morse code on my lady-parts. His hands moved to my rear end and tugged at me for a couple of seconds. I smiled as he kissed me. I did not expect him to be still standing here next to me. His tears became mine as we kissed!

I grabbed hold of his body, going out of my mind with passion. I knew that steam was coming off our bodies while I was beginning to sweat! I began to rub his crotch as he fondled my breast with a boldness, he had never shown me before. We pulled apart from one another then we collided towards each other once again. I unzipped his pants as he took off my top ... we were both getting carried away, while he smiled tenderly back at me.

I could not stop myself because I wanted to feel his body. I wrapped my legs around him as he dragged off his shirt. Akheem kissed my neck while removing my top and bra! Passion had overtaken us. I wanted his dick jammed inside of me, as my mind explored how this man made my body and soul mad with lust. I could hardly stand with the strain between both of us. I knew that I wanted and needed him all at the same time.

CHAPTER 25

ORAGAMI!

After several sexy kisses, we pulled away from each other once more. I wanted to stop but could not, as my body was weeping for him. I was longing to cradle him inside of my body. His body was offering me a promise to damn near destroy my pussy, as his kisses were almost bringing me to my knees! I could no longer pretend to be afraid of him for any reason. Mentally, I was walking around my mind examining my own thoughts. I smiled to myself as I clung to him for dear life. I knew that someone was about to be raped and it was not going to be me. I already knew that I wanted to fuck him as it felt as if he was already inside my body. I slipped my hands onto his chest. Emotion was taking the both of us as my pussy was turning into a wild river that wanted to be kissed or at least entered.

"Take off all of your clothes right now, Roxanne, so we can break in all of this new and expensive furniture!"

I just stood there with my breast hanging out inside my boardroom. I did not wish to understand his command. My body had reached such a high temperature maybe my hearing was affected. I wanted to run my hands up and down his body and rape the shit out of him, just not *here*. This was my workplace, where people respected me, and I wanted my standing to remain intact. I watched as Akheem began to take off all his clothing, telling me his body was longing for me to touch and taste him. I just stood there and looked at him while my mind was entertaining the fact that Sammi is right outside. He could walk in here at any time, catch me off guard and ruin our relationship with one another forever.

I did not wish for him to catch me like this. I became frozen as my eyes lingered on Akheem and his rock-hard body as he was setting it free from his clothing. I knew that I was no angel, but this was not the time or the place as my little glory was doing flips. There was a power struggle going on between us, even though my mind was already in the process of surrendering itself to him. The taste of consensual sex was floating around the room. It seemed like that he was eager to be raped by me. I could almost feel the both of us fucking right now, but my body would not move. I had too much to lose if I went out of character in my boardroom.

My mouth flew open as I wanted him inside of me, but I was at my place of business, dreaming of doing some really bad things to him. I had to take control of the situation, so I shook my head, no! This bronze-looking man began to move closer to me

"Let me see that beautiful body of yours, Roxanne! I plan on doing some harm to it *right* now!"

I was also longing to have him inside of me, but I could not give into his whims. I am the boss at this dealership, and I did not wish to lose my place in Sammi's eyes.

"Roxanne, what are you doing? Did I not use the magic words to have you remove your clothes? I'm sorry if I forgot to say the right words. Please take off all your clothes, Rocky!"

"Akheem, Sammi is outside and the conference room door does not lock. Maybe we could move to my office instead." Akheem smiled at me and said, "Doll, I gave your man $300.00

to not allow anything or anyone to bother us for the next three hours. We are down to two hours now because we spent one talking and hashing out this silly misunderstanding between the both of us. Come here, take off your clothes and get to the middle of that table. I promise you that no one will bother us at all. Your man will make sure that we are undisturbed, I promise you."

I removed all my clothes as Akheem just looked at me while I walked up next to him. I placed my hand over his heart while we kissed for several more minutes. Then when he lifted me off the floor, I knew that we were about to break in my new conference table, plus I was so wet and ready for him. My mind had already thrown away all my regrets about what I had said to him. My thoughts were already traveling through the clouds to have a massive orgasm and I so wanted it from him. I needed him to catch me because my mind was running around this room.

I could not get a clear thought about what was really going on, because this was like a spectacular dream. Akheem spread me out on that table as if I was on display before he devoured me. He walked all the way around the table, rubbing his hands together. He licked his lips several times before he attacked me.

He jumped on top of me with his imposing girth growing between his legs, saying, "It's Duck Season, Doll!"

I reached for him, and my Akheem entered my body. The sound effects of nothing but pure pleasure was streaming in and out of my conference room. Although his body was over the top eager to please me, my Akheem fucked me as if dancing to a Michael Jackson song! I felt like a human piece of origami while he folded me into many different positions! I was unclear as to what we were really doing. He entered me with such force that I thought that my conference table, with its clawed feet was about to get up and walk right out of the room!

We were both being rough with one another, as I demanded that he fuck me harder! We were both pulling at each other, and the sex couldn't be adequately expressed in words. If I had been a smaller woman, Akheem might have hurt me. I was built for the ride of pleasure with him as I began to smash my body into his. He was roaring in my ears as he kissed me.

I kept moaning all over that room. Akheem was in the process of special delivering his dick to me. I could not fake the passion I felt for him. Whatever pathway to passion we were walking on, I was no longer empty as I looked at him! Truly, I was *so* horny for this man. I might have entertained his whole body getting lost inside of me, with one single hard thrust! I smiled because I was moist enough inside to accommodate him without any form of struggle!

My vision became blurry as Akheem fucked me, as my mind and body becoming fully involved in us. This was the last thing that I thought I would be doing today, fucking my lover in my conference room at my dealership. He had my body all over that damn table as he kept doing this one thing to me that drove me crazy. He kept saying, "It's Duck Season!" as he would try to knock my little glory off the table, laughing our asses off as we fucked like rabbits. Finally, I guess he found the right spot inside me as he came.

My Akheem was sponsoring his dick to me and I was his number one supporter. My body was ticking away as he just kept placing all of himself in and out of me! The pleasure that we were giving each other had us sinking into of bliss. I was hanging onto every thrust as he pleased the hell out of me. He reached over to the sides of the table to help hold his body steady, because we were sweating all over one another. I held onto him as I began to beg him not to stop, because this was just what I really needed.

Once we were done with the first qualifying round of sex, we laid on that table smiling at each other. I could hardly believe that this was a real occurrence. I know I had a vivid imagination and I could make myself dream of anything or anyone. I reached over and pinched him because I wanted to make sure that I hadn't found myself in another fantasy. Once he flinched, I then pinched myself! I wanted to make sure that it was really me. I was no longer worried, as I'd damn near removed some flesh from my own arm. I almost made myself fall off the table as I became still and we remained silent. I was weak, but I loved the way that I was feeling at that moment.

Akheem said, "I think you have invested in some high-quality furniture, Doll, because it held up *well.*"

He swallowed me in his embrace, and we stayed locked inside of each other's arms for a while. Nine minutes passed before we found our voices again. I kissed him all over his face as we held each other. I placed my head on his chest, over his heart, because I loved to hear it beat inside of his chest! I had so much faith in this man because he had been good to me. He was

363

giving me a true sense of direction as I kissed him again. I touched his face and we just looked at each other for long periods.

I sat up on the table and asked, "Can we do that again?"

He shook his head yes, several times. I guess he wanted more of me as well, because that "rape" of one another was fun. I wanted to give him more than he could handle, as we combined our bodies! I was hopeful that he had forgiven me, because I had forgiven him, too. The fuck that he just delivered was a great sexual embrace. I needed to have sex real soon because I knew that I was a sexual junkie and he was my delivering my fix I had longed for.

"Doll, how about you come back to my suite with me, and I can promise you a night you won't forget? Because when I am with you, it is *always* Duck Season!"

ABOUT THE AUTHOR

Camille St. Charles Mississippi

Camille is a transplant make-up artist from Sacramento, California. Now nestled inside of irresistible Detroit, Michigan, she's found another part of her purpose in life as an author. It took patience and time for her to find the voice now weaving its way through all of the characters of her rather sorted and funny tales of The R Series: Rated R for Roxanne. Camille listened to the voice that told her to write what was stirring inside, excitedly growing, and soon bubbling to be released. Now she prides herself as a sweet-talking lady who enjoys dreaming up charming and sexy stories from her first book The R Series: Rated R for Roxanne, *Bring Your Boots!*, *An Uninvited Conversation*, and now the hilarious, *Ain't Got No Business.*

While she writes her tales, she falls in love with all of her characters over and over again. Camille enjoys the way her stories contribute to the fabric of her life. As her words pull together a masterpiece for her characters to thrive inside of, she gives her readers a little taste of sheer enjoyment with each page. Cozy up to the world of Roxanne, created by Camille St. Charles Mississippi. It will drive an assortment of smiles, secret giggles, drama and other sensational surprises your way.

Allow Ms. Camille St. Charles Mississippi to reach out and become one of your favorite authors as she transports you to the world of Roxanne! Not only is she a gifted storyteller, she also is a podcaster. Check out her Desert Novellas on podcast at http://dessertnovellas.libsyn.com/. You already know that she loves telling naughty stories that are hugely entertaining and hilarious, so be prepared to laugh your @#! off!

For more information about Camille go to http://www.TheRseries.com.